I0731059

JAZZY KITY PUBLICATION
PRESENTS

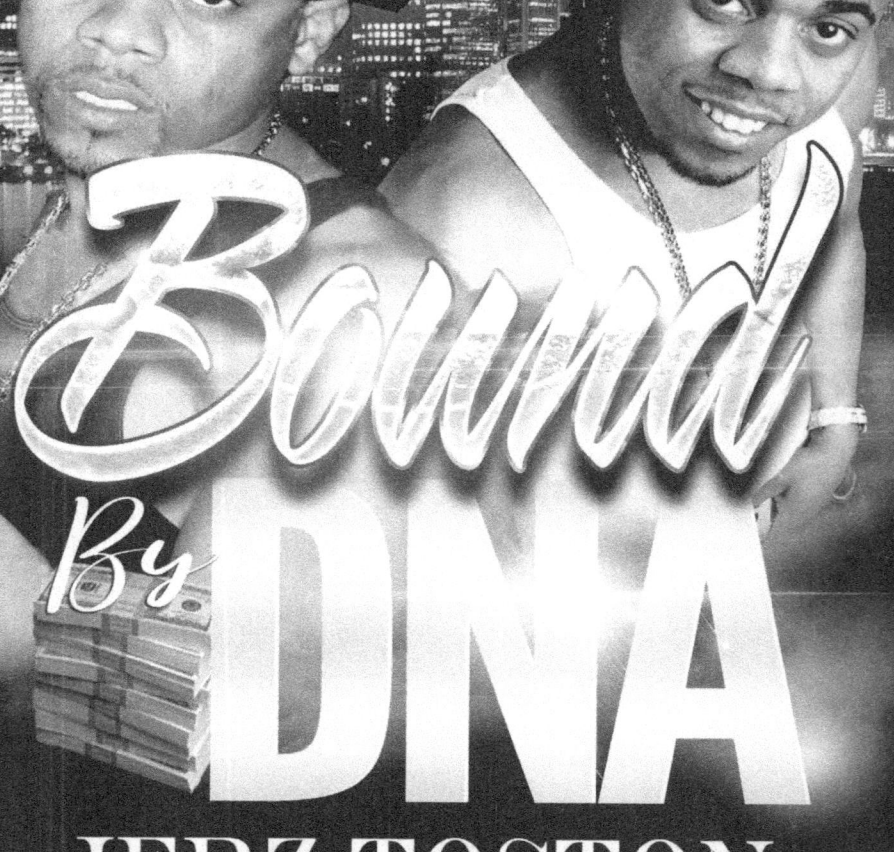

Bound By DNA

JERZ TOSTON

Bound By DNA

By Jerz Toston

Cover Art Created by KREATIVEGRAFIKS.COM

Logo Design by LeRoy Grayson

Editor: Anelda L. Attaway

Co-editor: Jerz Toston

© 2022 Jerz Toston

ISBN 978-1-954425-46-0

Library of Congress Control Number: 2022905671

ACKNOWLEDGMENTS

First and foremost, I to thx Allah (SWT) wit out Him; none of this would even be possible.

My kids, my ummi, sisters & brothers.

My wife for always having my back and pushing me when I didn't wanna be pushed.

DEDICATION

I dedicate this book to any & ery body that means anything to me.

Ya Fav Author!

TABLE OF CONTENTS

TABLE OF CONTENTS

INTRODUCTION

Urban Fiction at its best! This story is of two twin boys, Jah'ceer and Nah'ceer, who were separated. They desperately wanted to find each other again. Because for both of them, something was missing. Even though they thought they were far away, they were very close. So close that they could feel each other thoughts and feelings. The bottom line is they will find out at all times they were Bound By DNA

It's a journey of love, loyalty, family, friends, hatred, unloyal friends, murder and more.

CHAPTER 1

"Zeke, I just need a little something to get me off E, please."

"What I tell you about coming around here wit no money?"

"I know Zeke, but…."

"But nothing, no money, no drugs, now beat it!"

"A'ight, I'll scrape up a few ones and be back."

"Damn Zeke, she still phat to death; it's a shame Robby got her hooked on that poison."

"Roc, Robby's a weak ass nigga; he knew when Ash caught him wit that glass dick in his mouth, it was over."

"Yeah, but he didn't force her to get high."

"He might as well; he started lacing her blunts wit that shit."

"Zeke, I remember when you was geeked for her?"

"That was then, this is now, and I could never be wit her knowing she gets high."

But what Roc didn't know was Zeke had slept with Ash before and after she started getting high. Ashley hadn't told Zeke or Robby she was 3 ½ months pregnant wit Zeke's baby.

"So, how much did he give you?"

"Nothing."

"Bitch stop lying!"

"I'm not lying; he told me to come back wit some money." (SMACK)

"Stop lying to me; I know he has tha hots for you."

"AAAH! Robby, he did not give me anything."

"Strip!"

I didn't want to get hit again, so I stripped down to my panties and bra.

"Take it off now!"

"See, are you satisfied now?"

"See, you need to leave that shit alone."

"Don't tell me what tha Fuck I need to do. Maybe you should take your own advice."

Those drugs have him so far gone he hasn't even noticed I stop smoking that bullshit. Robby was cranky; he needed to get high badly.

"Ash, you might have to turn into a trick so we can get high."

"I know he didn't just say what I thought he said."

"Did you hear me?"

"Nigga you got me all Fucked up!"

"Bitch I ain't got u nothing!" (SMACK) "now get in there and put on something sexy!"

"Robby, I can't. I'm 3 ½ months pregnant."

"You're what?"

"3 ½ months."

"How do you know that?"

"I went to the doctors last week."

"I don't believe you."

"Robby, this isn't working for me."

"What isn't working?"

"This, us."

"It probably ain't even my baby."

I knew if I told him tha truth, he would beat my baby outta me.

"This is your baby Robby, so don't disrespect me like that."

"It better because if it's not, I'm gonna kill you and that baby."

From that moment, I knew tha only way to keep me and my child safe was to take who tha real father of my unborn child was to my grave wit me.

Three weeks passed by since I told Robby I was pregnant and he continued getting high. He graduated to heroin which always keeps him in a nod.

"I have to go get my ultrasound to see if I'm having a boy or a girl."

"You look like your more than some 4 months."

He was right; I looked more like seven months.

"I need bus fare."

"Bitch, you better walk; I need my money."

I just walked out before I said something I would regret. Zeke pulled up while I was waiting on my bus.

"Where you going?"

"To tha doctor's office."

"Would you like a ride?"

"Sure, if you don't mind."

"How far along are you?"

"4 months."

"Wow, I thought you were further along than that."

"I know, right?"

"Ash, you know that you shouldn't be getting high since you're carrying that baby."

"Zeke, I been stop messing wit that shit."

"Then why do you always come to cop?"

"Robby sends me to cop for him."

"What kind of nigga would send his girl to cop?"

"Tha kind that's embarrassed to let you see him at his lowest point."

"So, he rather let everybody think you get high, Fuckin' faggot. Why do you stay wit him?"

"Fear."

"I'll take care of you and ya child; you don't need his sorry ass." I could see the sincerity in his eyes.

"Thank you for tha ride," I said while getting out."

"You're welcome. Would you like me to come back to pick you up?"

"Not if it's going to inconvenience you in any way."

"Here's my number; just hit me up when you're ready."

I gave the receptionist my name and took a seat.

"Ashley Jacks."

"Yes, that's me."

"Follow me, please you can have a seat tha doctor will be in shortly."

After what seemed like forever, tha doctor walked in.

"Hello, Ms. Jack's," he said, looking at my chart.

"Hello"

"I'm Dr. Badur, if you can get up here, we can get started."

I had to pull my pants down so he could rub that gel stuff on my stomach.

"Oh my."

"What is something wrong wit my baby?"

"No, both your sons are fine."

"Sons?"

"Yes, you're having twin boys."

"Well, I guess that explains why my stomach is so big."

"Everything seems to be fine; stop by the receptionist desk so she can give you a prescription for some prenatal pills, and I'll see you in 30 days."

After getting my prescription I called Zeke, who said he was in route already.

"Why are you looking so sad? Is everything a'ight?"

"I just found out I'm having twin boys."

"No wonder you're so big."

"That's the same thing I said."

"My offer still stands."

"What offer is that?"

"Me taking care of you and tha twins."

I was tempted to just say fuck it and take Zeke up on his offer since the twins were his anyway.

"Don't answer, just think about it."

"OK."

"Let me take you out of that hell."

I should've chosen Zeke from the door, but no, I thought Robby was the money man. Boy, was I wrong.

For the next few months, it was pretty much tha same thing, verbal and physical abuse.

"Ashley... Ashley, bitch I know you hear me calling ya dumb ass."

"Robby, you need to get a grip." (SMACK)

"You dumb Bitch you better watch ya mouth."

(CRACK) Mafucka, don't keep putting ya hands on me," I said, still holding tha bat I had just hit him in tha arm wit.

"You stupid Bitch, you broke my arm."

"Good, I should break tha other one."

He went to jump up at me, and my reflect made me swing tha bat hitting him in tha same arm. "AAAAHHHHHH SHIIIIIT!"

I walked out tha door, and it was the last time Robby would see me until I had tha twins.

(KNOCK KNOCK)

"Who is it?"

"Ashley."

"Who?"

"Ashley."

"Hold up a sec. Yo put ya clothes on."

"Why, who is that?"

"Don't question me, just put ya shit on now! What brings you by Ash?"

"I was checking to see if ya offer was still good, but I see you got company."

He turned around to see home girl standing there shirtless.

"Bitch didn't I tell you to get dressed; now get outta my shit before I get pissed off even more." She threw her shirt on and ran out the door, nearly knocking me down.

"Zeke, I didn't mean to intrude or interrupt you."

"No Ma, you didn't do either."

"I'm sorry, I shouldn't have come." I turned to leave, but he grabbed me.

"Ash, wait, please don't leave."

"Zeke, I shouldn't have come unannounced."

"Ash, you're more than welcome here." Before I could say anything, Zeke kissed me.

"You don't know how long I've dreamed of this day."

"I need to get my things."

"No, you don't."

"All I have is tha clothes on my back."

"Come on, let's go."

"You don't have to go wit me; he should be in one of his deep nods.

"We're not going back there; he can keep that shit; we're going shopping.

Phone rings, "I don't know what trying to do, but I'm trying to bust moves and get that 36."

"Yo, what tha biz is Roc?"

"I just wanted to let you know we down to tha last 5 joints."

"A'ight, I got to meet wit Pablo in tha morning anyway."

"Cool, what you bout to get into?"

"Take Ash shoppin'."

"Oh, you bout to spend out on her, huh?"

"Yeah, she left that junky nigga."

"I know you're not about to wife her after all of that bullshit you was talkin'."

"Maybe."

"I knew you were still feeling her."

"Nigga you kno she's my boop boop."

"Awe shit, you bout to get all lovey-dovey on me."

"Fuck you Nigga."

"Ha Ha Ha! Nah, but on some serious shit, JoJo said he'll be ready after 8."

"I'll still be running around so you can handle it."

"I got you Homey."

"You always do, I'll hit you up when I'm done."

"Before you hang up, do you want me to deal wit Robby?"

"No, he ain't gonna make no noise."

"Don't sleep on that nigga Zeke."

"It's me you talkin' to Roc."

"A'ight, make sure you hit me up when you done."

CHAPTER 2

"Ash, you look like you're about to explode."

"I feel like I'm about to explode."

"Why are you looking at me like that?"

"I'm just admiring how handsome you are."

And he was. Zeke was 6'0, dark brown skin, hazel eyes wit long curly hair that he kept neatly braided, thanks to yours truly.

"Oh My God."

"What's wrong?"

"My water just broke."

"Stop playing."

"Does it look like I'm joking?" I said, looking down between my legs.

"Oh shit, oh shit."

"Boy, calm down, go get my bag so we can go to tha hospital."

Zeke was so nervous I couldn't help but laugh.

"What's so funny?"

"You."

"Me?"

"Yeah, I wish I had a camcorder. Help me to the car before I have these boys right here in tha living room."

By tha time we got to tha hospital, my contractions were three minutes apart.

"Can I get some help? My girl is in labor." Within seconds they were putting Ash on a gurney and taking her to the paternity ward. I didn't have kids, so this was all new to me.

"Just breathe like they showed us in class."

After about 15 minutes, the doctor said they were coming, and sure enough, they came 40 seconds apart. Zeke got to cut the umbilical cord. After seeing my sons, there was no way that Zeke wasn't tha father. Jah'ceer and Nah'ceer looked exactly like Zeke. Pretty hair, hazel eyes and they even had tha same birthmark Zeke had on his left foot. I could see what Zeke wanted to ask, so I just answered his question for him. "Yes, they are your sons."

"Why didn't you tell me?"

"Because Robby said he will kill me and my babies if they weren't his."

"I'll put that junky Mafucka in a box before I let him harm you and ours."

I knew Zeke meant every word just like Robby did.

"What are you doing?"

"Taking a picture so I can send it to Roc."

Zeke had an instant bond wit tha twins.

"Have you decided on any names yet?"

"Yes, Jah'ceer and Nah'ceer." So, let's call him Jah'ceer and him Nah'ceer," he said, pointing to each of tha boys.

"You're going to have a hard time telling them apart," tha nurse said, entering tha room.

"Nah, tha rest of tha world might, but we won't."

"When will I be able to take my babies home?"

"Two days," tha nurse answered wit out lookin' up from her chart, "I'll be back wit tha birth certificates in a few minutes."

I was happy and nervous at tha same time about leaving tha hospital. Happy because I would be taking tha boys home, nervous cause I didn't know what Robbie would do once he found out tha twins weren't his.

Zeke had turned his guest bedroom into a nursery for tha twins.

"Did you decide whether or not you're breastfeeding?"

"I'll stick to formula; I don't think I'll be able to handle it; I'll be sore."

"I guess I better stock up on baby formula, then."

"I'm going to sign up for tha W.I.C; that stuff is expensive."

"We not depending on the state for nothing." (KNOCK-KNOCK)

"Who is it?"

"Roc."

"Come in."

"What up, Homey?"

"I can't call it. What's good wit you?"

"Came by to see my nephews."

"They're in tha nursery go on in."

"Hey Ash."

"Hey Roc."

"How are you feeling?"

"Given tha fact, I just gave birth to twin boys, I'm fine. Zeke look after tha boys while I run to tha supermarket for milk. I might as well grab a few things for dinner while I'm there."

Once I had what I needed, I headed to tha checkout counter to pay for my stuff.

"Bitch didn't I tell you I will kill you and that bastard child of yours."

"Sir, I'm going to call security if you don't let her go and leave tha store now."

"I don't give a fuck who you call! Word on tha street is you had twins that look just like Zeke." I had to smile because tha streets hit it on tha nose.

"What tha Fuck you smiling for?"(SMACK)

I picked up a can of milk out of the cart and bust him in his head.

"Fuuuck You Dumb Bitch!" Before he could react, tha police had stepped in between us.

"Is this tha guy?"

"Yes, Officer," tha cashier answered, not giving anyone else a chance to.

"Officer, I want to press charges against this woman for assault."

"Officer, he came behind her and started putting his hands on her; she was just defending herself."

"Is that what happened Ms.?"

"Yes it is."

"Do you want to press charges?" I really didn't, but I knew if I said yes, they would haul his sorry ass off to jail, and it would get him away from me.

"Yes, I do want to press charges."

"You dumb bitch, Imma see you again, and next time they won't be there to help ya whore ass."

"You just added terroristic threatening to the list of charges."

"Fuck you and those charges."

Zeke, you couldn't deny those boys if you wanted to."

"I know, right? As soon as I saw them, I knew they were mines. Same hair, eyes and even tha same birthmark."

"You said you wanted a son to keep tha legacy going; now you have two."

"I'm about to put more money on my life insurance, so if anything happens to me, they'll be straight."

"What about setting up a trust fund for them?"

"First thing in tha morning."

"They going to be straight Uncle Roc going to see to that."

"I know you would; that's why I'm going to talk to Ash about putting you down as tha guardian."

"I'm cool wit that, but you not going nowhere."

"I know that, but Imma still put you down as tha guardian; I trust you wit my life, Roc."

"You should, I always got ya back."

"Now you sound like T.I. and Keri Hilson."

"Oh yeah, and you sound like Mike Epps."

"Ha! Ha! Very funny. Damn Ash ain't back yet? Let me call her to make sure see a'ight." Before I could finish dialing tha number, she was coming through tha door.

"What happened to you?" I asked, seeing her hair was all over tha place.

"Robby."

"I know that nigga didn't put his hands on you?" After Ash told me what happened, I was furious, to say tha least.

"I'll be back; come on Roc."

"He's at tha police station; one of tha employees called tha police while he was assaulting me."

"Roc, call see if he has a bail; if he does pay it."

"Zeke, I don't want you to do something that might land you in jail or dead."

"You don't have to worry about that, does she, Roc?"

"Ash, you don't get to be on top in this dirty game as long as we have unless you move swiftly."

"I hear y'all; just be safe."

"Always."

"Did you feed tha twins?"

"Yeah, and I burped them."

"Wit my help. What? Don't look at me like that, I know more about babies than both of y'all do."

"You should; you got 10 kids Nigga."

"Yeah right, I got two girls."

"That you claim."

"Nigga don't try to play me in front of Ash; you know I take care of mine."

"Damn, no need to get upset; you can't take a joke."

"Not when it comes to my seeds."

"You two act like brothers for real."

"Sometimes he forgets I'm older."

"By one month."

"Hey, I'm still tha oldest."

"Just like Jah'ceer is older than Nah'ceer by 40 seconds, but he's tha oldest."

"Point made Ash. I'll be back later."

"A'ight, should I make enough dinner for you?"

"Yup."

"She wasn't talking about you, Roc."

"I know, but I'll be back for dinner too."

"Well, in that case, I'll cook enough for three."

"Come on Zeke, let's go take care of ya boy so we can be back in time for dinner."

"Trails Bail Bonds."

"I need you to post a bond for me axel."

"Who and when?"

"Robert Jinkin and right now." He made a call to tha police station and just like that, it was done.

"Jinkin."

"Yo."

"Front and center, your bail has been posted."

"By who?"

That's none of my biz-ness; it's only my job to release you. So do you wanna leave or not?"

"Damn right."

"Then let's go."

I was given my property back and then released. As soon as I got outside, I lit up a Newport. I need to get myself together so I can get at that bitch and Zeke.

"Aye Yo Robby."

"What up Joe?"

"Where you heading?"

"I don't know."

"Get in; I'll give you a ride."

"Nah, I'm good; I need to clear my head."

"I got some get high Nigga, get in."

"Well, since you twisting my arm, I guess I can roll."

"I hope he hasn't left yet."

After waiting about 15 minutes, I decided to call to see if they already released him.

"Fuck!"

"What?"

"He already left. Ain't no telling where he at now."

"Let's swing by all of tha spots where a junky would go."

"He must got an angel on his side; we've checked all tha spots."

"He'll pop up and when he does, that's his ass. Ash should be done cooking by now."

"I hope so cause a Nigga hungrier than a homeless man."

"Yo, you stupid."

"Zeke, I love you like a brother."

"Roc, we are brothers. Answer ya phone."

"Hello."

"Yeah, meet me in 20 minutes."

"Swing by Stan's, I need to grab 2 joints for Kev."

"Did you ever get that money from him?"

"Nah, I thought you did."

"Nah, but he should have it now."

"Well, don't say nothing we gon' see if he can really be trusted."

"He'll say something."

"Want to put a friendly stack on it."

"Roc, you know I don't like to take ya money."

"I don't think you'll be taking it this time Baby Boy."

Kev was already there waiting when we pulled up.

"Unlock tha door, so he can get in."

"What up y'all?"

"Same shit."

"It's under tha driver's seat."

"I'll put tha money under there too."

"Hit us up when you ready."

"A'ight."

"I told you, let me get my stack."

I started to pull tha money out when Kev came back to tha car.

"My bag, I put the 15 grand I owe y'all in there too."

"Oh shit, I forgot all about that," I said, lying.

"Maybe, but I didn't, I been had it, but I wanted to wait til I copped to knock two birds wit one stone."

"You ain't gotta say nothing," Roc said, pulling out his money.

"You should know niggaz ain't fuckin' up our paper."

"Every now and then, we always get one."

"We better head to tha crib; Ash is blowing my phone up.

CHAPTER 3

"I've been in this rehab for 69 days and I think I'm ready to get out of here."

"You still have 51 days; this is a 120-day program; tha hard part is over."

"If I wasn't so far away, I would have left by now."

"Well, I guess that's a good thing then. People that try to rush back out there are normally tha ones to relapse."

"I ain't doing no relapsing; I just need to see some good friends of mine."

"Good friends, huh?"

"Yup, good clean friends."

"Robby, once you leave here, you're in charge of your own recovery."

"I know, but if I think of getting high, you're only a phone call away."

"True, now go ahead to your group before you're late."

I was in group physically, but mentally, I was someplace else. For tha past two months, I've been having tha same dream killing Ashley and Zeke. There was no way I could let either of them live after how they played me.

"Robby, Robby."

"Huh."

"It's your time to share."

I didn't like all that sharing shit, but I did so I wouldn't have to hear my counselor's mouth.

"My name is Robby and I'm an addict."

"Hi, Robby," everyone said in unison.

After I finished, everybody said, "Thanks for sharing, it works if you work it; keep coming back."

"Yo Robby, let's go out back for a smoke."

"Nah, Pete, I'm bout to take a nap; I'm tired as hell."

"A'ight, I'll see you at dinner then."

"Cool."

Even though I had plans to go to sleep, once I got to my room, I couldn't sleep a lick. (KNOCK KNOCK)

"Who is it?"

"It's Pete; you going to dinner?" I looked at tha clock it was 5:30. Damn, I didn't realize I dozed off.

"Yeah, Pete, give me a few minutes to get myself together."

Me and Pete gotton real cool since we been here. Our stories were tha same; he wanted to get clean, so he could get revenge on his son's uncle for turning him into a heroin addict. Nobody turned me into an addict, but I do have some plans of my own.

"Zeke, that nigga still ain't surface; maybe he overdosed somewhere."

"I heard he in rehab somewhere."

"What time you gotta pick tha twins up from daycare?"

"Oh shit, I'm supposed to pick them up at 2 o'clock for their doctor's appointment."

"Calm down Nigga; it's only a quarter after one."

"Imma go get them now, so I don't be rushing."

"Do you want me to come wit you?"

"If you want, but we both know you trying to run into home chick."

"All I gotta do is call her if I want to see her."

"So you already hit that?"

"Yeah, two months ago, there's this new broad that work there."

"Nigga you bout to get some shit started."

"No, I'm not. I don't mess wit Robin; we just friends."

"Does she know that?"

"We established that from tha door."

"Wait here while I run inside."

"Nigga ya sons is in tha daycare I'm going in wit you."

I didn't see Shorty at first, but that's because she was in tha twins' room.

"Now I know why they're so spoiled."

"I'm sorry, they're just so adorable, I can't help myself."

"They have that effect on people. I have to take them to tha doctors."

"Will they be coming back?"

"Probably not."

"OK do you want me to feed them first since that's what I was about to do?"

"We'll do it once we get to tha doctor's office."

"No problem. Just let me change them first."

"Be my guess."

"You need some help?" Roc asked her.

"If I didn't know any better, I think you were flirting wit me."

"Let me put ya mind at ease. I'm flirting wit you."

"If I wasn't at work, I might have responded to that."

"How about I'll give you my cell number and you can hit me up when you're not at work."

"A'ight, let me change Jah'ceer and Nah'ceer first."

Once she was done and Roc gave her his number, we headed out.

Zeke keep it 100, she Michael Jackson bad ain't she?"

"Let me just say this, you lucky I'm with Ash."

"No Nigga, you lucky I wouldn't want you to be mad when she chose me."

"What ever Nigga."

"Are they getting shots today?"

"Yeah it's their six-month checkup."

"Nah'ceer and Jah'ceer Abrams."

"Damn that was quick."

"There goes mommy's babies. How did the first visit go?"

"They troopers, they got two shots a piece and didn't even cry."

"Are you serious?"

"Yeah, it's surprise me too."

"Mommy's babies tough as nails," she said, kissing all over them.

Over tha next few months tha twins were getting bigger and I couldn't be more happier. Between Zeke and Roc, tha boys were always gone.

"Hello."

"Hey, Tae."

"Oh, what's up Girl?"

"What you up to?"

"Nothing probably about to hit tha mall up and do some shoppin'."

"It doesn't surprise me that you're doing what I was calling to ask you if you wanted to do."

"I'm not doing it; I'm about to do it."

"Bitch, you too damn smart."

"I know that's why I graduated at tha top of my class."

"Fuck you."

"No thanks, I'm Strictly Dickly."

"Where are my boyfriends at?"

"Wit their daddy and uncle."

"Who's driving?"

"You."

"Well, I'm on my way, so be ready slowpoke."

Tae was my childhood best friend who moved away but recently moved back. As I was about to go out the door, Zeke called to tell me I didn't have to cook because they would be eating out, which was cool wit me because I hadn't planned on cooking anyway.

"A'ight, I'm on my way to tha mall with Tae."

"If you see something for tha boys, pick it up."

"I always do. I go more for them than myself."

"Well, I'll see you later, love ya."

"You too."

"You was about to be left; I know you heard me blowing this damn horn."

"I was on tha house phone wit Zeke, my bag."

"So what's tha deal wit Roc?"

"Nothing, I told you I don't want you to talk to him."

"Stop Hatin and hook a bitch up."

"No, because he's not a one-woman man."

"I'm not looking to be his girl; I just want to get broke off proper."

"Broke off how?"

"Bitch I heard his sex game is off the meter."

"Next subject, I don't want to hear about Roc's sex game. So let me get this straight, you're willing to be his booty call?"

"Hell Nah, if the sex is as good as they say, he'll be my booty call."

"I know that's right," I said high, fiving her.

"So, you got me or what?"

"I'll tell him."

"My girl, I knew I could count on you."

"You're gonna owe me for this."

"Put it on my tab."

We did a lot of shopping; I ended up buying tha twins more stuff then I got myself.

"Make sure you holla at Roc for me," Tae said before I got out of tha car.

"If you tell me one more time, I'm not going to tell Roc shit!"

"Bye bitch."

"Bye, I'll hit you later."

When I got in tha house, Zeke was playing wit tha twins. Jah'ceer ran up to me, grabbing my leg.

"Mom Mom."

"Hey mommies baby."

Nah'ceer was too busy eating French fries to pay me any mine. When he noticed me, he dropped his fries and put his arms out.

"So now you want me to pick you up, huh?" He gave me a smile I couldn't and wouldn't resist.

"Looks like you bought tha whole mall."

"Nah, I just the things I liked."

"I hate to see tha things you didn't like."

"I know, right."

"Come give me a kiss."

"I thought you never ask."

CHAPTER 4

It was three days until Nah'ceer and Jah'ceer's first birthday and Zeke was going all out to throw down tha biggest party ever. I tried to tell him not to overdo it, but nothing was too much for his boys.

"Aye Roc, did you rent tha hall like I asked you?"

"Of course I did; I even called those party planner people for Ash so she won't have to tire herself out decorating."

"I know she'll appreciate that."

"Zeke, I don't know if I'm gonna bring Egypt or not."

"You might as well, all tha time y'all been spending together."

"I'll hit you up later. I need to pick up tha boy's gifts."

"What else did you buy them?"

"Don't worry about it; you'll see in a day or two."

"Roc, you got them enough stuff already."

"Nigga my nephews can never have enough stuff."

"Are you bringing Asia?"

"Are you kidding? She wouldn't miss her cousins' party for nothing in tha world?"

"I haven't seen her in a while. I know she's big as shit."

"Six going on 21."

"She gets it honest; look at her mom."

"Yeah, she's been on that you don't want me you won't see your daughter shit."

"I told you to go to tha courthouse and get visitation rights so you won't have to deal wit her dumb shit."

"I just don't wanna deal wit tha whole child support shit."

"As much as you do for Asia."

"I know and you know that, but tha White people don't and as long is it's not on record, they won't give a fuck."

"So, is she making you knock her down so Asia can come to tha party?"

"Hell Nah, I would never hit her off again."

"You better not, or you'll be in serious trouble."

"Tell me about it."

"Well, hit me up when you finish handling your biz-ness."

"No doubt, I got you My Nigga."

"Happy birthday Jah'ceer and Nah'ceer." Since they didn't understand tha whole birthday thing, they just kept eating their breakfast.

"Zeke, tha cake has to be picked up by 10 o'clock."

"I know Ash; you only told me six times."

"I'm sorry I just want to make sure everything is perfect for my babies first birthday."

"Ash, this will be a birthday to remember and it will be for tha rest of the twins' life."

"I need to go by tha hall to make sure everything is in order."

"Ash, just relax; they get paid to do this."

"Yeah, but I want to make sure everything is tha way I told him I wanted it done."

"I know you didn't bother them after I told you not to?"

"I told Roc you would say something anyway."

"Well, if you knew I would, why tell me not to?"

"Good question."

The party started at one, but we didn't arrive until 2 o'clock.

"We were starting to think you wasn't coming," Tae said.

"Oh my, look at you too handsome or should I say, fine brothers." I had to smile because tha twins were sharp in their Gucci blazers, jeans and sneakers.

"If I didn't know any better, I think they were twins," some lady from Ash's job said with a smile.

"Hello, Miss Ebony, I'm glad you could make it."

"Chile, I wouldn't miss this for the world."

"Are those your grandkids over there by tha moon bounce?"

"Yes, them my grandbabies."

"They look just like you Miss Ebony."

"Chile, everybody says that."

"They do."

"That's because me and her mom argued tha whole time she was pregnant wit both of them."

"I put tha gift over on tha table with tha rest of em."

"Thank you Miss Ebony."

"Chile, you supposed to bring a gift to tha birthday party."

"As long as you bought ya grandkids, that was enough for me."

All in all, the party was a huge success. Nah'ceer and Jah'ceer had so many clothes I wouldn't need to buy them any for tha next three months, at least.

"I almost forgot this gift," Roc said, handing me a box.

"What's this?"

"Open it up."

When I did, there were two necklaces wit two charms that read Bonded By Blood.

"Damn, I'm feeling this; you must've paid a grip for them?"

"I'm not Jay Z or Jermaine Dupri, but money ain't a thing."

"Those are real nice Roc."

"I know, but they won't be able to wear them for another 12 years, at least."

"It's cool; they can wear these until then," he said, holding up two smaller versions of tha same chains.

Rock between you and Zeke, y'all gotta stop spoiling these boys."

"Like you should talk."

Zeke put tha chains on tha twins and I hate to admit they look good on them.

"Y'all trying to get my babies robbed wit all this ice on."

"Mafucka's not crazy; they value a life too much."

Around 8 o'clock, tha party was winding down.

"Look at them; you would think they would be tired by now."

"Yo, you sure you want to do this?"

"You damn right, I'm sure, and if everything goes they way I hope we'll be paid."

"Now that's what I'm talkin' bout My Nigga."

"Why don't we just go inside and wait for them to come home."

"Because we don't know tha alarm code, they should be home in a little and if they're not, we'll wait."

I screwed tha silencer on my pistol and laid my seat back just in case we were there for a while.

"Yo, Yo."

"Huh."

"Wake up; I think this is them pulling up." I looked at tha clock on tha dash.

"Damn, it's almost 12 o'clock; I was sleep that long?"

"Nigga you was snoring like a bear in tha winter."

"I haven't been getting too much sleep lately."

"Damn, that's not even them."

"Maybe they're not coming home tonight."

"We'll sit here and wait, but if he doesn't show before tha sun starts coming up then we roll out."

Before we knew it, tha sun was coming up, so we rolled out.

"Oh Shit!"

"What's up?"

"Man, we was on tha wrong Fuckin' block."

"Say word."

"Word, that's tha block; there's his car right in the driveway."

"Fuck it, let's go in."

"No, I know tha neighbors will call tha cops; will come back tonight."

"Hello."

"Hey bitch."

"Takes one to no one."

"I just called to say thanks."

"For what?"

"Giiiiiirl let me tell you, his shot is off tha phone."

"Eeeeeeewww Tae T.M.I. (too much information).

"I'm sorry, but he has it going on."

"So, does that mean he threw it on you?"

"We threw it on each other."

"What ever sounds like you got tha bad end of tha stick. I hope you're not going to be another falling victim of Roc's."

"You better check wit him then asked yaself who's going to be tha victim."

"Well, I'll call you later. I'm about to fix breakfast for my family."

"Bye Bitch!"

"By Hussy."

"Ashley."

"Yeah Babe."

"I just got off tha phone wit Roc and it sounds like Tae gave him a taste of his own medicine."

"That's a coincidence; Tae just hung up bragging about her night wit Roc."

"I never seen Roc like this over any broad before."

"What do you mean?"

"He's never called to tell me about some pussy."

"Zeke."

"Ow Ash, why you hit me?"

"Watch ya mouth in front of the twins."

"Shit, my bag."

"Shit," Jah'ceer and Nah'ceer repeated.

"Boy you better watch ya mouth."

"See, that's why I tell you be careful what you say around them."

"They're so smart they pick up on everything."

"They get it from they mama."

"They said you would say that."

"Did they?"

"Yup."

"I hope it wasn't a mistake hooking those two up."

"I know, cause if it doesn't work out, I'll have myself to blame."

"Better you then me."

"Ha! Ha! Ha! Very funny Smart Ass."

"If it doesn't work, you can't blame me cause I told you not to get involved and let Tae do her own shit."

"I know, but that's my girl and you would have done tha same for Roc." Ash was right, but I would never let her know it.

"No, I wouldn't cause Roc knows not to involve me in his females."

"Zeke save that for somebody who don't know no better."

"Ash, you swear you know me."

"I do before we started messing we crept for 2½ years and we been officially messing for 18 months, so that's four years; I would say I know you."

"Since you put it like that, maybe you do."

"Maybe?"

"A'ight, A'ight you do know me."

"That's what I thought," she said, balling her fist.

"What you gonna do wit them," I asked, pointing to her fist.

"Go upside ya big head."

"It is pretty big, isn't it," I said, grabbing my shit.

"You wish."

"Oh, you talking Shit, are you?"

"No, No," I quickly said last time I did, he made me pay. He had my shit so sore we couldn't have sex for two days.

"I thought you changed ya mind."

"Put tha boys in their highchair so they can eat."

When everybody was fed, bathed, and clothed, we decided to head out for tha day for some fun.

CHAPTER 5

I was trying to decide if I should call Roc or not.

"Yo."

"Hey Roc."

"What up? Who is this?"

"Damn, that many Bitches got ya number that you don't know my voice?"

"Didn't no name show up on my caller ID."

"Well, when you figure it out, you got my number."

I hung up before he could respond. I don't know why but I was salty he didn't know who I was. After taking a shower, I had to laugh at myself. It's not like Roc didn't have a gang of bitches, so how was he supposed to know my voice. When I checked my phone I see I had one missed call when I saw who it was I couldn't help but smile.

"Hello."

"I hope you're not mad at me."

"Who is this? Your name didn't show up?"

"A'ight, I guess I deserved that."

"I see you called Ash to verify my number."

"Actually, right after you hung up, I picked up on tha voice."

"Tell me anything Roc."

"Only tha truth Rachael."

"Who?"

"I'm just joking Tae; pump ya brakes."

"Nigga you was about to get cursed all tha way out."

"You and Ash are just alike."

"I know we don't take no shit."

"So, what's good Ma?"

"I figured I'd call you since you wasn't going to call me."

"Who said I wasn't going to hit you up?"

"Nigga it's been damn near two weeks."

"Tae, I'm a busy guy, so bear wit me."

"You can make it up to me wit lunch."

"I would love to but…"

"I knew a but was coming."

"But I had to tie up some loose ends, so I'm a be ripping and running all day."

"A'ight, just hit me up when you have some time."

"How about we do dinner tonight instead?"

"Sure, I'm game."

"I'll make reservations for 9 o'clock. Is that cool for you?"

"Yup."

"It's an upscale place, so…."

"You don't have to finish tha sentence. I'm a classy chick, so it ain't nothing for me to look tha part, trust me."

"Well, I'll see you around eight."

"I'll be waiting."

"I'm sure you will."

"What is that supposed to mean?"

"Nothing, see you later."

"Mmmm hmm."

I couldn't wait for tonight hopefully; it would end wit me on top of Roc in every other position possible.

"Is it all here?"

"Come on Roc, since when did you need to start asking me that?"

"Nothing personal; I always ask everybody that, but you wouldn't know that since you don't fuck wit me like that no more."

"Nah, you know I be in New York doing my thing."

"So, what brings you to these parts of tha woods again?"

"It's a drought up my end."

"Oh, so you're using me?"

"Come on Roc; you know you still my peoples."

"If I was ya peoples you would stay in contact Nigga."

"If you ever go to N.Y.C you'll understand."

"I'll probably never understand because I don't plan on ever going to N.Y.C unless it's to shop."

"So, you gonna let me get that work or not?" I couldn't put my finger on it, but something just didn't seem right wit Fish.

"I ain't making no noise, Fish I been chilling."

"Come or Roc, just because I live in New York doesn't mean I don't know what's going on down here in tha 'A'."

"You can't always believe what you hear."

"You can when tha source is reliable."

"How long are you in town for anyway Fish?"

"Two weeks, my mom is in tha hospital."

"Take my number and hit me in a few days; I might be able to do something for you."

"A'ight bet Roc."

What Roc didn't know was that dealing wit Fish would haunt him for years to come.

"Roc, make sure you call me; my money still green."

"I heard that; like I said, I'll hit you in a few days."

"Hello."

"Hey, I'll be pulling up in five minutes."

"A'ight, just hit tha horn and I'll come out."

Damn, look at her; she know she bad. Look at him checking me out. I knew I was looking good in my cream Michael Kohr dress wit my Christian Louboutin sandals to match.

"You look nice Tae."

"Thank you, I hope I'm not overdressed?"

"Nah, not at all."

"We didn't do too much talking on tha way since he was bumping his system."

"Valet, this must be a really nice spot."

"You've never been here before?"

"No."

"Well, you'll enjoy their food; it's delicious."

"I hope so cause a sista love a good meal."

"Hello, I'm Marc and I'll be your waiter for tha evening. Would you like something to drink while you browse tha menu?"

"Yes, could I have a bottle of Louis tha 13 please?"

"Sure, I'll be right back."

"I see you have good taste in champagne."

"Stick around and you'll see I have good taste in a lot of things."

"Here you go Sir."

"Thank you, we'll be ready to order in 10 minutes."

"OK. I'll be back in 10 minutes."

"This stuff is expensive."

"You have a lot to learn."

"Excuse me, but what is that supposed to mean Roc?"

"There is no price when you're wit me."

"Exxxcuse me."

"Don't worry about it; you didn't know, but now you do."

"Are you guys ready to order?"

"Yes, I have the Asian lobster tail with the Baltic steak and shrimp."

"White or dirty rice?"

"Dirty."

"Anything else?"

"No."

"And you ma'am."

"I have tha um grill salmon wit tha stuffed lobster, fried cabbage and steamed shrimp."

"Will that be all?"

"Yes."

As Marc started to walk off, Tae called out to him.

"Yes."

"Could you bring me a shot of Bombay?"

"Sure."

"Nah, Marc, just bring tha whole bottle, please."

"Certainly."

"I have to make sure I tip him good."

We talked tha whole time during dinner and found out how much we actually had in common.

"So, you're really a diehard Nets fan?"

"Yeah."

"Wow, you get props from me; not too many people would admit to that."

"I don't care how sorry they are; that's my squad."

"Hey, no need to get uptight; that's ya team and I respect that."

"You better wit ya big head self."

"I gotta use tha bathroom; I'll be right back."

"Sure, go ahead and call ya broads back ya phones been blowing up all night."

"I really gotta piss; I'll leave my phone here."

"Boy, go use tha bathroom. I'm just playing wit you."

"Hey Ma'am."

"What's up Marc?"

"Here is your check," he said, handing me the little black book.

As soon as he stepped off, I looked at tha check.

"Damn, no wonder they don't put tha price on tha menu."

I slid tha check over in front of Roc's chair.

"You must of had to shit."

"Ha Ha, very funny. I see Marc brought tha check. How much is it?"

"How would I know?"

"I know you looked at it."

"Damn what, you was watching me."

"No, I just know if it was me, I would've."

"Next time, we can go to Daddy's House to save some money."

"What did I tell you?"

"Ooh yea, there's no price wit you."

"Right right, you'll get it together."

He paid the tab and left Marc a $50 tip.

"Excuse me Sir."

"What's up Marc?"

"You left a $50 bill on tha table."

"I know it's yours for tha good service you provided for us tonight."

"Thank you."

"Nah, thank you Marc. Next time we come, I'll be sure to ask for you."

"Once again, thank you for tha tip and enjoy tha rest of your evening."

"You do the same," I said, waving bye.

"So what time is your curfew?"

"Boy pleeeease I'm grown, I make my own curfew."

"Good, that means you can stay tha night wit me then, right?"

"Did you not just hear me say I'm grown?"

"What do you want to do now?"

"Let's see how about swinging by my house so I can get my over night bag and that movie King Richard."

"I got that already."

"Well, I'm a grab For Colored Girls."

"That Tyler Perry flick?"

"Yup."

"Got that too."

"When do you have time to watch them?"

"I don't really; I just got a connect wit movies, so I always have tha latest ones."

"You can come in if you want."

"If you only grabbing some stuff, I'll wait here."

"A'ight I'll be right back."

"I hope I didn't take too long?"

"I was about to pull off."

"I wasn't that long; I had to find my hair cap."

"It's gonna get fucked up anyway."

"Boy, I just got my shit done this morning. I need this to last all weekend."

"Well, you better make an appointment for tomorrow, then I'll pay for it."

"In that case, you can fuck it up all you want to."

"I'd planned on it."

Three hours and eight orgasms later, we both lay there exhausted and sweaty.

"I have to get in tha shower."

"I think I'll join you."

"A brother could get use to this."

"You're not tha only one."

We took turns washing each other up only to get out and go right back at it until the sun came up.

"Tae, if I didn't know no better, I think you was trying to get a brother hooked."

"I could say tha same about you."

"Well, you'll be on tha money."

"Roc, you got too many Bitches to be trying to wife somebody."

"That's only because I haven't found tha right one yet."

"Now you have?"

"I think Tae, I been feeling you for a minute."

"Why didn't you say anything then?"

"That's not me; I don't holla; I get hollered at."

"Wow, you something else."

"So, I've been told."

Little did he know he already had me wifed, but I wouldn't tell him that.

I woke up to tha smell of pancakes, eggs and bacon. Before I could get out of bed, Roc was walking in with a tray in his hand.

"Breakfast in bed?"

"Yeah, you should feel lucky I've never cooked for a broad before, let alone serve them breakfast in bed."

"I bet."

"Seriously."

"In that case, I feel honored."

"You should."

"A'ight, A'ight, I get tha point don't overdo it."

"Don't you forget to make that hair appointment."

"I don't need to. I can fix this myself."

"Fine by me; I don't mind saving money."

"Is it safe to eat this food?"

"I would never poison you; after all, you just might be my future wife."

"I hear you sounds good. Oh, shit, I was supposed to call Ash this morning so we could get our nails done."

"So, call her."

"I will after I eat and get myself together. Umm, Wow, you can really cook."

"I know, I learned from the best, my mom."

"I'm really impressed now."

After I was dressed, I called Ash.

"Hey Ash."

"Damn Bitch you was suppose to call me two hours ago."

"I know; I had a late start this morning."

"So come pick me up so we can go."

"I'm not home, so you need to pick me up."

"Where you at Tae?"

As soon as I gave her tha address, she yelled, "You at Roc's house!"

"Just come pick me up."

"On my way."

"Zeke, I'm on my way out."

"So, Tae stayed at Roc's house last night, huh?"

"Sure did, she just called for me to pick her up."

"Well, at least you know why she didn't call."

"I know, talking about she had a late start, I bet she did."

"I don't know why Roc couldn't just drop her off, he's on his way over anyway."

"I don't know, but I'm out. I'll see you and tha boys later."

"Don't we get a kiss or something before you leave?"

"Awe, come here, mommy's other baby." I grabbed Zeke's face and kissed him how I knew he'd love to be kissed.

"You better go before this turns into something more."

"By Zeke, Nah'ceer, and Jah'ceer." They all waved bye.

"So, boys, what do you want to do today?" They both shrugged their shoulders.

"Come on, let me get you dressed before Uncle Roc gets here." Upon hearing Roc's name, they went berserk.

(BEEP-BEEP)

"Wow."

"What's that supposed to mean?"

"You didn't have that on yesterday, so that could only mean one thing."

"I'm listening."

"You had a overnight bag that you left to have a reason to come back."

"Ash, you something else you know that, don't you?"

"So I've been told."

"Ash, I can't lie, I've fallen for Roc and I've fallen hard."

"Tae I just don't want to see you get hurt you are my best friend."

"I know what I'm doing and it goes both ways wit us."

"Are you sure?"

"Bitch, after countless and I do mean countless orgasms, I woke up to breakfast in bed this morning."

"Bitch shut up!"

"I'm serious Ash."

"Oh shit, Roc has finally met his match."

"Do you think?"

"I've never, never, never seen or never heard of him cooking for any of his broads, let alone serving them breakfast in bed."

"He told me the same thing, but I didn't believe him."

"It's true."

"Yeah, I know now."

"He even invited me to tha Divas and Bosses party tomorrow night."

"I was going to ask you if you was going because me and Zeke are in tha building. We can hit the mall once we leave tha nail salon."

"You know I could see myself wit Roc."

"Unh, Unh, Unh"

"What's that supposed to mean?"

"He must've really put it on you."

"No Bitch, we put it on each other."

"Hold up this Zeke calling me."

"Hey baby."

"Ash, what tha hell did Tae do to my boy?"

"What do you mean?"

"He hasn't stopped talking about her since he been wit me."

"Him too?"

"You going through tha same thing, huh?"

"Yes I am."

"I got a idea; where are y'all at?"

"Leaving tha nail salon on our way to tha mall."

"That's where we headed; we'll meet you at tha food court."

"A'ight."

"What he talkin' bout?"

"Nothing, come on, let's get to tha mall."

"I hope tha Gucci store has some new stuff; I'm trying to be tha baddest diva in tha building."

"Second baddest next to me."

"Fuck you Ash."

"No, thank you I'm Strictly Dickly."

"And so am I Bitch."

"Damn, I hate when it's packed like this."

"Everybody in town must be shopping for tomorrow's party."

"It's a major event, all tha who's who will be in attendance for this so bitches better come wit they A-game."

"We not gonna have to worry about that, look what stores they going in."

I spotted Roc, Zeke and tha twins.

"Come on Tae," I said, walking towards them.

"Mommy!" they both yelled, running up to me.

"Hey mommy's babies."

"Did you know they were going to be here?"

"Yes, she did; I told her to meet us here so you two could hang out because we're both tired of you to talking our heads off about the other."

"Come on Ash."

"Damn Zeke, you gonna put me on blast like that?"

"Oh, so you was talking Zeke's head off about me?"

"Probably the same way you was talking minds off about him. It's obvious tha two of you are definitely feeling each other."

"Hey Roc." We all turned around to see who was talkin'.

"What up Cherl?"

"You must of lost my number; I haven't heard from you in a while."

I could tell Tae was about to say something, so I said, "Didn't lose it; just didn't have tha need to use it."

"I know you not trying to get new."

"Cheryl."

"Let me handle this Roc. Listen, whatever y'all had is tha past; as you can see, he's upgraded from an Escort to a Maybach."

"Excuse you, Roc, you better keep ya new puppy on her leash."

"It was never nothing wit me and Cherl; I had to find out tha hard way she's a stalker."

"I don't want no problems, so it would be best if you left."

"Roc, you know tha number; when you get tired of her, call me."

"Before he gets tired of me, we'll be married wit children, you dumb bitch."

Zeke, Rock, Ash and even tha twins all looked at me. Shit, I surprise myself wit that comment.

"Married with kids huh?"

"I don't know where that came from. I just wanted to get under her skin."

"Bitch, you did a good job at it."

"Well, we gonna let you two do y'all thing since y'all can't stop talkin' about one another."

"Y'all don't have to do that; we can shop together."

"Are y'all sure?"

"Yes, unless y'all want some alone time."

"We'll get that later tonight," Roc quickly said.

"Who said she was staying wit you tonight?"

"Ash, mind ya biz-ness."

"I'm just playing Zeke."

When we walked inside the Gucci store, one of tha sales ladies walked up to us.

"Hello, welcome to Gucci. My name is Janet; if you need any help wit anything, please don't hesitate to ask."

"Do you have any new arrivals?"

"As a matter fact, we just got three new pieces. I haven't put them out yet."

"May I see them?"

"Sure, I'll be right back."

"So you really feeling Tae, huh?"

"Yeah it's like we connect on so many levels."

"I feel you on that; that's how me and Ash are."

"Nigga I knew you was creepin' with her tha whole time."

"Why didn't you say something?"

"Wasn't my place too."

"Imma grab this pink and cream linen set wit those pink Gucci slip-ons."

"I'm gonna grab something from tha Prada or Ralph Lauren store." I put my stuff on tha counter, then made my way to where tha watches and shades were.

"Now, what kinda luck is this. Let me get that watch and those frames right there," I said, pointing to tha cream Gucci watch wit pink diamonds and frames wit pink tint.

"Damn baby niggaz gonna have to step up they game way up. Look at you trying to dress like ya man."

"This just came in and I had to have it."

"Why you buying those shoes? Why don't you just wear tha ones at home you've been wanting to wear?"

"Oh shit, I forgot about them they'll be perfect wit this dress."

By tha time we got home tha twins were knocked out sleep.

"Ash grab tha bag, I'll get tha boys."

CHAPTER 6

"Tonight is the night."

"You been saying that for tha past few weeks."

"I know, but tonight is it."

"Awe Nigga I think you having second thoughts because of that Bitch."

"Nigga I could care less about that Bitch; she ain't no kin of mines."

"We'll catch him coming in from tha party that's been tha talk of tha town."

"How do you know he'll be going?"

"Trust me, he wouldn't miss this party for tha world."

"I just hope he takes us to tha money wit no problems."

"Don't worry, he will."

"You sound real confident."

"Because I am."

"Maybe we should check this party out if all tha big fish are going to be in tha same pond."

"No, we don't want him to get suspicious."

"Nigga we going to blend in wit everybody else."

"You can go; I'm chillin'."

I don't know what it is, but there's something he wasn't telling me. I would hate to rock his ass to sleep if he crosses me, but I will.

"Damn Baby, you look good; every Nigga in tha building going to be on you."

"They might, but I belong to you."

"Do you?"

"Oh, you don't know by now?"

"Well, in that case." Zeke dropped down on one knee.

"Baby, we don't have time for that Roc and Tae will be here any minute."

"Ashley, I loved you before you knew I did and I knew one day you would be mines and now that you are I don't plan on being wit out you, so will you marry me?"

"OOOH My God, OH My God, OOOH My God."

"Umm, wouldn't mind an answer so I can get off this floor."

My mouth was open, but nothing was coming out.

"Ash."

"Yes, Yes, Yes, Yes I'll marry you Zeke."

I couldn't believe the size of tha diamond Zeke was sliding on my finger.

"Just so you know you're doing all tha planning and I'm just providing tha money and showing up at tha altar."

"Fine by me, I'll get Tae to help me. Before I forget, I put more money on our life insurance tha other day."

"Why you plan on killing me?"

"Not unless you give me a reason to."

I could hear Roc pulling up. "Come on before he starts blowing tha horn." Beep-Beep "Too late."

"Imma follow you," I said, hitting tha alarm to unlock tha doors on my Maserati."

"Pulling out all tha stops tonight, I see."

"So are you," I said, referring to his powder-blue Bentley.

"They ain't ready for us."

"Well, I suggest they get ready cause here we come."

Rick Ross, track 7, volume 15 "Here I am I gotta bunch of dollars to spend on her she can be ya friend or ya lover."

"This still my cut right here," Ash said, bumping her body to the beat.

There were cars everywhere when we pulled up to the valet. "Zeke, what up My Nigga?"

"I can't call it."

"Damn, what's up Cuz?"

"What tha deal Lil' Eddie?"

"Man, you better stop by and see my moms she been worried about you."

"You know I'm good."

"She had one of her dreams."

I took a mental note to go see my aunt tomorrow. I'm not one of those superstitious people, but my aunts' dreams or visions as she calls them are normally on tha money.

"Who is shorty? She's Michael Jackson Bad?"

Tae was bad at 5'6, Coco skin complexion, long shoulder length hair, hazel eyes and to top it off an ass like Nikki Minaj but hers was real.

"Yo watch yaself Cuz."

"Must be something serious because you never defend any of ya female friends."

"Yeah Cuz, this is my future wifey." I caught Tae smiling.

"You two Niggaz cheating?

"How's that Lil' Eddie?"

"Y'all got these two fine ass women on y'all hips."

"I heard that and I must agree wit you."

"I'll see y'all inside I'm waiting on my mans."

"First round on me Little Cuz."

"No doubt, I'll see y'all inside."

"You ladies do look nice."

"Thank you Zeke."

"Bitch what's that on ya hand?"

"Oh this?" I said, holding up my hand, "my fiancé gave this to me tonight."

"Roc, did she just say her fiancé?"

"Yup, I sure did, were engaged."

"Bitch, why didn't you tell me?"

"Because he just proposed tonight."

"I thought you never would," Roc said, dapping Zeke.

"I was waiting for tha right time."

"I see all tha ballers out tonight." Zeke and Roc both looked at one another then smirked.

"I see you done fucked up somebody's paper to get an outfit."

"Nah, I'm still spending ya paper I won at tha crap house."

"Damn, you still holding on to that 10 grand from two months ago?"

"Come on, I done flip that numerous times; actually, that 10 grand put me in tha game."

"I heard that. What you drinking?"

"Patron."

"Here, next ones on me," Roc said, passing him a c-note.

We stopped at tha picture booth to flick it up a little.

"Tae these bitches ain't saying shit to us."

"You don't have to tell me."

"Roc's little fan club is heated."

"Cause they know it's a new bitch in town."

"I know that's right and they better not get it fucked up because I got this pretty ass face."

"Bitch you so conceded."

"And you not?"

"No comment."

"That's what I thought."

"Look at those bitches."

"Tae, I don't worry about that cause Zeke ain't stupid; why would he go from steak and shrimp to peanut butter and jelly?" (Ha! Ha! Ha!)

"Bitch you stupid."

"What we miss, what's so funny?"

"Inside joke."

"Put these in ya purse," Zeke said, handing me tha pictures we just took.

"Let's head to tha bar. I need a drink."

"Me too." Zeke took my hand and led me to tha bar.

"What are you drinking Babe?"

"Bombay and pineapple."

"I should've known; I don't know why I even asked."

"Because you loooove me, that's why."

"Can't argue wit you on that."

"Give Mommy a kiss."

"Save that shit for when y'all go home."

"Mind ya biz-ness," I said, turning to see who was talking.

"Cat what's up Girl? When you get in town?"

"Last night."

"Why didn't you call us?"

"I was busy," she said, clutching Trey's arm.

"Mmm-hmm, I bet she was," Tae said.

"You know a sista gotta get a tuneup every so often."

"Somethings will never change."

"And you know this man."

"How long are you in town for?"

"A few weeks, I'm doing some promotion for my job."

"We got plenty of time to catch up then."

"We sure do; how are my two little men?"

"Girl bad as shit."

"Don't be talkin' bout my sons."

"You know they bad."

"So, what, they boys they suppose to be."

"I know that's not what I think it is on ya finger?"

"Depends on what you think it is," I responded, holding my hand up so tha light could reflect off tha diamond.

"What's tha date and I know a bitch is in it."

"We haven't come up wit one, yet he just proposed tonight and of course, you're in it."

"Let's get together and do lunch tomorrow, tha three of us."

"Works for me."

"Me too."

"A'ight, I'll call y'all."

After we had our drinks, we headed to tha VIP section.

"Heeeey Roc haven't seen you in a while; where you been hiding?"

"My girls been keeping me occupied."

"Oh, that's ya girl; I'm sorry I didn't mean any disrespect."

"None taken," Tae said wit a smile.

"Roc, you got a hell of a fan club."

"I've never been in a relationship, so I didn't have to have one female."

"Do you honestly think you'll be a'ight wit just one female?"

"There's only one way to find out unless you're not willing to give us a chance."

"Us, chance? Hold on, who are you and what did you do to Roc?"

"Fuck you Zeke."

"Tae, you better not let this Roc slip away cause if I didn't know any better, I'd say he's catching feelings already."

"Roc, if you're really serious, then I'm willing, but on one condition."

"What's that?"

"Change ya numbers."

"Huh?"

"You heard me; change ya numbers."

"Tae, I got a lot of important people."

"Save it; once you change ya number, all you have to do is text them all wit tha new number."

"You've got it all covered; there's just one problem."

"I'm listening."

"I've never text before, so I don't know how."

"You're in luck; I do." Zeke tapped me.

"What Boy?"

"She reminds me of you."

"That's why we're best friends."

We partied for tha rest of tha night until we were ready to leave.

"Mafucka, if you ever disrespect me like that again, I will kill you."

"I wasn't trying to disrespect you." (SMACK)

"Nigga shut up, ain't nobody tell you to say shit. Yo Bask, hand me that pistol."

"Hold up; we don't have to take it there." (SMACK)

"Didn't I just tell ya punk ass not to say shit, didn't I?"

I could see he was trying to reach for his pistol. POP! POP! POP!

"What tha fuck you do that for Pete?"

"You rather let him shoot you?"

"He wasn't gonna shoot me."

When Pete turned him over, his gun was in tha Clearview.

"Are you sure he wasn't gonna shoot you?"

"Damn good-looking Pete, I owe you big-time."

"Nah, that's a down payment for tha doe will be getting soon. As a matter of fact, we need to go; come on."

"What about his body?"

"Fuck him, by tha time they find him won't be nothing left."

"You sure?"

"Yeah." I went to get tha bag outta tha trunk.

"What's that Robby?"

"Something to help identifying him a lot harder."

"Baby, I had a ball tonight."

"Ash, you were by far tha baddest female in attendance tonight."

"You think?"

"Yup, me and all tha other niggaz that were eyeing you all night."

"Oh, so you did see that?"

"I don't miss much."

"Neither do I; I saw your little fan club."

"I'm glad tha boys are at tha sitters house."

"I know; I can be as loud as I want tonight."

As soon as we got tha door open, two guys rushed us.

"Don't say shit; just walk in."

"What tha fuck is this?" (SMACK)

"Now I didn't I just tell ya dumb ass not to say shit, huh, didn't I? I'm going to ask you one more time and depends on ya answer whether you live or die. Oh yeah ya bitch too. Now where is tha money?" When he didn't answer, it pissed me off. (SPIT)

"AAAAAH SHIIIIT!"

"You dumb Mafucka, you told him not to say shit."

"Oh yeah, I did, didn't I?"

"Ha! Ha! Ha!" tha other masked gunman started laughing.

"Where's tha money? Speak.

"No real paper here but a few petty grand."

"It better be enough cause we ain't got time to be running around town to get no paper."

"I need to show you where it is."

"Nah, ya bitch will show us."

"I don't know where it is." (SMACK)

"Bitch don't lie to me."

"She's not lying and please don't put your hands on her again."

"Or what?"

"Listen, if you want tha money, then I need to show you."

"Stay here wit her while I go see if it's enough money to save their lives." The handcuffs were so tight I knew there was no way I could get to my pistol I had inside my safe.

"Sit down right there."

"What's tha combo?"

"42.17 23." When I opened the safe, I couldn't believe my eyes.

"This is what you call a couple grand?"

"Yeah, that's chump change to me, but it'll probably make you feel like a millionaire."

"How much is it, or do I have to count it?"

"300,000 give or take."

"You got some nice jewels in here too."

I grabbed a Gucci bag and stuffed everything inside.

"Get up, let's go."

"Did you get enough to spare lives?"

"Yes."

"Let's get out of here then."

"Hold up." Before I walked out, I stopped and kissed Ashley.

"Oh My God, Robby. What tha fuck was that about?"

When I didn't respond, Zeke said, "Nigga you gonna die."

At that point, I took my mask off.

"Only person that's gonna die is you," I said, putting my pistol to his head.

"No, please don't do this Robby." (SMACK)

Pete smacks the shit out of her, "Bitch shut up!"

"Robby, what is all this about?"

"It's about was inside this bag."

"Nigga you better use it to get as far away as you can."

"That's tha last time you gonna threaten me."

"What are you going to do kill me? Nigga you don't have no heart; you never did."

SPTT, SPTT, SPTT

"NOOOOOO, NOOOOOO ROBBY WHHHHHY!"

Ash jumped up and my reaction made me shoot her in tha head and chest.

"A dumb bitch see what you made me do. Pete, check tha rest of tha house for any more money."

I couldn't believe that I just killed the only female that I had actually loved at one point in time.

"Ashley, I'm sorry it had to end like this. I hope one day you can forgive me."

"Robby, I found about 10 grand in the kid's room."

"Shit, I forgot about the kids!" At that point, anger took over me.

SPTT, SPTT, SPTT, SPTT

"What tha fuck was that for?"

"For her being a whore. Come on, let's get outta here.

CHAPTER 7

"AAAAAAAAH, AAAAAAAAH OH MY GOD, OH MY GOD." The sitter couldn't believe what she was seeing.

"Mommy!" Jah'ceer yelled.

"Daddy!" Nah'ceer also yelled, running to Zeke.

Tha sitter was so hysterical on the phone wit tha police. As soon as she hung up, she called Roc, who's number she knew because they had a fling or two.

"Hello."

"Roc come quick, please, come quick."

"Hold up, calm down Shorty and tell me what's going on."

"Ashley and Zeke have been shot."

"Where you at?"

"I'm at tha house wit tha boys."

"I'm on my way."

"Yo, come on Tae, we gotta go now."

"Why, what's going on?"

"Ash and Zeke have been shot."

"Oh My God, are they a'ight?"

"I don't know."

Roc did a buck tha whole ride. When we pulled up, there were police everywhere and tha whole house was taped off.

"Roc, this doesn't look good."

"I know."

Before we could get to tha house tha paramedics were bringing two bodies out in black bags.

"NO, NO, NO, PLEASE DON'T TELL ME!" Tae yelled out.

"Officer, are they dead?"

All he could say was, I'm sorry Mam. At that moment, Tae broke down. I was hurt, but I knew I had to be strong for tha boys.

"Where are my nephews?"

"Over there wit her," he said, pointing to tha sitter.

Once they seen me, they came running full speed. I knew I would have to raise them as if they were my own.

It was tha day of tha funeral, and I was in no mood to go, but I had to be there for tha boys Ash and Zeke.

"Who would do such a thing like this to them? They were loved by everyone."

We decided to wear white instead of the traditional black to celebrate their life and not mourn them. You would've thought it was Tupac or Biggie Smalls funeral how many people showed up. I walked to the podium to give tha eulogy. I got a little choked up seeing Tae and tha boys sitting there so innocently. The twins were dressed in all white linen wit Zeke's face airbrushed on tha front wit Ash on tha back of their shirts.

First of all, I want to thank all of you for coming today. I wrote something down, but I'm just going to speak from my heart. I knew Zeke for 21 years and Ash for 10. They were like, no, they were family to me. They leave behind two beautiful twin sons who are too young to understand what's going on and who will grow up mother and fatherless.

By tha time Roc was done wit tha eulogy tha whole church could be heard crying. The hardest part for me was watching Ash and Zeke get lowered into tha ground, knowing I would never see either of them again. Nah'ceer and Jah'ceer both started crying out for their mommy and daddy. I was strong up unto that point. Watergates flooded open, seeing my nephews in such pain. I made a promise that tha person or people responsible would pay dearly.

It's been six months since tha murder of Zeke and Ash; I still had no clue who was behind it. Biz-ness has picked up and I couldn't front Fish was definitely doing his thing in tha big apple (NYC). I've been dealing wit him for tha past three weeks; even though I never met wit him personally, he was definitely handling his biz. I had my young boy Sharky dealing wit him. My phone started ringing and by tha ringtone, I knew it was Fish.

"Hello."

"What up Roc, you ready for me?"

"Holla at Sharky."

"Why you keep throwing me off on ya peoples?"

"Everything proper, ain't it?"

"Yeah."

"Then what's the problem?"

"I just rather deal wit you."

"Holla at Sharky."

"A'ight but in a little Imma need a few and I'm only dealing wit you fuck this middleman bullshit."

"What ever, holla at Sharky."

"Roc, I don't know why you deal with that Nigga anyway."

"Fish was my man when he lived in tha 'A'."

"Hey, as long as you say he cool, then he cool."

"I'll get up wit you later. I'm bout to take Tae and tha boys to dinner."

"A'ight hit me up later."

Sharky was my young boy. I've been grooming him for tha last three years.

"What's tha deal? Is he coming this time?"

"Nah, he sending his people again."

"You need to get him to come your time is running out."

"He won't unless it's worth it."

"Well, we'll just have to make it worth it then."

"Let's just take what we have on his people and run wit it."

"That's not tha deal we made; now here's tha money for what you're about to purchase."

I swear I hate working for these pigs. If I could go back, I would've listened to my girl and not took that trip to the Big Apple.

"We decided to give you six more months, then we're pulling tha plug and you're going to serve that 15 years."

Little do these pigs know they'll have to find me before I let them throw me in jail!

As we sat there eating our food, I couldn't believe how much tha twins look like Zeke.

"Baby what's wrong?"

"Nothing."

"They look just like Zeke, don't they?"

"That's all I see when I look at them with a trace of Ash."

"Uncle Roc."

"What up Nah'ceer?"

"More," he said, pointing to his chicken tenders.

I motioned for tha waitress and ordered more.

"Me, Me, Me," Jah'ceer said, flapping his arms.

"Make that three orders, please." Ash loved their tenders too.

"Tae, I've been thinking."

"About?"

"Retiring from tha game, I have to be around for tha twins and I can't do that if I'm dead or in jail."

Hearing Roc say that brought a smile to my face; that's something I've been wanting him to do but felt he had to make that decision.

"Tae, I know that we have only been together for seven months, but it feels like years."

"Hmm, that's funny you say that because last night while we were in bed, I was thinking tha same thing."

"It feels like we have been in this relationship for many years."

"Roc, I can't speak for you, but I can see me wit you for tha rest of my life."

"Well, in that case, let's get married," I said, now holding a ring in my hand.

"Are you proposing to me?"

"Let me think about it."

"Boy you better stop playing."

"Then don't ask no stupid question that you already know the answer to."

"In that case, I'll gladly marry you."

"A'ight we can go to tha Justice of the Peace first thing in tha morning."

"I know you didn't just say Justice of Peace?"

"Sure did."

"Be serious Roc."

"I am we'll still have a big wedding too."

"Oh well, I guess we can do it like that."

After eating and playing video games, tha twins were exhausted.

"Come on, let's get them home so they can get a bath and go to bed."

"Uncle Roc me tired," Jah'ceer said wit sleepiness showing all over his face.

"I know we're going home now." Nah'ceer was already asleep and Tae's arms.

"WE STILL HUSTLE TIL THA SUN COMES UP CRACK A FORTY WHEN THA SUN GOES DOWN"

"Yo."

"I hollered at ya boy Fish."

"You know where to put tha change. Everything was straight?"

"Yeah, but I did have to remind him that he's a fish and I am a shark."

"Ha! Ha! Ha!"

"Sharky, you wild as shit."

"Nah, that nigga was talkin' all this he shouldn't be dealing wit no middleman shit. I wanted to say nigga you not even buying enough work to be dealing wit tha boss."

"Sharky, let me get tha twins ready for bed and I'll hit you up later."

"No problem."

"Sharky, make sure you leave ya phone on because I need to holla at you about some important shit."

"My phone always on Big Homie."

"Roc, Roc."

"A'ight, let me get off this phone before she has a fit."

"Damn, you already bathe them."

"Yeah and they in tha bed knocked out."

"So why you was calling my name all crazy like that?"

"Cause my car needs to be serviced," she said, dropping her robe to tha floor, exposing her nude body.

"You're in luck. I just got my mechanic license."

No more words were exchanged tha only sound that could be heard were tha soft moans of Tae and grunts from me.

"So, what's the deal?"

"Imma have to introduce you to tha plug cause in another few months, I will be done wit this shit."

"Why? Are you serious?"

"Yeah, I have to think about my nephews."

"I definitely respect that."

"Plus, I'm set, I have more than enough paper."

"I'll pick up where you leave off."

"Do you think you can handle it?"

"Can I handle it? Come on, I'm all tha way in now."

"I know that's why I've been letting you run tha show."

"Sort of like transitioning me, huh?"

"Exactly."

"I'm most definitely feeling that Big Homie."

"Sharky, let me make myself clear. If I didn't think you were ready or couldn't handle it, I would never put you in this position."

"Roc, tha same way I move now will be the same way I move once I'm the H.N.I.C. (Head Nigga In Charge)

"Have you been stacking ya money over tha past three years or bullshittin'?"

"I've got a little something saved up for a rainy day."

"Well, it's a rainy day, so how much do you got?"

"Damn, Big Homie you need some doe?"

"Nah, Imma match you and you can start from there."

I wasn't prepared for what I was about to hear. Sharky was only 17, so I only counted him for 50, no more than 60 grand.

"I got 350 grand."

"You can get 18 easy, so wit my match, that'll start you wit 36 birds."

"How much will I owe you?"

"What I put in plus 36 grand."

"That's all?"

"That's all and you can keep using my money to flip."

"Wow, it's a win-win for both of us."

"I would say so."

"I really appreciate this Big Homie."

"You've earned it, so be ready tomorrow morning by 8 o'clock."

Tha meeting wit tha plug went better than anticipated; he ended up fronting Sharky an additional 24 birds. I knew he was going to front him 10 because we had already talked about it, but he said he see something in him and that's why he hit him with the extra 14. Pablo knew if I was introducing him, not only did he have potential, but he could be trusted as well.

"Big Homie, I wasn't expecting him to front me wit no work."

"That's nothing; depending on how fast you move it, he'll hit you with 100."

"100?"

"Yeah, that's how he moves."

"Ya boy, Fish has been calling all morning."

"He's probably ready for you."

"I am not going to be able to get at him today because my old head had to handle something today."

"You haven't been meeting wit him?"

"Hell Nah, I'll be watching from a distance. I get a bad vibe of him."

I was really impressed wit Sharky.

I started doing tha math in my head. Big Homie always hits me with 20 at 22 apiece, which is 440 grand wholesale equals 500 grand, which nets me a 60 grand profit. So off the 60, once I pay Big Homie is 368 and Pablo is 528, I should have 654 grand for myself, probably more, since I'll break a few down for my foot soldiers. All I could see was tha dead presidents.

"Look, go ahead handle ya biz when my folk call I'll hit 'em wit ya digits so I can fade out."

"Big Homie, I want you to know I always have your back."

"That goes both ways."

The next few months were lovely for Sharky; he was seeing more money than PNC, and Pablo had upped his order to 50 birds.

"Money, Power, Respect is what they need in life."

"Yo, what up Big Homie?"

"Did Fish call you?"

"Yeah, but I sent him to voicemail."

"This nigga keep calling my phone."

"What he say?"

"I didn't answer." BEEP BEEP

"This him now, hold on."

"Hello."

"Damn, My Nigga I been calling you; all I need is 20 bricks of cocaine."

"Hold on, let me call my man."

"Hello."

"Yeah, I'm still here Big Homie."

"He said he needs 20 birds that nigga ain't never purchase more than one now all of a sudden he needs 20."

"I know, right."

"He working for them alphabet boys."

"We'll find out; hold on."

"Hello."

"Damn Nigga I thought you forgot about me."

"Nah, I had to make a call."

"Can you handle it?"

"When do you need 'em?"

"ASAP."

"No problem, he'll meet you tomorrow at noon."

"That's what's up."

"Fish."

"Yeah."

"He'll be in a blue Taurus."

"Ok, I'll holla after the deal is done."

"Sharky."

"Yeah."

"This is what's going down," I explained everything in full.

"Big Homie, you know if he's workin' he'll be swimming wit tha fish foreal."

"As he should, Death B-4 Dishonor always.

CHAPTER 8

"Why go through all this? If you don't trust him, then don't deal wit him."

"You're missing the whole principal Tae."

"Tell me tha principal then Roc."

"Trust, disloyalty, need I say more?"

"No. Just be careful Baby."

"They won't even know we're there. He wants 20 birds; that's what he's going to get."

"Why would you take that chance selling him anything if you think he might be workin'?"

"Tae, trust me on this."

"I do; I just want you to be safe."

BEEP BEEP.

"That's Sharky. I'll see you later tonight."

"Will you be home for dinner, or should I just put you a plate in tha microwave?"

"If I'm not going to be home in time to eat wit y'all, I'll call to let you know."

"Make sure you do that," she said, giving me a soft passionate kiss.

"Whoa, Whoa, keep that up and I won't make it nowhere."

"Hmm, would that be so bad?"

"Under other circumstances, I will put what I have to do on hold."

"But."

"But this needs my immediate attention, so like I said, I'll call you if I can't make it."

"I love you Roc."

"Ditto."

"Damn Big Homie, did I interrupt something?"

"Naw, I was just bustin' it up wit Tae."

"Did you find somebody to drive tha car?"

"Yeah, I'm bout to pick her up now."

"Oh, you got a broad?"

"Not just any broad this my ride or die chick; she trained to go Big Homie."

"I trust her because I trust you."

"She more thurl than most niggaz."

I stopped by Man's house to grab a quarter of sour diesel for the 2-hour ride we had to take. When we picked up Lassy, it was hard to believe everything Sharky had just told me about her.

"Big Homey, don't let her face and tha way she looks fool you."

To me, Lassy looked like she just stepped off a runway; she was nothing short of a dime piece.

"Hello Sharky and you must be Big Homey," she said wit her hand extended.

"Roc," I said as I took her hand and carefully shook it.

"Ha! Ha! Ha!"

"Did I miss something?"

"I'm not a china doll; I won't break."

"Sorry if I offended you."

"No sweat, so who needs to be killed?"

"Nobody as of now."

"Well, let's get this party started."

"Lassy, let me get ya heat."

"Hell no, I'm not parting wit my Baby."

"Listen, if it is a setup, I don't want you to get caught wit ya pants down."

"I understand that, but if it's something else, I don't wanna get caught wit out my panties on."

"We got ya back, Lassy, you have nothing to worry about, I promise."

"If you say so, I trust you."

Halfway there, Fish was blowing my phone up.

"What up Fish?"

"Where you at? You still coming?"

"I'm in route now."

"You in that blue Taurus?"

"Yeah."

"You by yaself?"

"Yeah."

"You bought 20, right?"

"Yeah, what tha fuck is all tha questions about? Damn nigga what you wired?"

"N-N-N-OO I ain't wired."

"I'll call you when I get close."

"We meeting at tha same spot I meet Sharky?"

"Yo, I think this nigga trying to line me up."

"I heard him askin' a million questions."

"He even stuttered when I asked him was he wired."

"Maybe we should just say fuck 'em and not deal wit him anymore."

"I need to know so I can handle it so he won't try to line nobody else up."

Once we were in position, I called Fish to let them know where to come.

"I am on my way."

"They change tha location."

"So what? He still going down."

"Are you guys going to wait for tha transaction to go down?"

"Hell no, we're just going to swarm tha car since we already know he has tha work. We should be good right here; we can see them, but they can't see us."

Three minutes later, all you could hear and see were tires screeching and Feds everywhere.

"Don't move! Put ya hands where we can see them!"

Agent Rayner walked to tha driver's side wit a big smile on his face, which quickly vanished when he saw Lassy sitting behind tha wheel.

"Where's Roc?"

"Who?"

"Play dumb if you want."

When she started smiling said, "You won't be laughing when you get a hundred years."

"For what? I haven't done anything wrong."

"Haven't done anything wrong. Let's start wit tha 20 birds you're carrying."

"I could be wrong, but I don't think it's a crime to sell 20 birds asshole!"

"You wanna be a wise ass; get out tha car."

They handcuffed her and proceeded to search tha car.

"May I ask what you are looking for?"

"Where are they?"

"Where's what?"

"Tha drugs, tha 20 birds?"

"Since you're not blind, I know you can see those 20 canaries in tha cage sitting in tha back."

"Ha! Ha! Ha!"

"Look at their faces."

"I know they pissed."

"I knew that nigga wasn't right Big Homey. That's why I always sent my old head to deal wit him."

"So he never seen ya face then, right?"

"Yup."

"Listen, I suggest you take these handcuffs off me."

"We're taking you to headquarters, where you're going to tell us everything you know about Roc."

"Who?"

"Roc, don't play dumb wit me."

"I don't know any Roc. All I know was I was paid 5 stacks to deliver these birds to some guy named Whale."

"You mean Fish?"

"Whale, Fish, What ever."

Agent Best looked at his partner and nodded.

"We're going to let you go for now."

"I need to meet wit Fish to give him these birds and get tha money he was suppose to have."

"I doubt you'll be doing that," Agent Rayner said, opening tha cage and letting tha birds go.

"I hope you have tha money for those?"

"You're lucky we're not locking you up."

"No, you're not locking me up because you have no reason to."

"Are you sure about that?"

"Positive."

"Put tha cuffs back on her."

"I wouldn't do that. I have three years of law under my belt and you would be violating my constitutional rights, but if you don't mind a lawsuit, be my guest," I said, holding my hands out, daring them to arrest me.

"You have one minute to get outta here."

"Listen, Agent Rayner, is it?"

"Yeah."

"What you're doing is considered harassment; matter fact, let me get your badge number so that I can let Mr. Ramsy know about this."

Tha look on his face said it all.

"That's right; my Uncle David will be hearing about this."

"T-T-T T-here's no need to take it there, especially since I was already on his shit list."

"Well, you have a nice ride back Ms. Ramsy."

Once I was back in tha car, I called Sharky.

"Yo."

"Hey you good?"

"Always, you know that."

"I'll meet you back at tha spot."

"Cool."

"Big Homey, you know what has to be done."

"Yeah, but we have to move swiftly since we know tha Feds are probably watching over him."

"Fish, what tha fuck was that?"

"How should I know?"

"You tipped him off?"

"No, I didn't, but thanks to you, he knows I tried to line him up."

"Fuck, we almost had him!"

"We still might; I think we can get him for conspiracy to sell."

"You think that will hold up in court?"

"We gonna find out you know how tha Federal court system does."

"A'ight, let's get tha warrant ready."

"What about him?" Agent Best asked, pointing to Fish.

"What about him?"

"Yeah, what about me?"

"Do you want to throw him in lock up?"

"Hold on; I did my end of tha deal."

"Nah, we'll put somebody on him just in case he thinks he's going to run before he testifies."

"Testify?"

"That's right."

"Y'all didn't say nothing about that. I'm not getting on no stand."

"You will get on the stand or go to jail; you make the choice!"

"I wonder if I could get away with killing an FBI agent," I thought to myself as I stood there pissed off.

CHAPTER 9

"FBI, nobody move, everybody down!"

"What tha hell is going on?"

"Give me a fuckin' reason," Agent Rayner said wit his pistol pointed at Roc's head.

"POW-POW POW-POW," tha twins said, not realizing tha seriousness of tha situation.

"Jah'ceer, Nah'ceer come over here," Tae said wit tears in her eyes.

"Taroc Smith, you have the right to remain silent; anything you say can...."

"Yeah yeah, I know my fuckin' rights," Roc said, cutting tha agent off. Rayner kept going til he was finished.

Now that we have that taken care of, you better pray they don't find so much as a crumb."

"Listen, Agent."

"Rayner."

"Yeah, what ever, I'm a legit biz-ness man who pays his taxes just as you do."

"Are you sure about that?"

"I'm pretty sure you've had one of Rocco's Steaks and if I'm not mistaken, my cleaning company has a contract with tha bureau."

Agent Rayner hated to admit it, but he loves Rocco Steaks in fact, he has at least two a week.

"All that sounds good, but it doesn't negate the fact that you've been selling drugs."

"Nah Man, you got me mixed up."

"Sir."

"Yes Agent."

"Can I speak to you for a sec?"

"Excuse me, don't go anywhere."

"Sir, all we found was this," he said, holding a half of a blunt.

"That's good, well, Mr. Smith, or would you prefer me to call you Roc?"

"Listen, if you're charging me wit something, do it; if not, take these fuckin' cuffs off me now!"

"Sure, put him in tha car."

"What are you charging him wit?"

"Possession of marijuana, conspiracy to sell 20 kilos."

As soon as he said that, I knew this was all Fish's work, but since they had nothing, I wasn't tha least bit worried.

"That's Bullshit," Tae said, getting into his face.

"Agent Bell cuff her."

"For what? She hasn't done shit, you Fuckin' Cracker."

"Assault of a Federal Agent and somebody call Social Services for these kids."

"Nooooo!" Tae screamed, causing tha boys to cry.

"Agent Best, let them ride wit you."

While they were putting me in tha car, I spotted Sharky standing among the other spectators. We nodded because no words needed to be spoken. By tha time we reached our destination, my lawyer was already waiting on us.

Roc, are you a'ight?"

"Yeah, I'm cool, but I need you to see what's up wit Tae and tha twins first.

"No problem, just don't say anything wit out me present."

"You know me better than that." As soon as they put me in their interview room, Agent Rayner walks in wit tha biggest smile on his face.

"So Roc, Rocky, Rocco what ever it is they call you, do you have anything you want to see for yourself?"

"No, he does not."

"Well, Well, Well, if it isn't Piranha Pete."

"In tha flesh."

"Not even you will be able to get ol' boy outta this."

"What's he being charged wit?"

"Possession of weed and conspiracy to sell 20 kilos of cocaine."

"Ha! Ha! Ha! Are you serious?"

"As a heart attack. He'll go in front of tha judge first thing in tha morning, until then he'll be spending tha night in our hold area."

"Fuck that, Pete I need bail."

You can forget about that you'll be in tha detention center til trial."

"You'd like that wouldn't you?"

"Well, I'll let you talk to ya lawyer now, but before I go, just remember there are bigger fish in tha sea."

He turned to walk away, "Agent Rayner."

"Yeah," he said all happy as if I was about to tell him something important.

"Fuck you!"

He turned blood red and slammed the door shut, almost breaking tha glass.

"What do you think Pete?"

"I really won't know till I look over the discovery."

"What about Tae and tha boys?"

"I'm afraid they booked her on assault which I'll beat hands down, but Social Services took tha boys."

"Fuck!"

"Calm down."

"How tha hell can I calm down when them Crackers got my nephews Pete?"

"I am on my way to see what I can do now."

Tha next morning, when they came for me, I was more than ready to go. When I got into tha courtroom, Tae was seated next to Sharky. I could tell she had been crying all night because her eyes were puffy as well as red.

"Your Honor, case number 41562009. Mr. Smith, you're being charged wit possession of marijuana and conspiracy to sell 20 kilos of cocaine. How do you wish to plead?"

"Not guilty, Your Honor."

"Mr. Anderson, what's bail on this matter?"

"Your Honor, we request that bail be denied."

"Objection, Your Honor!"

"Your Honor, the defendant has a capias history and would be a flight risk."

"Excuse me, Your Honor, all these things Mr. Anderson are talking about is juvenile; my client has a clean adult record."

"Mr. Brown, that may be true, but it's still a fact that he skips bail, so I have no choice but to deny bail."

"That's Bullshit!" Roc shouted.

"Mr. Smith, I'd advise you to settle down."

"Why should I y'all on some straight bullshit!"

"I'm holding you in contempt."

"Fuck that contempt!"

"Mr. Smith, I'm goin to make sure I'm tha judge on this case."

"Why so you can rail road me?"

"So that I can see justice served."

"I bet."

"Bailiff, take him away." I felt bad seeing Tae cry like that.

"Pete, you need to make sure that bitch isn't my judge!"

"I'm already on it."

"Let Tae know I'm a call her first chance I get."

Tha next few months were really stressful. Social Services weren't trying to give tha boys back until this case was resolved. They would not even let Tae visit. Most of our conversations always ended tha same wit Tae crying.

"Smith, your attorney is here to see you."

"About fuckin' time! Pete, tell me something good."

"I have good and bad news; which do you want first?"

"The good, of course."

"I got you a new judge."

"That's what I'm talkin' about; I knew you would."

"Ready for tha bad news?"

"Give it to me."

"They assigned her husband to your case."

"Hell Nah, ain't that a conflict of interest?"

"I argued that, but they told us to be lucky they did that for us."

"This shit is un fucking believable."

"Trail starts in three days."

"Make sure you get my black Gucci suit from Tae."

"I already got it."

"My man."

Later that evening, after talking to Tae, I went to my room to relax.

(KNOCK KNOCK.)

"House, what's up Homey?"

"Can I come in?"

"Always."

I met House when I first got here; we hit it off from tha door.

"I just bucked up on some good green. Do you want to blow it with me?"

"Sure, why not? I need to ease my mind for tomorrow."

"Man, you should be a'ight I heard about ya lawyer Piranha Pete they say he that nigga."

"Yeah, he make it do what it do; he's never let me down yet."

"Neither did my lawyer, but some Crackers had it out for a Nigga."

"You'll get 'em on appeal."

"I hope so, but I'm not counting on it. I'll probably do 10 of this 15."

"I'm hoping to get moved out in tha next couple weeks, especially after you roll."

"If I do beat this, Imma hold you down."

"That's what up cause I'm not going to front between my kids and my mom my doe gonna be gone in 5 to 6 years."

"Don't worry; I got you my money long like tha Atlantic Ocean."

"I'm out; go head get some rest for tomorrow."

As soon as I closed my eyes, I was out like a light.

"Smith, Smith."

"Yo."

"This ya wake-up call for court."

"I'm up."

"I'll be back to get you in 25 minutes."

"A'ight."

Tha ride to tha courthouse was quick and quiet. By tha time I got up to court, it was 10 o'clock. After the Federal prosecutor gave his opening argument, it was Pete's turn. I couldn't help but smile to myself after hearing his opening argument. All in all, I believe the first day was a win for us. I just hoped tha rest of tha trial would be tha same. I was so exhausted by tha time I got back to tha jail.

"How did it go Big Homey?"

I was so tired I didn't feel like talking, so I just gave House tha thumbs up.

"A'ight, get ya rest. I'll get at you later."

Little did I know when I opened my eyes, it would be time to go back to court. The next few days, I could tell that tha judge was being bias; he was overruling all our objections but sustaining theirs. The jury kept coming back deadlock and the judge just kept sending them back.

"I need to holla at tha Judge. I'll be back."

(KNOCK KNOCK)

"Come in."

"Your Honor."

"Mr. Brown, what can I do for you?"

"Your Honor, I think you're forcing tha jury into a guilty verdict."

"How do you figure that Mr. Brown?"

"Because you keep making them go back in instead of declaring a mistrial."

"No, Mr. Brown, I'm trying to help them make tha right decision."

"Tha right decision would be to declare a mistrial."

His next statement threw me off.

"Your client is going to jail for a long time where he'll be able to reflect about disrespecting my wife."

"So you've made this case personal against my client?"

"You damn right I have!"

"I'm putting in a request to have you removed for conflict of interest."

"Mr. Brown, I'm sorry, but I'm totally bias," he said wit a smile.

"Sharky, why doesn't the judge just declare a mistrial?"

"Because that Cracker is trying to force them into a guilty verdict."

"How?"

"Tha jury is going to get tired and just say guilty."

"I doubt it."

"Well, Pete should be able to beat them on appeal."

"Wit out a doubt."

"Pete, I already know they gonna find me guilty."

"Roc, I just was in wit tha judge and I gotta be honest, he's on some bullshit."

"I know Pete, I know."

"He told me that he's gonna make sure you go to jail for disrespecting his wife."

"I'm about to file a motion to have him removed."

"No."

"Huh?"

"We can use that as one of our grounds on appeal."

"Yeah, you're right."

"Mr. Brown, tha jury is in."

"You ready?"

"Yeah, let's get this over wit so we can start my appeal."

I looked at Sharky, who just shook his head.

"Has tha jury reached a verdict?"

"We have Your Honor."

The Bailiff took tha judge tha paper as soon as he read it a smile crept across his face.

"On tha charge of possession of marijuana, how do you find tha defendant?"

"Not guilty."

"On tha charge of conspiracy to sell 20 kilograms of cocaine, how do you find tha defendant?"

"Guilty."

"Noooooo, Nooooo, that's not right!" Tae yelled.

"Order in tha court, order in tha court!" tha judge screamed while banging his gavel.

"Mr. Smith, I'll set sentencing for two weeks."

"Yeah What ever."

Even though I had prepared myself for this, it still felt like a truck hit me head-on.

"Mr. Smith, do you understand that you face up to a minimal of 10 years but a maximum of twenty?"

"Yeah and I also understand that I was railroaded by you."

"Sentencing in one week, bailiff take him away."

"Your Honor, you said two weeks tha first time."

"Did I? Well, I changed my mind."

When I got back to tha prison, I didn't feel like being bothered; not even by House.

"Big Homey, I had that same look when I got found guilty, so I'm gonna give you your space. Holla at me when you feel like talkin'."

That's why I fuck wit House; he knows when to fall back. For tha next couple days, I stayed in my room, only coming out to shower and eat.

"Smith mail call!" one of tha officers yelled out.

All tha other inmates were in tha Day Room waiting to see if their names would be called. Roberts, Jackson, Snell, Pickney, Smith. As soon as he called my name House said, "I knew most of that was for you."

Tae always sends me at least three letters or cards every day, but today, she sent me some pictures. When I pulled them out, I couldn't put them back fast enough.

"Ha! Ha! Ha! Big Homey you should've seen tha look on ya face."

"She didn't tell me she was sending no flicks like these."

"Go on back to ya room, just don't hurt yaself."

"House, you a funny dude."

"We gotta keep our spirits up some kinda way in this place."

"I definitely feel you on that."

I had to look at tha pictures before I read tha letter that was in tha envelope.

To tha Love of My Life,

Hey, you, I know that you're not in a good place right now and neither am I that's why I try to keep you wit letters, pictures as well as cards. Baby, I'm not going to lie. I cry myself to sleep every night; between you and the twins not being here, I don't know what I'm going to do. No matter how much time that judge gives you, I'm not going anywhere and I will be faithful. I promise you that.

Love your wifey, Tae

After reading Tae's letter, I had more respect for her.

"Big Homey, you good?"

"Yeah, come on in House."

"Check these Flicks out Tammy sent."

"She really loves you."

"For now, anyway; once this shit start kickin' in she gon' bounce that's why I keep a few of them on tha team."

"I just read wifey's letter; she said she gon' ride, but Imma be a man and let her go."

"Damn, Big Homey you better than me."

"She shouldn't have to put her life on hold because of me; I'm not selfish."

"I hear you, but judging by tha way you talk about her, she ain't gonna be hearing that."

"She ain't got a choice."

"Aye Man, don't say I didn't tell you."

"House, don't get me wrong, I love her to death, but I love her enough to let her be free."

"What if that's not what she wants?"

"I don't know House; I really don't know."

"You might wanna think about that."

When I walked in tha courthouse, I wasn't surprised to see Tae even though I told her not to come.

"All rise, tha Honorable Judge Frankowski presiding."

I didn't bother to stand since I already knew what he was about to do to me.

"Mr. Smith is there something wrong wit your legs?" I didn't answer him which really pissed him off.

"Hmm well let's get this over wit I have a lunch date wit my lovely wife."

"Ha! Ha! Ha!"

"Something funny Mr. Smith?"

"Yeah you."

"Let's see if you find this funny. On tha charge of conspiracy to sell 20 kilograms of cocaine, I hereby sentence you to 20 years."

"NOOOOO, NOOOOO, NOOOOO!" Tae screamed out, not letting him finish.

As soon as she stood up, she fainted. It broke my heart to see her like that, but I kept my eyes glued on tha judge.

"As I was saying before, we were rudely interrupted."

"We heard what you said."

"In that case, Bailiff, please take tha prisoner away he said wit a smirk.

"Roc Baby, I love you and I'll be here for you."

"Dumb Bitch," tha judge thought to himself.

Even though I was mad as hell, I was more hurt seeing Tae in so much pain. By tha time I got back to my cell, I had made my mind up to let Tae go so she could live her life. That night I had so much on my mind I didn't get a wink of sleep. I was wondering what was going to happen to tha boys since I had 20 years, even though I'm sure to give it back on appeal, but that is going to take at least five years.

"Pete, is there anything you can do about getting me custody of tha boys?"

"I have to be honest; it's not looking good."

"Why is that Pete?"

"Roc is their legal guardian, but since he's incarcerated, tha state has guardianship over them. If you two were married, you'd probably have a better shot."

"I might be able to make that happen."

"You need to get back to me A.S.A.P."

"I'll call you after my visit wit Rock tomorrow."

"A'ight and tell him all tha paperwork on my end is done."

"All visitors, please step through tha metal detector put all objects inside tha tray."

I walked into tha Visiting Room to find Roc already seated. He stood to hug me and I just broke down in his arms.

"Oh Baby, I miss you so much."

We sat down and for tha first time in my life, I realized I loved another woman besides my mom.

"What's wrong? Why are you staring at me like that?"

"Tae, I love you."

"I love you too."

"But I have to let you go."

"What!" she said loudly, causing everybody to look at us.

"I said."

"No, I heard what you said, but you don't get to make that choice."

"I don't want you to put your life on hold for me."

"Roc, I'm doing this because I love you, not because I have to. Listen Roc, we need to get married if we want to have any chance to get tha twins back."

"Is that what Pete said?"

"Yes, he said it's not a sure thing, but it may help." I had no choice if it was going to give us a shot at getting my nephews.

"How soon can we do it?"

"Tomorrow, I already talk to tha prison."

"Well, tomorrow it is then."

"I have to call Pete as soon as I leave here."

Tha next day me and Roc got married in tha prison chapel.

"We're now married, so hopefully Monday, I'll be able to get custody of tha twins."

"Don't we get a conjugal visit now?"

"I'm afraid not; it has to be approved by tha warden first."

That night I couldn't stop looking at my ring.

Damn I'm really married. I would have love to do it under different circumstances and in a real church, but some things are beyond our control.

"So, how does it feel to be married Big Homey?"

"Weird."

"I could be wrong but wasn't it me who said that she wasn't going anywhere?"

"We just tied tha knot so we could have a better chance to get my nephews back."

"That just sped up tha process up."

"What ever Nigga."

"Aye House, you and Roc what to lose some of that good money y'all got at tha spades table?"

House looked at me to see if I wanted to play. I looked at my watch, then let him know I would play till 8 o'clock.

"That's good time; I have to call my Shorty too."

"A'ight, Redz we'll take some of that money off your hands."

CHAPTER 10

I couldn't believe that judge denied me custody of tha twins even though tha bogus assault charge was thrown out.

"Pete, can we appeal that decision?"

"Already on it."

"These Crackers make me sick; can I at least get visitation?"

"That shouldn't be a problem."

"Pete."

"Yes."

"Thanks for everything you're doing for Roc and tha boys."

"Roc is not only my client; he's also my friend."

"I have to get to work, so please keep me updated."

"I will."

I wasn't in tha mood to deal wit work, so I called off then headed home for some much, much needed rest.

"Mr. Smith, you're free to go and I do apologize for tha actions of my colleague."

"Oh My God, Oh My God," I screamed.

I couldn't believe that after six years, they were finally letting Roc out. I ran into his arms and squeezed him with all my might. It felt so good to hold him again, knowing this time I wouldn't have to say goodbye. I opened my eyes to see that I was having another dream.

"Damn," I yelled, letting go of tha pillow that I was holding.

My dream felt so real I had been holding my pillow so tight I thought it was my Roc. I was so lonely and it had only been six months since Roc had been locked up. I heard my phone ringing, so I ran to tha living room to answer it.

"Hello."

"This is A.F.D.C wit a collect call from Roc to accept this call dial 0, to refuse this press 5 then hang up, to block future calls press 77."

"Thank you."

"Hey Baby."

"Hey."

"I got some bad news."

"I already know; Pete came to see me; hopefully, we can win on appeal."

"I hope so; I'm so stressed out."

"What are you doing?"

"I just got up."

"You're not at work?"

"No, I didn't feel like dealing wit them after court, so I called off."

"Baby, don't let this shit stress you out. I'm doing enough of that for tha both of us."

"I know; I just can't help it."

"They'll probably ship me to another jail soon."

"I hope it's not far away."

"I got Pete working on that for me."

"Roc."

"Yeah."

"No matter where they send you, I'll be to visit."

"Tae, you don't have to and if you want, we can get this marriage annulled."

"What is that what you want?"

"I don't want to hold you hostage or stop you from being happy."

"You're not holding me hostage, but if you want to end this marriage, then you will stop me from being happy. So, since you said you want me to be happy, then we should stay married, case closed. Did you get tha money I left on your books?"

"Yeah."

You have one minute remaining on this call.

"Tae, I have more than enough money on my books, so you don't have to put any more on there till I tell you I need more."

"Ok, if you say so, I love you."

"I love you." (CLICK)

Tha phone hung up before he could get the last word out. Since he didn't say he was calling back, I decided to jump in tha shower. I couldn't control my emotions and tha flood gates came pouring open. I set down in tha tub, balled up and let the water beat down on my body as I cried for my Roc.

"You a'ight Big Homey?"

"I don't know House."

"Remember do tha time, don't let tha time do you."

Tha time ain't shit, even if I have to do all of it; I'm more worried about wifey."

"If she's anything like you say, then you have absolutely nothing to worry about."

"Make no mistake, her cheating or doing her is the last thing I'm worried about."

"I know that's right because if the shoe was on the other foot, you'd be damn sure doing you."

"Yeah, you're probably right."

"Probably."

"Yeah probably Nigga."

"Ha! Ha! You never like to tell me I'm right. It's your turn to cook. I could go for another one of those buna's."

"I was hoping you would make one of those good wraps."

"Nah."

"Smith, Anderson."

"Hey, what's up Cooley?"

"You're both being transferred tomorrow."

"Are you sure?"

"Yeah, I just seen tha list."

"Fuck."

"Don't worry; you're both being transferred to tha federal jail here in Atlanta."

"Oh shit, that's what's up," House said, dapping me.

"I better call Tae and let her know."

CHAPTER 11

Ten years later and I was still trying to appeal my case. Pete found out that tha higher uppers were in cahoots wit tha other judges.

"Damn, Big Homey I would be going home today if I didn't get tha additional two years for assault."

"I told you that that nigga was going to tell."

"I know, but I couldn't let him get away with that shit."

"House, we've been boys for 10 ½ years now and if nothing else, you should know I'm not going to steer you wrong."

"True dat true dat."

"Tae is bringing my nephew up to see me today."

"That's what's up; you still haven't found out where your other nephew is yet?"

"No, but I'm not giving up."

"Aunty Tae, are we going to see Uncle Roc today?"

"Yes Jah'ceer. I haven't seen him in a while, so I'm glad I get to see him."

"Aunty Tae, when is he coming home?"

"Soon, Jah'ceer soon."

"Aunty Tae, you been saying that for tha past five years."

"There's a process he has to go through."

"My friend's dad got locked up and they gave him 10 years, but he told on his boy and they let him out. Why don't Uncle Roc just tell on one of his friends?"

"Jah'ceer, look at me," I said wit a stern voice so that he knew what I was about to say was serious. What your friends dad did is called snitching."

"Aunty Tae, he told us that it was called being smart."

"He lied, and if you ever put yourself in a situation like that, you better never ever tell. Do you understand me?"

"Yes."

"No man should ever tell on another man for his mistakes."

"My friend always tells on me."

"Because it's in his bloodline and he's not really your friend."

I thought about what my Aunty Tae was saying and it made a lot of sense, so I made up my mind right then that I would never snitch.

We were the first ones inside the visiting room. As soon as Jah'ceer saw Roc, he jumped up and ran to him.

"Uncle Roc."

"What up Little Man?"

"Nothing chilling."

"Are you still playing ball?"

"Sometimes."

"All that talent you got and you wasting it."

"How do you know I got skills?"

"Well, for one, you told me and two, it's in your blood; me and you pop handled that peel like Pistol Pete and Bob Cousy."

"Who?"

"They were before your time, but let me give you some names. You know LeBron and Kobe?"

"My dad don't play no ball; he plays golf."

"That Mafucka ain't ya dad!"

"Roc!" Tae yelled.

"My bag."

"He is my dad, he told me and mom said it too."

Now it was Tae's time to snap, "That Bitch is not ya mom!"

Jah'ceer looked at both of us puzzled.

"It's time that somebody told you tha truth. I was under tha assumption that you knew, but it's painfully obvious that you have no knowledge, so let me break it down for you."

By tha time I finished, Jah'ceer was in tears.

"I'm sorry, but you need to know tha truth since those people have lied to you for tha past 10 years."

"Ten years."

"I knew it was something I didn't like about him." We both looked at him.

"What?"

"What do you mean?"

"I love him because I thought he was my pop, but it's just something about him that I can't explain."

"He's not putting his hands on you, is he?"

When he didn't answer, I knew the answer.

"Tae, I need you to have Pete come see me today, not tomorrow to fuckin' day!" Ceer asked if it was Ok if he asked us a question.

"Yes."

"Why did those men kill my baby brother?"

"What?"

"Jah'ceer, I've never said anything because I thought you knew but just never wanted to talk about it."

"I only knew what they told me; we even visit his grave every year on his birthday." I was pissed off, to say tha least.

"Jah'ceer, you have a twin brother named Nah'ceer. I had custody of both of you, but when I got railroaded tha state took y'all. Eventually, you both got adopted. You were in Atlanta, your brother we don't know; my lawyers been trying to find him for the past 10 years." I could see tha rage in his eyes.

"Aunty Tae, I don't want to go back there." Tae looked at me to say something.

"Ceer, you have to until we can get a judge to give custody to Tae."

"A'ight, but if it's not soon, I'm up outta their word on my pops and moms." I could see Zeke all over again.

"Big Homey, how was tha visit?"

I explained to House what went on.

"What kind of people would lie to a child?"

"I don't know, but he's going to pay."

"You going to chow they got cheesesteaks tonight?"

"I wasn't, but since they got that on the menu, I am."

On the way to tha chow hall, we ran into this loudmouth nigga named Pete who had stories for days. "House there go to ya boy Pete."

"My boy, huh?"

"He always bustin' it up wit you."

"More like telling me one of his body stories. He's a dumb Mafucka he'll learn when he's on death row or dead."

"Aye yo House what it do?"

"Same shit, different year."

"Man, I don't know how tha two of you pulled that dime."

"Not like we had a choice."

"Yeah, true."

"Y'all don't mind if I walk to tha hall with y'all do y'all?"

"Suit yourself."

"I see you had a VI today," I said, pointing at his Kevin Durrant's."

"Yeah my man Robby hit me off."

"Robby wit tha mole on his face?"

"Yeah, you know him?"

"Not really," I said, lying.

"He used to get money before he started getting high."

"That's where I met him at a rehab center; I use to fuck wit them E-pills really heavy. I could tell y'all a few stories about some capers we did together."

"Hit us wit a few."

House looked at me because I normally wouldn't want to hear his stories. I would never want to be called in to testify. I was trying to see if they pulled any capers or any of our spots. After two stories, I was about to step off when he said a name that caught my attention.

"Then there was this one time when we did this one job wit his ex. I think her name was Ashmere no, no, it was Ashley. Yeah, that was one of the fiesty ass bitch. Her nigga he was holding a little bread and jewels. I did feel sorry for them having to lose their money and their life."

"At that point, all I could see was Pete dead, but I had to do it smartly."

"House, I'm bout to go back to tha Tier."

"Me too, Pete, we'll get up wit you later."

"I'll see y'all later. I'm about to head to tha gym they got that game B-Tier versus D-Tier."

"Ain't them Niggaz beefing?"

"Yeah, but they hoopin' for that cheddar."

"You know they gon' to get to rumbling."

"Hey, long as nobody don't swing my way."

"A'ight we'll holla at you."

"House, I'm going to tha game."

"Huh?"

"I'm going to tha game."

"You must got some doe on it?"

I didn't answer I just went to tha room to get my wack.

"What up Big Homey? Is everything good?"

"That nigga killed my brother."

"Who?"

"Pete."

"You lost me."

"Ashley is my nephew's mom."

"Oh shit, it didn't even register."

"Probably cause you wasn't paying attention."

"I rarely do when he starts to babble."

"I'm wit you," he said, grabbing his wack also.

"I don't want you to get involved."

"Yeah right, Nigga talk that shit to somebody else. I'm wit you, so let's go."

Tha game was already underway when we got there.

"House, Big Homey over here."

Just seeing him made my blood boil. One of tha partners got fouled and didn't like it. Wit in seconds, it was an all-out rumble.

"Let's get outta here!" Pete yelled.

I didn't say anything; I just pulled out my wack and started hitting him up.

"AAAAHH, AAAAHH!"

I put my hand over his mouth and continued to poke him up. House joined in. When we were sure he was done, we slipped outta there as if nothing ever happened.

"Let me get that wack House."

"I got 'em; you just get rid of that shirt."

"A'ight, I'll meet you back at tha hut."

Since I was one of tha maintenance men, I had access to tha basement, where I threw my shirt inside tha inferno. I strolled into the Day Room like everything was cool, which it was.

"Bout time you got up, we trying to win some of that commissary you got."

"You should be tired of losing that money by now."

"My shit like a rainbow, I'm spending 88 money."

"I heard that we might as well play for pay-to's."

"If you think you can handle it."

"Tunk or Spades?"

"Spades, hundred a man, another hundred a set."

"Bet."

"Two sets is game, Boston any time during the game triple, 10 from the door double and game."

"I know all tha rules. Are you going to play or talk?"

CHAPTER 12

"I hate both of you, y'all ain't Shit but liars!"

"Jah'ceer, you better watch ya damn mouth. Matter fact, go to ya room."

"Gladly," I said stompin' up tha stairs.

"I told you it was a bad ideal to let him go wit that girl."

"Sandy, we had no choice tha judge gave her tha right to keep him every other weekend."

I had a feeling they would be making me go to bed hungry, so I went into tha closet and pulled out tha chicken I had gotton from Ms. Lee's earlier. Little did they know this would be my last night in this house.

"Hello."

"What kind of bullshit you been filling my son's head wit?"

"It wasn't bullshit; it was tha truth he need and had tha right to know since it's quite obvious tha two of you weren't going to tell him!"

"You don't have to worry about seeing him anymore once tha judge finds out that you've been taking him to see that bum in jail."

"Bitch you better watch ya mouth before I drive over there and kick ya stuck up ass!"

"Come try it; I'll have ya ass locked up faster than you can say my name, you Fuckin Hood Rat!"

"You'll be hearing from my lawyer in tha morning so hood rat that Bitch."

"No, she didn't just hang up on me."

I couldn't help but smile when my Aunty Tae told her off. I slid under tha covers, acting like I was sleep. Once Sandy looked in, I knew neither one of them would be back until tomorrow, where all they would find is my note that I was leaving them.

"Jah'ceer, Jah'ceer, I know he hears me calling him."

"Just go wake him up; he's probably too tired to get up."

I threw my robe on, then walked to his room.

"Jah'ceer, Jah'ceer, I'm not going to call you again," I said, snatching the covers off his bed only to find a pile of clothes wit a letter attached to them.

"Ed, Ed, come quickly Jah'ceer's gone!"

"Gone? What do you mean gone?"

"He left this," I said, handing him tha letter.

Don't try to find me. I'm not over my Aunty Tae's because I know that's the first place you assholes will look. Oh yeah, fuck you and fuck off!

Ceer.

"I'm going to break my foot off in his butt. Who does he think he is talking to us like that?"

"I don't know but hand me tha telephone."

"Who are you calling tha police?"

"Not yet, I'm calling that aunt of his."

I had to call four times before she finally answered.

My phone was ringing nonstop, so I turned tha shower off. It was only 8 o'clock so I knew it couldn't be Roc.

"Hello," I said wit out looking at tha caller ID.

"Well it's about time."

"Excuse me."

"Could you tell Jah'ceer we're on our way to get him?"

"Jah'ceer?"

"Yeah, I know he came over there."

"Jah'ceer is not here."

"Listen, I'm not in tha mood to play games right now."

"No, you listen, where is my nephew?" I could hear Sandy in the background.

"Ed, tell that ghetto bitch to stop playing games, or we're sending tha police."

"Ed, you better put ya bitch in check."

"You're tha only bitch!"

"You don't have to call tha police because I am," I said, disconnecting tha call.

I have never been disrespected by a man like that; if Roc was home, he would never talk to me like that. I decided to call Pete first.

"Hello."

"Hey Pete."

"Hey Tae."

"I have a situation that needs to be dealt wit ASAP."

"What's going on?" I explain tha situation to him.

"That's good."

"How?"

"Remember I told you that tha judge was considering you for custody?"

"Yeah."

"Well, if this along wit Jah'ceer's testimony doesn't do it, then I don't know what will. I left you a message about our court date; did you get it?"

"No, when did you leave it?"

"A half-hour ago."

"I was in tha shower and when I got out, Ed was blowing my phone up."

"Has Jah'ceer tried to call you?"

"No, but I'm going to call him as soon as we hang up."

"Call me and keep me updated."

"Ok." No soon as I hung up, my phone started to ring again.

"Hello."

"Aunty Tae."

"Boy, where are you at and why didn't you come here?"

"I'm around tha corner."

"I'm coming to get you."

"No, just unlock tha back door."

"Ceer, you do not have to come through tha back door."

"I don't know if they're watching your house or not."

"It doesn't matter if they are or not."

"Here I come Aunty Tae."

I was waiting in tha door by tha time he came.

"How long have you been out in those streets?"

"Since four this morning."

"I know you hungry?"

"Not really; I had a bag of chips and a quarter hug."

"Boy, that's nothing to eat. I'll make you some breakfast."

"Aunty Tae, don't you have to be at work?"

"I took off; let me find out you're trying to get rid of me."

"No, I just didn't want you to be late because of me."

"Ceer you come first always, know that. For somebody that wasn't hungry, you sure did dog that food."

"Sandy can't cook; all her foods always taste burnt."

"Ha! Ha! Ha! Boy you crazy. So do you wanna tell me what happened?"

"It started because I asked them why they lied to me. All they could do was asked me if I was going to believe you and Uncle Roc."

"Imma end up busting that bitches ass."

"Aunty Tae, I'm not going back there."

"You don't have to; what do you say we go do some shopping?"

"You know I'm down wit that." We were shopping, buying everything that wasn't nailed down, when my phone went off.

"Here it's your Uncle Roc." I had to wait for the automatic lady to finish her speech so I could push zero and talk.

"Hey Babe."

"Whoa miss me wit tha babe thing Unc."

"Jah'ceer."

"Yeah."

"What are you doing wit Tae you're suppose to be in school."

"It's a long story."

"I got plenty of time, talk."

I hit him with tha short version of it.

"Put your aunt on tha phone." I could tell that he was pissed off.

"Hello."

"I don't want him to be going back over there, so you tell Pete I don't care what he has to do, just get it done!"

"He's already 10 steps ahead of us."

"How's that?"

"I have a court date in two weeks for custody."

"In tha meantime, I don't want him staying there wit that punk and his bitch of a wife. Is that understood?"

"First, I'm not any of your workers. I'm ya wife, so don't talk to me like that; is that understood?"

"My fault. I'm just upset."

"I know and so am I."

"You may need to get Pete to draw something up just in case they try to get tha police involved."

"Already on it."

"What are y'all doing now?"

"Shopping, he needed a wardrobe update."

"The phone about to hang up. I'll call you later. I'm bout to go to the gym and shoot around for a little while.

"A'ight, I love you."

"I love you too."

I hereby award sole custody to Natae Smith.

"Yeeeeeeeees!" Jah'ceer screamed out.

Ed and Sandy looked pissed, probably because they knew they wouldn't be getting no more money for Ceer. Once outside, Sandy tried to speak to Ceer, but he just ignored her. She looked at me and mumbled Bitch, wit out thinking, I punched her in tha mouth, knocking her to tha ground. Ed acted like he wanted to hit me.

"I wish you would," Pete said, stepping up in my defense.

"Thanks Pete."

"No problem, call me if you need anything."

"Will do."

"This is my song right here; turn it up Aunty."

"Would've been right for you. I just needed time to do what I had to do. Caught in tha life, I just can't let it go. Whether it's right, I may never know Aston Martin Music."

"Look at you over there bumpin'."

"I can party."

"So could ya mom." Ceer got quiet.

"Aunty, are we ever gonna find my brother?"

"I hope so; I promised ya mom I would look after tha two of you. What do you want to do for your birthday next weekend?" He looked at me like I just asked him tha dumbest question.

"Come on Aunty."

"Come on what?"

"You know I want to do some more shopping."

"I don't think they'll have any new stuff."

"Well, I just wanna see Uncle Roc."

Tha look on his face just broke my heart; that's when I decided to do something big for him.

"A'ight, I'll call and make tha proper reservations."

"Damn Babe, I can't believe he'll be 15 next week."

"I know, right. I've been in this hell hole for 13 years, shit I don't need no appeal; I max out in seven years. Actually, two, since only 15 was mandatory. I didn't think about that; my good time will knock the last nickel off."

"We'll be to see you next Friday."

"That's what's up. I told Pete to try harder to locate Nah'ceer."

"I've been all on Facebook trying to find him."

"I got a letter and some flicks from House today."

"Oh yeah, how's he doing?"

"He said he's trying to chill, but it's hard out there."

"Why don't you give him my number and I can put him in one of tha shops."

"Damn, I didn't think about that."

"That's why I'm here."

True dat you definitely been holding me down that's what a wife is suppose to do hold her husband down and keep tha Punanny tight. Why are you smiling?"

"How do you know I'm smiling?"

"Oh, so you're not?"

"Yeah, but."

"That's what I thought."

"Tae."

"Yes."

"I love you."

"I know you do and I love you too."

"I know you're proving that in more ways than one."

CHAPTER 13

"Nah'ceer Shorty wanna holla at you."

"Tell her to take a number like the rest of them."

"Nigga you crazy Shorty a dime all day."

"Man, I'm trying to get at a dollar. I don't got time to be dealing wit no stuck-up broads."

"Um, excuse me, but I'm far from stuck up." I had to turn around to see who was talkin'.

"Damn, this bitch is bad," I thought to myself.

"So, what's tha deal Ma?"

"Heaven."

"Excuse me."

"Heaven is my name."

"My fault Heaven."

"Even though you're sexy as hell, I'm not trying to get at you but wit you."

"I'm not following you."

"I'm trying to get at this paper."

"What that got to do with me?"

"I've been peeping you for a few weeks now and you have a lot of potential. You just don't have tha resources."

"And you do?"

"Yup."

"Then what do you need me for?"

"He's my uncle, so he won't sell me nothing, that's where you come in."

"I'm still listening."

"We can put our money together and grab something nice."

"How you know I got money?"

"You not out here 24.7 for nothing."

"Heaven, if you don't mind me askin' how much money do you have?"

"Enough."

"Truth be told, I only grab 4 ½ off my peeps."

"If tha work was better, you'd grab more."

"My work is fine."

"Is that why you give up so much?"

Before I could even answer, she said, "I've sent somebody over to buy some of your stuff."

"So you get high?"

"Hell no, tha person I sent tasted it."

"How much does ya cuz charge?"

"22,000 for tha whole pie."

"So we gone split tha cost of 2 ½?"

"Whoa, I don't have that much money; I thought we could split tha cost of one."

"We can do that, but I want another one."

"Let me call him to set it up."

"Use my phone."

"Got my own," she said, pulling it out.

"Hello."

"Who's this?"

"It's Heaven, Uncle Ross."

"Oh Hey, what's up? Is everything a'ight?"

"My peoples need two pies."

"Ya people who?"

"Nah'ceer."

"I don't know him."

"He's on tha up and up."

"You sure?"

"Positive, I've never stirred you wrong before, have I?"

"No, you haven't."

"Ok then."

"When is he trying to holla?"

"When ever is best for you."

"A'ight, meet me at my spot in an hour."

"A'ight." (CLICK)

"What he say?"

"We gotta meet him in an hour."

"I need you to go pick my money up; I'll be back in a few minutes."

"Me too, so I'll meet you back here."

"Nah'ceer you gon' trust her wit ya bread?"

"Kool, I don't know why but I do trust her."

"That's all it is then."

By tha time we got back, Heaven was already there.

"Come on, let's go meet my uncle and remember this is all your money."

"If you tell me that one more time."

"Turn here, now park behind that black SUV."

"Y'all go ahead and will wait out here."

Heaven did some kind of special knock and within seconds, tha door came open.

"Hello Heaven."

"Hey Big Mike."

"He's in tha back waiting for you."

I didn't have to ask why they called him Big Mike at 6'6, damn near 300 pounds his name spoke for itself.

"Uncle Ross."

"Hey, how's my favorite niece."

"Considering I'm your only niece, I'm good. Uncle Ross, this is my friend Nah'ceer I was telling you about."

"Heaven, he's a child."

"No offense, Mr. Ross, but what does my age have to do wit my money as long as I come correct? There shouldn't be a problem."

All Ross could do was smile. "Nah'ceer, I like you already; we could become good friends."

"I'd like to keep it strictly biz-ness when people friends while doing biz-ness they tend to get comfortable." From that moment Ross knew he had something special in Nah'ceer.

"I respect that, but in this biz-ness we all need friends to remember that and never let tha money go to your head."

I took heed to what he was saying because you don't get to be in this game as long as he is wit out knowing what's going on. He handed me a bag which contained what we came to get.

"This is the best work on tha East Coast it could stand a 8, but I never put more than a five."

I knew I would only put a 2, 3 at the most on it. Once we got back to the spot, I handed Heaven hers.

"Nah, we in this together what ever you do wit that is on you," she said, pointing to tha other brick.

"Look Nah'ceer, I figured we could run this in shifts so that neither of us have to be on tha block all day."

"I don't mind being out there all day."

"You don't want tha Jakes to see you all day; always avoid tha heat if you can."

I could tell that Ross had schooled her. Once we turned 36 into 54, we bagged tha whole thing up; if everything went tha way I had planned, we should come out with $81,000, which would give us a profit of $59,000. I tried to contain my excitement. I've never had that much money. In fact, I was spending everything I had so I could come up. Who would've ever thought that at 15, I would be making this type of money?

Over the next few months, things couldn't have been any better but you know there's always somebody trying to test you.

"Nah'ceer since we got this block jumpin' Niggaz been trying to get a piece."

"I'm not having that; Mafucka's is gon' respect us."

"Don't worry about it. I'll handle it." Me and Kool both looked at her.

That's why those other niggaz are in tha boneyard." Kool busted out laughing.

"Yo you crazy Heaven."

"Nah, I'm serious."

"Yo, is that dude right there?"

I got this," Heaven said, walking toward dude.

"Excuse me."

"What up Shorty?"

"This ain't gonna work."

"What's that?"

"You hustling on this block."

(Ha! Ha! Ha!)

"Shorty, I'd advise you to keep it moving before we have a problem."

"Yeah I guess you're right." Heaven turned around and turned back around wit her .45 in hand.

"The only problem I see is you, so I'm going to do everybody a favor and get rid of tha problem."

Before he could say anything, boom, boom, boom, boom, four shots sent him to the boneyard.

"Oh Shit, she earthed that nigga." Damn was all I could say.

"Come on, let's bounce before tha Jakes come."

"What the hell?"

Two guys were putting dude into a black van while another was pouring something where tha body once was.

"Don't worry about them; that's my cleanup crew."

Tha funny thing is tha police never ever came.

"If we didn't have it before, we got respect now."

"Nah, Heaven has it and I refuse to let anyone think I'm hiding behind you, no offense."

"None taken, I definitely hear you and feel what you're saying."

"Do you think we need to worry about his folk?"

"Fuck his folk!"

Little did I know I would catch my first body later that night.

"Aye yo, My Man, let me holla at you for a sec." I could tell the way he was walkin' he was holding heat.

"What up?"

"Were you out here earlier today?"

"Why what's up?"

"I'm looking for tha bitch that killed my cousin."

"Nah Peeps, I don't know what you're talkin' bout."

"Well, if you see her give her…"

Pop, Pop, Pop, Pop, I hit him four times before he could finish this sentence or let off a shot. Before I realized what I was doing, I was standing over him, letting my .40 Cal sing his face a lullaby.

"Nah'ceer, Nah'ceer, Nah'ceer." When I came out of my daze, Heaven had my arm.

"I had a feeling something was going to pop off tonight; that's why I came back."

"Tha same dudes from earlier were there to do what they do."

"Now, you'll be respected."

CHAPTER 14

"Listen, either you wit me or against me and trust me, you don't wanna be against me."

"Come on Jah'ceer, don't even try to play me like that; you already know I got ya back 100 percent."

"Then next time them niggaz act like they want it give it to 'em."

"They ain't want no smoke; they was scared to death, stutterin' and shit."

Over tha last year, I've earned respect and a name for myself. My auntie Tae didn't want me in tha streets, but Uncle Roc let her know tha streets was in me. I loved and had a lot of respect for Uncle Roc he always put me on to tha real shit and never kept anything from me. When I first stepped to him about trying to get at a dollar, all he said was, "are you sure this is what you wanna do?" He also let me know what comes with tha game. I took everything he said into consideration, but at tha end of the day, this is what I wanted to do. He gave me his boy Sharky's number and it's been on since.

"Yo, here come ya aunt."

"Hold this shit down; I'll be back."

"Damn Nigga where you going now?"

"To see my uncle."

"Let him know I said what up."

"No doubt."

I walked over to tha car, took a couple more pulls from my Dutch then threw it down.

"Spray yaself wit this before you get in my car."

"Damn Aunty."

"Watch ya damn mouth."

"My bag."

"Boy, what am I going to do wit you?"

"I'll be 18 next year."

"Don't remind me."

"Did I tell you I be seeing Ed?"

"No, is he bothering you?"

"Yeah, for drugs, he's a smoker."

"Stop lying."

"I'm not."

"Unh, Unh, Unh."

"I don't sell him shit and neither does my team. He didn't even know who I was at first."

"Oh, he knew, he probably just didn't want you to see him."

"Yeah, cause he did have somebody scoring for him."

Uncle Roc was already sitting in tha visitor's room when we got there.

"What up Unc?"

"I can't call it; what's good wit you."

"You know me trying to stay focused."

"Sharky told me you doing it real big out there."

"Did you get that change and flicks I sent you?"

"Yeah, but I told you I don't need no money."

"I spoke to ya folks too."

That was code for a hit his man with tha pack and he got it yesterday.

"Pete told me he got me a court date in seven months."

"Yeah he came up here."

"You don't sound to happy."

"Should I be?"

"Yes, considering you might be coming home."

"Tae, I'll be finish my time a few months after my court date anyway, so it really doesn't matter if I get out then or not."

"I feel you on that Unc you done gave these Crackers 14 years of your life and they didn't have no case."

"It's all part of tha game."

"Well, that's one part I wanna avoid." I looked at Aunty Tae, then smiled.

"What you smiling at Boy?"

"You Uncle Roc lucky to have a wifey like you."

"Is he?"

"Hell yeah, I hope I can find me a woman like you."

"Don't count on it Neph; she's a diamond in tha rough."

"She better be lucky she's my aunty." We all started laughing.

"Damn Neph, I know them young girls all over you."

"Unc them broads straight smuts."

"Boy, you grew up fast; it seems like just yesterday you was runnin' around in diapers."

"Now I'm on my grown man shit."

"OOW!"

"What I tell you about that mouth of yours?"

"My bag."

"Yeah, ya bag."

"Unc, you still haven't heard anything about my brother?"

"Nah, but Pete is still on it; don't worry, we'll find him if it's tha last thing we do."

"15 minutes left on visits!" tha guard yelled out, "Imma let y'all talk for this last few minutes."

"Baby, one more year of this and you'll be home; I can't wait."

"I can't wait to be able to eat real food, wear my own clothes."

"You're gonna need a whole new wardrobe."

"You gonna make sure I'm straight."

"Don't I always?"

"Yup, that's why I love you so much."

"Jah'ceer, remember what I told you." I just nodded my head up and down.

"See you, next week Baby."

"No doubt, love ya."

"Love you too."

After my aunty dropped me back on tha block, I headed to one of tha trap houses.

"The count is off; count it again," I heard Jizz say when I walked in.

"How much?"

"Huh?"

"How much is it off?"

"$2,500."

"It's not off. I forgot to tell you I hit Jonas wit some work."

"Oh, that's why he told me to tell you to get at him."

"That nigga know my number."

"He's been calling, but it's been going straight to voicemail."

"Shit, I never turned it back on when I left tha visit."

"What up wit Roc?"

"Same song, different station."

"I heard that."

"He schooled me to a few things."

"Don't he always?"

"I look forward to it every time I go."

"Man Roc get big respect; he been down 14 years on some bullshit."

"Tell me bout it, and he don't even complain about it."

"He'll be home next year. Imma throw him tha biggest party tha ATL has ever seen or had."

"We should get Jeezy, TI, and Luda to perform."

"My Aunty got connections; she can probably make that happen."

"Aye Ceer, let me ask you something."

"I'm listening, go head."

"You know how they say, twins feel each other."

"Yeah."

"Do you ever feel ya brother?"

"It's funny you asked me that because at times when I feel mad, sad or happy for no reason, I be thinking it's Nah'ceer."

"That's deep."

"Imma find him."

"He's probably a square."

"Hell Nah, if he has tha same bloodline and he does, he's somewhere fuckin' it up like me."

"Yeah, you're probably right."

"Nigga ain't no probably, I am right."

Meanwhile, in North Philly, Nah'ceer was meeting wit Heaven's Uncle Ross.

"Ceer we have been doing business for tha past two years and it has been beneficial for tha both of us, don't you think?"

"I couldn't agree more."

"And that niece of mine, she's one hell of a shot, wouldn't you say?"

The look on my face must of said it all.

"Come on Ceer; this is my city. You don't think I know about tha body count tha two of you have racked up over tha past two years? Now don't get me wrong, everything tha two of you have done, I would've handled tha same way. Heaven's a lot like her mother rest her soul. My sister was a hit woman, contract killer or is you kids these days say she was a gun."

"Heaven told me that."

"She's been bitter since her mom was killed."

"I could understand that my moms and pops were killed in a home invasion."

"Sorry to hear that."

"It is what it is."

"I called you here to discuss some biz-ness."

"I'm always gamed for that."

"I know you've been content wit purchasing 5 kilos, but I think it's time to step it up a few notches. How bout you?"

"I was just talkin' to Heaven about this."

"Good, Good."

"Ross, I know that tha number you're giving me is good, but I was hoping it could be better if I could grab more."

"Tha price drops to 19,000 for 10 or more."

"I'll take 15 then."

"Plus, Imma hit you wit 35 for 22,000 apiece."

"I'm cool wit that."

"A'ight, you know what to do."

As I was leaving tha restaurant, Heaven was pulling up.

"Is everything cool?"

"Yeah, follow me."

"Imma leave my car and ride wit you."

"A'ight, jump in."

"What was my uncle talkin' bout?"

"I'm buying 15 for 285,000 and he's fronting me 35 for 775,000."

"We just talked about doing more."

"I know, tha time couldn't be better."

"Pretty soon, my name will be ringing all over tha East Coast."

"I got family in Atlanta; he says tha money down there is serious."

"Is he major in tha "A" or just getting by?"

"He's doing a'ight for himself but wit us backing him."

"Say no more, get in touch wit him, find out what his numbers are and when we can come down and check shit out."

"My aunt is sick, so he went down New Orleans to look after her."

"He'll probably be there for a while."

"I don't know, but I can find out."

"Do that."

Back in the ATL, Jah'ceer and Jizz had just finished putting in some work on two females.

"Aye Ceer, let's drop these boards off so we can hit tha block."

"You can go ahead. I'm a chill for tha night."

"Do you want me to drop shawty off too?"

"It doesn't matter."

"A'ight, I'll hit you up in the morning then."

"Come on y'all we out."

They both grab their purses, but when shawty that was wit Ceer seen he wasn't coming ask, "You not leaving?"

"No Imma chill."

"Well, Imma chill too," she said, putting her purse back on tha chair."

"Nah, shawty we out."

"It's cool Jizz; she can stay if she wants."

Her friend had that look that said you lucky bitch. Once they were gone, we both jumped in tha shower, where I wasted no time digging her back out.

"OOOOOOOH DADDY this dick tha bomb!"

Hearing that only stroked my ego and made me go extra hard on her. I turned tha shower off so we could get out.

"Let me dry that off," she said, pointing at the 9 inches that was swinging between my legs.

"Help ya self."

That's exactly what she did as she dropped down and put my penis in her mouth bringing it to life. I had to admit her head game was off tha chain. Three hours later, we were both laid out sweaty and exhausted.

"Damn Jah'ceer, you got a bitch all the way fucked up putting it down like that."

"You weren't so bad ya self."

"Boy pleeeeeeease."

"What?"

"I know my shot tha bomb."

"Ha! Ha! Ha! You funny."

"Am I?"

"Yeah."

"What ever Ceer."

Even though she was right, I would never admit it to her, but she would definitely be my jump-off.

"Why are you lookin' at me like that?"

"No reason," I said, lying while I was thinking that eventually I would be wifey.

"Here Nya, roll this up."

"I don't know how to roll."

"Stop lying."

"I'm serious."

"You smoke but don't know how to roll; I don't believe it."

"For real, Charnise always does tha rolling."

"What do you do when she's not around?"

"My brother and if he's not around, my next-door neighbor does it for me."

"Ha! Ha! Ha! Yo that's some sad shit."

"Works for me."

I tossed her tha wrap I had.

"I just told you I can't."

"I ain't trying to hear that; you about to learn."

"Ten wraps and an hour later Nya knew how to roll a blunt."

"A little more practice and I'll be a beast."

After we smoked, we were at it again. When we finished this time, we both fell asleep.

CHAPTER 15

"Nigga I don't give a fuck who you are or how much money you claim to have!"

"Listen, all that loud Hollywood shit you on save it for one of them other niggaz you accustom to dealing wit."

"Bet a stack."

"A stack?"

"Yeah, a stack."

"All the mouth you got and you only want to bet a stack?"

"What ever you want to bet, we can bet."

"Nah, how much can you afford to bet?"

"Bet 10 grand."

"Oh shit, damn, it's on now," those were some of tha comments from tha onlookers.

"Nigga I got that on my books."

"Me too; you want to check?"

"For what? If you say you got it, then that's all it is."

"Shoot for ball."

I looked around before saying, "I'm taking all side bets too."

"Damn Roc, let's get some of this free money."

"A'ight y'all can take tha side bets."

"Aye yo Nice, let me holla at you for a sec."

"What up Zac?"

"I heard Roc can ball."

"So what, I can't?"

"I'm just saying."

"Zac that Nigga is always trying to tell somebody how to play but never gets on tha court."

"Fuck him, then I'm wit you; I got two stacks on my man Nice."

"Bet, anybody else like Nice?"

After all tha bets were in, we shot for ball, which I missed on purpose.

"Are we playing to 32 or 16 by ones?"

"You got ball, so you call it."

"32 check rock."

Since I knew Nice could only go right, it was easy to defend him.

"Let me get that," I said is he tried to blow past me.

"Come on, you gotta make it a little harder than that."

"What ever Nigga, play ball."

I hit him wit a head fake that he fell for, then blew pass for tha easy windmill dunk that sent tha gym into a frenzy.

"This Shit is too easy My Man!" Rich yelled.

"Awe Nigga, that's only one bucket."

"Yeah, but that was a hell of a bucket."

My next 10 points came from jumpers.

"Damn Nice, you'll be lucky to score."

"Imma score and win."

"Bet three stacks you don't score over 10," I said.

"Nigga bet it."

I knew that he would not even touch tha ball again on some real shit.

"Aye Roc, don't let that nigga touch tha ball again unless he checkin' it up."

"Ha! Ha! Ha!" Rich couldn't control hisself.

"Point check rock."

"I didn't want to do this to you, but you asked for it." Nice threw tha ball kinda hard, which only pissed me off. He was all up on me.

"It's a little too late to try to play me like this."

"Rip that nigga Nice."

"He can't."

I jabbed step causing him to back up enough to cross him one way, then dip back tha other way, making him fall, setting me up for tha perfect 360 dunk. Tha whole gym went berserk, even his boys.

"Game, I trust by tha time I get out tha shower tha money will be in my account."

"Not to be funny, but I don't think you got another 10 in ya account."

"I don't, but one phone call and I will."

"Check this out, you already know how tha Feds be about more than 10 grand on the books, so after I win this 10 have ya folk wire it to this account," I said, writing it down on paper.

"No problem if you win."

This time Nice came out aggressive and scored tha first 12 points.

"I knew he couldn't hold you Nice!" his boy yelled.

I smiled to myself, knowing that I could turn it up at any time. Before I knew it, Nice had me 28 nothing.

"That's right Nice, give it back like he gave it to you."

"Aye Roc, if you don't stop playing and end this shit so I can shut this clown ass nigga up."

"Say no more Rich final score 38 to 28 me."

"Ha! Ha! Ha! If you think Imma let you come back, you crazy as shit."

"Check rock."

As soon as he tried that bullshit ass cross, I ripped him step back then drained my jumper.

"Two and rising."

"This game is over."

Slowly but surely, I climbed back into the game.

"26 check rock."

"Damn Zac, you awfully quiet over there."

"He still gon' win."

"Nigga this shit over he ain't even gon' touch tha rock again only to check it up."

I hit two deep jumpers giving me point.

"You can just give me five and call it off."

"Yeah right, Imma win."

"A'ight, but I tried to save you some money."

"Check rock."

He threw the ball at my feet, causing it to roll to him; he then turned around and laid it up.

"Tie score."

"Nigga you crazy check tha ball."

"I just did."

"Nice we ain't doing it like that."

"We playing straight or win by four?"

I started to just knock him out but decided he wasn't worth tha hole time.

"Straight," I said, giving him a hard chest pass.

"Fuck that nigga Roc," Rich said walking on tha court.

"Rich, it ain't bout nothing. Imma still win."

Nice tried to slip by while my head was turned, but I saw him and ripped tha ball.

"Damn you a desperate nigga, here take this," I said, shooting a deep jumper, "all cotton like I said tha money should be in that account by tha time I get out of tha shower."

"It'll be there; I don't get down like that."

"Anytime you want to donate some more of that good money, just holla at me."

"Nice you really gonna pay him?"

"Of course, that couple of ones is nothing to me."

"I would've let that nigga smell tha smoke."

"That's tha difference from you and me, I honor all bets and debts."

"Aunty Tae you home?"

"I'm in tha bedroom."

"You decent?"

"Yeah, come on in."

"Are you busy?"

"No."

"Can you throw six braids in my hair?"

"Go get tha big comb out tha bathroom. And grab those black rubber bands too. Have you talk to Uncle Roc today?"

"Not yet."

"He won 20,000 on a basketball game."

"Was it that Lakers Heat game?"

"Nah, he played some dude for 10,000 a game; he just called for me to make sure tha money was in tha account."

"Was it?"

"Yeah, it was there. I swear ya uncle has won over 200,000 since he's been locked up. He's proof that you can get at a dollar no matter where you at."

"You not done yet?"

"I'm on my last one. So who's tha girl that's been coming around so much lately?"

"What you spying on me now Aunty?"

"Boy please, every day I get off work, I ride thru there."

"Oh yeah, well, she ain't nobody, just a friend."

"MMM HMM, friend my ass."

"For real, her name is Nya."

"Anya James?"

"I don't know all that."

"I thought she looked familiar; that's Sissy's daughter."

"Who?"

"Sissy, somebody that use to hang out wit me and ya mom sometimes. There I'm done."

I got up to look in tha mirror.

"No wonder it took you longer," I said, looking at tha 10 braids she put in my hair, "thank you."

"You're welcome."

"When you talk to Unc, tell him to call me."

"Ok. And you be careful out there."

"I will."

"Speaking of tha Devil."

"What?"

"You forgot you told me to come thru when I got off work."

"Oh Shit, I did; never mind, I had my aunty hook me up."

"I wish you would've called me."

"My bag."

"Sure is."

"Hey, is ya mom name Sissy?"

"Yeah, how you know that?"

"My aunty says ya mom use to hang wit her and my mom sometimes."

"What's their names?"

"Tae and Ash."

"Oh Shit, my mom got pictures of tha three of them together; talk about a small world."

"Tell me about it."

"I hope this doesn't mess up my chance to be his wifey."

"You cool wit my moms knowing ya aunt?"

"That shit don't mean nothing to me."

"Good."

"We just friends family anyway."

"Yeah, you right," I said, holding back what I really wanted to say.

"Well, I need to get to tha store before they close."

"A'ight hit me up later."

"Damn Ceer, did you see tha look on her face when you said y'all were just friends?"

"It was tha truth."

"Well, you might need to stop spending so much time wit her."

"Jizz, she good peoples."

"I know, just like I know you're not going to admit ur feeling her."

"If you don't know nothing else Jizz you should know I would never lie to you."

"So I'll take that as a yes."

"I didn't say that; I said I would never lie to you."

"Well, let me ask are you feeling Nya?"

"Yeah."

"So why don't you let her know?"

"Imma let her be tha first to say something."

"Nigga you crazy, not only is she thurl, but she Michael Jackson bad."

"She is, ain't she?"

"Something like that, be a shame for somebody else to get a hold of her."

"You suppose to be my boy."

"I am that's why am telling you all this, Ceer don't be no fool."

"Did Champ call you?" I asked, switching tha topic.

"Yeah, and don't try to switch tha topic."

"All I'm saying is let me deal wit this my way."

"I always do."

"You gonna be a'ight out here I need to handle something."

"I hope it's Nya."

"You're not going to let this go are you?"

"I just don't want to see you let a good thing getaway."

"If it will make you happy, I'll call her."

"Don't do it for me, do it for you."

I went to my contacts, found Nya's name then pushed send.

"Hello."

"Hey are you busy?"

"Never too busy for a friend."

I knew she was being smart, but I paid her no mind.

"Would you like to grab a bite to eat?"

"Wit you?"

"No Jizz smart ass."

"Sure, why not."

"Cool, I'll be by to pick you up in 20 minutes."

"Call when you get close so I can be out front."

"A'ight, see you in a few."

"You gonna tell her, right?" I didn't respond; I just walked to my car.

"Don't let a good one getaway!" I heard Jizz yell before shutting my door.

"I'm already there."

Nya was standing there like she just got off tha runway. 5'6, bronze skin tone, shoulder-length curly hair, hazel eyes and a ass like Nicki Minaj, that Ralph Lauren dress wasn't doing her body any justice.

When Jah'ceer pulled up, I could tell my outfit done its job.

"As always, you look good."

"Thank you."

His smile alone had my panties wet. I decided I would tell him over dinner how I felt.

"What do you have a taste for?"

"You," I said wit a smile."

"That's dessert," he said in response.

"I could go for some steak and shrimp."

"Sounds good to me, Ralph Steakhouse it is then."

"Isn't that place expensive?"

"Does it matter?"

"You too damn smart."

That's twice today I've heard that; I'm actually starting to believe it myself.

When we got to Ralph's tha wait was 45 minutes just to be seated.

"Do you want to go somewhere else or what?"

"That's up to you; it doesn't matter to me."

"Fuck it, we'll wait."

Tha hostess gave us this device and told us when it lights up our table is ready.

"Come on, let's go smoke some of this good Sour D."

As soon as we got in tha car, Jah'ceer passed me tha wrap and weed.

"Roll up, or did you forget how?"

"Boy pleeeeease, I'm tha best roller in tha ATL."

"I'll be the judge of that."

"Maybe he was adopted in another country."

"I'm starting to think that we've been trying to find him for tha past 14 years wit no luck."

"I'm not giving up until we do."

"Me either, Baby me either."

"Tae I have to admit, I didn't think you would be able to do this bid with me; shit I didn't think I would even do 15 years."

"Only tha strong can survive."

"Tae you can put me in tha ocean wit killer whales and Imma survive, believe that."

"I don't doubt it. Six more months and you'll be able to get out of this nightmare you've been in for 14 ½ years."

"You know tha funny thing is they didn't even give me no probation."

"That's a good thing, ain't it?"

"Hell yeah."

"Well, I'll have you a nice blunt of that Sour D you be smokin'."

"Now that's what I'm talkin' bout. Oh yeah, before I forget, I had to fire Skunk."

"Why?"

"Customers were complaining about things missing from their cars."

"How do you know it was Skunk?"

"Because it was only tha cars he was detailing, not to mention a few items were in his locker."

"Did you tell Sharky?" I gave him a look that said yeah, right.

"You know I hate a thief."

"Roc, you know if I would've told Sharky, he would make Skunk disappear permanently."

"My point exactly."

"If he would steal petty shit like that, then you know he'll take anything."

The guard announced that tha visit was over.

"I love you and I'll see you next week."

"OK, Damn, you picking up weight," he said, grabbing my ass.

"Nah, I'm just back in tha gym; I got to get this thing back tight for you."

"Girl stop, it's already right. I can't wait to dive face-first in it."

"You gonna make me go home and pull out my toys."

"Six more months and you won't need no toys."

"I know that's right."

All I could do was stare until she was out of my sight completely.

I can't wait to get into her when I get out. Rich was on his way to tha gym when I got back to tha cell.

"Hold up, let me change. I wanna hit some steel too."

"How was ya visit?"

"You know how those visits are; you're happy while they're there but sad when they leave."

"It's over for you now you did yours."

"Yeah, more like I did somebody else time."

"I definitely feel you on that."

"These Crackers ain't never gotta worry about seeing me no more."

"Man, I got 60 months left, then I'm moving up north."

"I wish I could move; all I know is tha 'A'."

"Roc, I'm telling you all you gotta do is pack up and go anywhere you want especially since you got tha funds to do it."

After about a 1 ½ of hitting the steel, I was ready to bust a grub then hit tha shower.

"Hello."

"Yo who this?"

"It's ya cuz down in tha ATL."

"Oh shit, what up Bake?"

"I was calling to let you know I'm back from Aunt Liz's."

"That's what's up; Imma fly down this weekend."

"You gonna bring some of that work wit you so I can see what it's hittin' for?"

"Imma have to drive down wit that."

"Damn, I was hoping to put it out so people can see what we gonna be workin' wit."

"Don't worry, I'll have somebody drive it down."

"A'ight what time is ya flight coming in?"

"I don't know; I'll hit you later wit all tha information."

"That's all it is then, talk to you later." (CLICK)

"Ceer that was my cuz from Atlanta."

"Oh, he back?"

"Yeah, Imma fly down Friday."

"You need me to go wit you?"

"Nah, but Imma get Dooby to drive down wit 3 birds."

"Why not just drive down wit him?"

"Cause, Imma tell him to take his wife wit him so it won't look obvious. Imma have them leave at one in tha morning, so they'll get there around tha same time as me."

"How long are you gonna be down there?"

"Just for tha weekend, I'll be back first thing Monday morning."

"You make sure ya peeps got some heat for you when you get down there."

"Now you know I'm already two steps ahead of you on that."

"I figured you would be."

"Come on, it's me, why wouldn't I? Shit, if I could get on tha plane with mines, I would."

"Yo Wiz, what time her flight come in?"

"It should be here by now; let me hit her cell phone."

"Leave it."

"It went straight to voicemail."

"We been here for an hour already. Are you sure she's coming?"

"She'll be here."

"Wiz ya awareness is shot."

They both jumped then turned around to find me standing behind them.

"How long you been standing there?"

"About an hour."

"Why didn't you say something?"

"I wanted to see how long it would take for you to spot me."

"Had we been on tha block you might of gotton shot."

"Nigga if we was on tha block, both of you Mafucka's would've been dead!"

"What ever," Wiz's boy said.

"I'm not ya average bitch, Wiz you better tell him about me."

"I already did."

"Where is my pistol I told you to bring?"

"In tha truck."

"Fuck is it doing in ya truck?"

"Damn Heaven, we in tha airport."

"Fuck that mean?"

"It means ain't shit going down."

"Better safe than sorry."

"Man, come on so I can give you ya pistol."

I turned my phone back on only to find I had two messages. The first was from Nah'ceer.

"Just checking to make sure you made it in one piece." (message deleted.)

"Hey, we made it; we're at tha Marriott on Peach Street, Room 441. Call when you get this."

"Wiz swing by at tha Marriott on Peach Street."

"You not staying at no hotel."

"I know, I need to pick up something."

The phone rang two times before Dooby answered.

"Hey Heaven."

"I'm on my way."

"We're parked on tha fourth level and tha door is already unlocked."

"A'ight, you and tha wife enjoy tha rest of tha weekend."

"Thanks to you and Nah'ceer, we will."

"Have fun and I'll see you back home."

Pull up to tha fourth level. Stop right here." I hopped out, grabbed tha bag out of tha back of Dooby's car then got back in.

"A'ight, let's go."

"Where to?"

"Wherever we can cook this up," I said, opening tha bag so they could see tha three bricks of fish scale.

"God Damn, that's some real shit there."

"Tha best."

"How much you bring down?"

"Three bricks."

"That's all?"

"You can turn it into five and still have grade a work."

"Nah Cuz, that thing ain't like that."

"I'm done talkin'."

"In that case, Khalif, get us to tha spot."

Fifteen minutes later, we were pulling up to this red brick house.

"Let's get down to work so these birds can fly."

The whole time Wiz was whippin', his phone was blowing up.

"Damn, Khalif finish this why I answer my phone."

"Yo who this?"

"Mike, what's up Peeps?"

"Yeah but tha number is a little higher."

"Huh, of course, tha work is official for that number."

"A'ight, give me 30 minutes and I'll meet you at tha usual spot." (Click)

"That was Mike, he needs a half."

"Did he complain about tha new number?"

"Nah, he just said it must be official for that number."

"What are you charging him Wiz?"

"We was letting them go for 700 apiece, but wit this, I need 900. By tha way, what's tha damage for these?"

"24,000 apiece."

"Wow, that's all?"

"Yeah that extra two is all you."

"Say word."

"Word."

"Damn, I'm going to give you an extra 10 grand to show my appreciation."

"You don't have to do that; we family and family always look out for one another."

"I know, that's why I'm giving you tha extra 10,000."

"Let's go get this money."

"I need to hit tha mall; all I have are tha clothes on my back."

"I was wondering where your bags were."

"We're gonna hit tha block for a little while, then we can hit tha mall up."

That was cool because I wanted to see how they were runnin' their block anyway. We pulled up and it was total chaos; workers were running up to cars. Nobody was looking out; I couldn't believe how unorganized Wiz block was.

"What's up Cuz my block Jumpin' ain't it?"

"Do you want tha truth?"

"Of course."

"Wiz this shit is straight up chaotic." He was about to speak but I cut him off.

"If you're gonna do any biz-ness with us you gotta get this block in order."

"What are you talkin' bout it's mad doe out here," Khalif said.

"Nigga Fuck tha money, what good will it be if nobody's out here to get it?"

"What you mean by that Cuz?"

"At this rate, they'll all be locked up. Does everybody out here work for you?"

"Most of 'em."

"First off, nobody that doesn't work for you shouldn't be out here, point-blank. I have no doubt that this block does numbers; that's why y'all should get it all. Call a meeting wit all ya workers."

"When?"

"Right now."

"Yo listen up, I need everybody to go to tha basement; emergency meeting."

As all tha workers start walking to this one house, I noticed three stragglers still hustling.

"I take it they not on ya team?"

"Nah."

"Well, they either need to get down, or they gotta go, point-blank."

"Y'all go in tha crib; I'll be right behind you."

Khalif looked at me like I lost my mind. Once they were inside, I walked over to tha trio.

"Damn what up Ma?"

"Would you fellas mind joining us for a sec?"

"We gotta get this paper Ma."

"It's only gonna take a sec, I promise."

"Well a'ight, but if it's longer than two minutes, we out."

"That's cool."

When everybody seen them wit me they got quiet.

"Fuck this shit about?" one of them said.

"I'm about to explain."

"Well, you better talk cause you only got about a minute left."

"First of all, that shit y'all doing out there stops right now."

Hell no, who is this Bitch? You crazy where some of tha comments made.

"Shut tha fuck up and listen," Khalif said wit attitude.

"That shit don't apply to us, we not on tha payroll."

"That's why I asked y'all to join us."

"Oh Hell Nah, we straight Ma, we doing us."

"Well, actually, you're not, either you gon' join tha team or pump elsewhere."

"Yo, this Bitch talkin' real dumb right now!"

"Who tha Fuck you calling Bitch?"

"You," he said steppin' closer to me.

"Whoa, hold up y'all."

"Nah, Fuck her."

"Like I said, ya punk ass either gon' get down wit us or."

"Or what Bitch," he said, cutting me off.

I knew from past experience that he was just all mouth.

"You know what, I'm tired of ya mouth; this is a man's game so Wiz you need to tell your peeps to sit down, or shit may get ugly for her real fast."

Khalif was about to say something, but Wiz motioned for him to fall back.

"You're a Pussy!"

"What?"

"Nigga you heard me, you a Pussy."

"I had enough of this bitch."

He walked up to me but was met by my .40 cal to his face. He backed up a little.

"Nah, don't back up now."

"I-I-I."

"Stop all that stuttering you was talkin' straight a minute ago, tough guy. Where I'm from, we nip a problem in tha bud before it gets outta control and you're a problem Pop, Pop, Pop, Pop, Pop, Pop! Six shots, one to tha forehead and tha other five to his chest.

"Now, like I was saying, there are about to be some major changes anybody else got a problem wit that?"

Everybody, including the two dudes that was wit dude, shook their head no. After I laid tha game plan out, I let Wiz and Khalif figure out who would work what shifts and who would be tha lookout as well as tha guns. "Wiz, I got to admit at first I was skeptical, but now I see us really making money."

"Do you think Jizz and his peeps will be on some bullshit once we start taking over?"

"They don't want to end tha truce."

"If things go tha way I'm projecting, I think they might."

"Damn Ceer that's a nice chain you rockin'."

My uncle had this made when I was one."

"What ever nigga."

"Real rap, he had it made for me and my twin brother."

"I still can't believe it's another one of you out there somewhere."

"What's that supposed to mean?"

"Nothing, but if he's anything like you were in trouble."

"Fuck you Jizz!"

"Nah Fuck her," he said, pointing to Nya, who was pulling up.

"That's not a bad ideal."

"Hey Boo."

"Boo, awe hell no let me find out you going soft on a nigga."

"Ain't nothing soft bout me."

"That's right, only thing soft on him is his thing before I bring it to life."

"I did not need to know that."

"Ceer I'll be right back I gotta run across town for a minute."

"I'll be here; I'm not going nowhere." Ever since Nya let me know how she really felt about me, I had no choice but to keep it 100 wit her.

"Jah'ceer, I was thinking about you all day at work."

"Now you got me blushing. Truth be told, you've been on my mind too."

I had never been in a relationship before, so this was all new to me.

"Remember I told you about that house I was trying to get?"

"Yeah, what about it?"

"They finally called me to go look at it tomorrow morning."

"What about work?"

"I took tha day off."

"Maybe we can get some breakfast when you're done."

"I was kind of hoping you would go wit me."

"You don't need me."

"Your opinion matters especially since you will be spending a lot of time there."

"I might as well move in."

"That's not a bad ideal."

"I don't know; a lot of people can be together but not live together."

"True, but we damn near live together now; we're always at each other's house, so what's the difference?"

"The difference is if either of us get mad, we can always go home."

"Jah'ceer, look and get it."

"Get what?"

"You're not ready for a full commitment and I understand that, I really do."

"Nya, that's ya shit, I'll go wit you to look at this crib if that's what you really want."

"Jah'ceer, I don't want you to do anything you don't want to do."

I had to laugh to myself tha way she emphasize tha word anything.

I didn't want to make her upset, so I just said, "I do want to go wit you."

"You sure don't act like you do."

"Nya, us moving in together would be a big step and I don't want us to regret it."

"We won't know unless we give it a try; if it doesn't work out we could always go back to this."

I looked her in her eyes before answering.

"Well, I guess I'm willing to give it a try if you are."

At that moment, she grabbed my face and kissed me passionately.

"Y'all need to do that in tha house and not on tha street. I turned around to see my Aunty Tae getting out her car.

"Hey Aunty."

"Hey, Mrs. Tae."

"What a tell you about calling me Mrs.?"

"My bag, I keep forgetting."

"Where are you coming from Aunty?"

"Seeing your uncle and making sure everything is in order for his welcome home party."

"I can't wait til he comes home."

"Three more weeks, that's all."

"I know he's ready to get out of there after 15 long years."

"Aunty, did Jeezy ever get back at you? My cousin said he would be able to perform."

"How much did he want?"

"Nothing."

"Huh?"

"He knows Roc, so he said he would do it on tha strength."

"Damn Uncle Roc that nigga."

"Yeah, anytime you can get Jeezy and T.I. at ya party to perform for free, you are that dude."

"That's my Uncle Roc."

"I can't wait to meet him."

"He said tha same about you."

"He did?"

"Yeah, he wants to meet tha woman who made his nephew settle down."

"What's that supposed to mean Aunty?"

"Neither of us thought you would ever settle down wit one woman."

"I've been known to have that kind of effect on people."

"You are most definitely your mother's child."

"I'll take that as a compliment."

"Well, I had to make a few runs so I'll see you later."

"A'ight Aunty."

"Nya ya mom said you're about to get ya own place."

"Yeah, I'll go look at it tomorrow morning."

"I guess I won't be seeing much of you anymore Ceer."

"Why you say that?"

"Boy, you know damn well you're moving in wit her."

"Uncle Roc will be home, so you won't miss me too much."

"Of course, I will miss you nephew."

"Don't worry Tae, I'll take good care of him, I promise."

"I know you will, or I wouldn't be letting him deal wit you."

"Jah'ceer remember when we were at tha visit and you told me and Roc that you wish you could find a woman like me?"

"Of course, I remember."

"Well, you found her; I love you and will see you later."

"I love you too Aunty."

I looked at Nya and thought to myself, *"Damn, I bucked up."*

CHAPTER 16

(SMACK)

"What tha fuck did I tell you about tha next time you fucked my paper up?"

"I'm not tha one who fucked ya paper up."

"Who did then?"

"I ain't no snitch." (SMACK)

"Then you'll die right here, right now!"

"You're gonna have to kill me cause I'm no rat."

"Let me get this straight you'd rather die than to tell me who's been Fuckin up my paper?"

"Yes."

"I have to admit I admire your loyalty."

"Ceer you know me, I ain't never messed up no paper in tha whole three years I been down wit you now all of a sudden money coming up short."

He did have a point; this problem just started when Kool put his man on.

"Heaven get Kool on tha phone and tell him to come here wit his man."

Twenty minutes later, Kool and his man came walkin' in wit out a care in tha world.

"What it do Ceer?"

"Sit down!" Kool looked at me like I was crazy.

"Sit tha fuck down!" They both sat down.

"Not you Kool, ya man."

"What's this shit about?"

"Mafucka don't say shit!"

"Hold up Ceer what's tha problem?"

"Ya man here seems to have a Fuckin problem takin' shit that doesn't belong to him."

"Whoa, what you talkin' bout Homey?"

"Nigga don't play fucking stupid with me," I said, pointing my pistol at his head.

"I told you it was Ali who was takin' that money."

"He seems to have a different story." I signaled for Heaven to get Ali.

"Mafucka what lies you spreading?" Kool asked, charging at Ali, who sidestepped and caught him wit a right hook.

"Nigga Imma kill you!"

"Hold up, you niggaz need to chill."

"Nah Fuck this Nigga!"

"Nah Fuck you!"

"Listen, all I want is tha truth."

"I gave it to you."

"Kool, I understand that's ya man, but if you think Immy bite tha bullet on this, you crazy."

"So what tha fuck you trying to say Ali?"

"I'm not trying to say shit; I'm saying before you came on board, we never had this problem."

"I have to agree wit him," Heaven said while pulling her .45 out.

Since Jab seen her work first hand, he knew she wouldn't hesitate to kill him.

"H-H-H-Hold on, let me explain." I caught tha look Kool gave him.

"You got five seconds to explain, starting now."

"It wasn't my shit, it was his," he said, pointing at Kool, "he set it all up; he said he was going to take over and I could be his right hand all I had to do was take a few thousand here and there."

"You lying Faggot!"

"Look you my man and all, but I'm not willing to die for you."

"Ceer I told you he couldn't be trusted."

"Damn Kool, we like brothers; how could you steal from me?"

"You gonna believe him over me?"

"Kool don't try to flip this on me, you said and I quote, "Ever since that bitch came along Ceer been on some bullshit. Imma make both of them pay."

I was so hurt that wit out thinking, I pulled my pistol and emptied the whole clip into Kool's chest.

"After all tha shit I've done for him and this is how he repays me. Ali, I owe you an apology."

"It wasn't nothing personal, so I understand completely."

"What about him?" Heaven asked, pointing her pistol at Jab. Before I could respond, Ali took Heaven's .45 and emptied it in his face.

"He can't be trusted; if he would rat his man out, just imagine what he will do for one of us."

"I couldn't agree wit you more."

"Why are you looking at me like that?"

"You just killed your best friend wit no remorse."

"Because I don't have any."

"I've created a stone-cold killer."

"Nah, you just brought it outta me."

"Ali, you're now in charge of all the spots Kool was runnin'. Do you think you can handle it?"

"Of course, I can handle it."

"Let's get outta here so tha crew can do their job."

"Hello."

"Hey Cuz, it's me."

"What's up Wiz?"

"I need you."

"Damn already, I just sent you ten."

"I know, but this shit selling like hotcakes."

"Look, let me make a call and I'll hit you right back."

"A'ight."

"Ceer that was Wiz he's done already."

"I guess it really is jumpin' down there."

"I know, right."

"Let's send him 30 this time; see how long it takes to move that."

"I was thinking maybe we should go down for a week or two."

"That might not be such a bad ideal. Ali can hold shit down while we're gone."

"Let me hit Wiz back and let him know we'll be down in a few days."

"You need to get at Dooby also."

"I thought ya peoples name was Bake?"

"It is, but he told me he rather be called Wiz now. We gave him that name Bake because he always wanted my aunt to bake cakes and pies."

"Instead of 30, we gon send 50. We can make a killing from them niggaz

Ceer."

"I was thinking more on tha lines of Virginia, North and South Carolina."

"I know some folk in those states."

"Me too."

"You know a lot of people Ceer."

"You forgot I been in a few foster homes."

"How come you don't try to find ya real family?"

"They haven't tried to find me, so why should I?"

"Maybe they have tried to find you."

"I guess they haven't tried hard enough then. Lately, I have been thinking about tha brother and uncle I never knew."

"My uncle can help you find them; he has tha East Coast on lock, so if they in tha game, he's probably their supplier."

"Nah, Heaven I'm good."

"You sure?"

"Positive."

"Well, that's all it is then, but Ceer know I always got ya back no matter what."

"Vice versa."

"I think we should take care of that situation before we leave town."

"Great minds think alike."

Meanwhile, at tha A.F.D.C, Roc was saying his last goodbyes.

"Aye, you be easy out there; a lot has changed in 15 years."

"Nothing I can't adapt to."

"I don't want to see you back in this Mafucka."

"One thing for sure, two things for certain you'll read about me in tha obituary before you see me back in here."

"A'ight just be safe."

"Rich, don't worry. Imma hold you down until you touch."

"That's all it is."

"I'm not none of them other Niggaz that say they going to do something when they get out then you never hear from them again. I might even send a couple broads ya way."

"You know a nigga could use that."

"Smith, if you want to leave, I suggest you put some pep in ya step."

I gave Rich a hug and some dap before steppin' out tha cell. I know how he feels because I felt tha same way when House maxed out. When I got to intake, they already had my stuff waiting.

"Y'all can donate that stuff to Goodwill; I'm rockin' this sweatsuit out."

"All we need for you to do is sign this paper and you can go." I couldn't sign that paper fast enough.

"Roc, it was nice knowing you even though I wish I could've met you under different circumstances."

"Likewise, Cpl Taylor."

As soon as tha door clicked, I was thru it. I had to walk down this path to get to tha gate that led to my freedom. Tae was standin' there looking beautiful as ever. She ran up to me and jumped into my arms.

"Oh My God, it's over; it's finally over!"

"I would've never made it wit out you Tae."

"Didn't I tell you I wasn't going no where?"

"Yes, you did and for that I will always remain faithful to you."

"You better because if you don't, I'll be tha one in jail for murder."

"Ha! Ha! Ha! You crazy."

"No, I'm dead serious."

"Where's Jah'ceer?"

"He had something to do."

"More important than seeing his uncle released after serving 15 years?"

"I think he had to pick a shipment up."

"I don't care all that could've been put on hold."

I didn't want to ruin tha surprise, so I kept it going.

"If you were him, you would've done tha same thing."

"Let me see ya phone."

"Here, this is ya phone."

I knew when he called, it will go to straight to voicemail.

"Fuck!"

"What's wrong now? You still remember how to use one of those don't you?"

Yeah, I just got his voicemail."

"Baby, you can't be mad he has things he has to take care of."

"Tae I'm not mad just a little disappointed. I really wanted to see him."

"And you will get to see him later on."

"You're right. I can't expect him to put everything on hold just because I'm home." I could hear the sarcasm in his voice.

"Why you smiling?"

"I'm just happy you're home."

"Me too, now, let's get away from this place."

I hit tha alarm on my car.

"I know you not driving no Honda?"

"Boy ain't nothing wrong wit my car, I like it."

"Is this tha only car you have?"

"Yup."

"Well, take me to tha Benz dealership. I'm not driving no Honda."

"Ain't nothin' wrong wit Honda's."

"If you a female, ain't no niggaz driving 'em."

"Yes they do."

"Not no real Nigga, me and Zeke always had a no Honda rule."

"Don't you want to change clothes first?"

"I'll do that afterwards."

Thirty minutes later, we were pulling into tha dealership.

"Now, this is what I'm talkin' about."

"Oh shit, is that my boy Roc?"

"Who else would it be?"

"They finally let you out."

"I should've never been there in tha first place."

"True dat, what can I do for you?"

"I need a whip; what you got for me?"

"All I need to show you is this 2021 S600 fully loaded."

"Lead tha way."

As soon as I saw it, my mind was already made up. Roger showed me all the features; after that, there was no way I wasn't driving off this lot wit that car.

"Hey Rog, do you have it in any other color besides this green?"

"Actually, we have platinum, blue, and cranberry."

"I'll take cranberry."

"Let's get tha paperwork started."

Forty-five minutes later, I was pulling off tha lot in my S600 headed straight to the rim shop.

"Hey Aunty, where y'all at?"

"I'm following Roc to tha rim shop."

"Rim shop?"

"Yeah, he just bought a car."

"I told you he wasn't going to drive that Honda."

"Ain't nothing wrong wit my Honda."

"I know, but it's a girl car."

"Boy, if you don't sound like Roc."

"I know he was mad I wasn't there."

"Mad isn't tha word, but I told him you had to handle ya biz-ness."

"He'll be okay. Did you finish?"

"Yeah, I already dropped it off at tha crib."

"Ok, I'll see you tonight then."

"Nya, is ya mom coming to tha party tonight?"

"Does a bear shit in tha woods?"

"Ha! Ha! Ha! You funny."

"You know she wouldn't miss this party for tha world."

"I can't believe it; after 15 years, my uncle is finally home."

"I know tha first thing he did was get his thing off."

"Nope, he went to buy a car."

"Are you serious?"

"Yeah."

"Tae better than me he would've had to knock me down right there in tha car."

"Cause you a freak."

"Yup, only for you."

"I'm bout to take a shower."

"Me too."

"You might as well get in wit me."

"I planned on it."

Pop, Pop, Pop, Pop.

"Awe shit I'm hit."

"Come on, let's get outta here."

"I can't get up."

"Here they come."

"Go head, Imma slide under this car."

"Nigga I'm not leaving you."

"We'll both get killed if you don't."

"I told you this was a bad ideal."

He picked me up and threw me over his shoulder.

"There they go up there."

Tat-Tat-Tat-Tat-Tat-Tat-Tat-Tat-Tat-Tat-Tat-Tat-Tat-Tat-Tat-Tat-Tat-Tat-Tat-Tat-Tat-Tat-Tat-Tat Jizz let tha Mac Ring dropping them like a boxer in a heavyweight fight.

"Come on let's make sure they dead."

When we got up on 'em their bodies look like Swiss cheese.

"Take those mask off so I can see who it is."

Oh shit, was all I could say. Don and Steph both had a look of surprise on their face.

"Dumb ass niggaz fuck were they doing trying to rob us? Get everybody together right now!"

"Yo."

"Where you at?"

"Getting dressed for my uncle's party."

"Shit, I almost forgot about that."

"Nigga you better get ready."

"We have a serious situation; I just called a meeting."

"What's going on?"

I explained what just went down wit Don and Steph.

"I'm on my way."

Since I knew it will take him at least an hour, I decided to go get dressed.

One hour later, me and Ceer were both pulling up at tha same time.

"Is everybody inside?"

"They should be."

"Let's make this quick."

"Look, I'm not going to waste a whole lot of time, so let me get straight to tha point. I'm sure y'all know what went down tonight." Everybody just shook their heads.

"I hate a liar and a thief. For some reason, Don and Steph thought they could try to steal from us; that's right, I said us because we're in this together. All of you in this room make more than enough money to survive off of, so you have no reason to steal anything. Let what happened to them be an example for anybody who thinks they can get away wit it. With that being said, go get that paper."

"Look at you; Nya must of picked that out for you."

"How do you know?"

"You don't own no shoes, so you wouldn't know tha first thing about buying any."

"I actually pick these out Nya just showed me a few pairs."

"So Shawna didn't pick that out for you?"

"Nah."

"What ever Nigga."

"Real talk, you know I do tha Shoe thing occasionally."

"Speaking of Shawna, I have to go pick her up."

"I'll meet you at tha club. I have to pick Nya up then handle a few last-minute things."

CHAPTER 17

"Is Wiz going to be at tha airport when we land?"

"I told him to meet us there with two pistols."

"Good cause I already reserved us a rental."

"You could of saved some money; we could have use one of Wiz's car."

"It ain't about nothing."

"I spotted Wiz as soon as we stepped into tha airport."

"Cuz here I go."

"Wiz this is Murder, Murder this my folk Wiz."

"What up Murder?"

"I can't call it."

"Heaven speaks highly of you."

"Murder you get tha car while I go get tha guns."

"I know y'all didn't rent no car?"

"Yeah we did."

"Come on Cuz, now you disrespectin' me, why don't you use one of my whips and cancel that rental?"

"Nah."

"Are you sure?"

"Yeah plus ain't no telling what you done in it."

"Nah, Nah, I'm just playing. I know you wouldn't give me no hot car."
Ceer pulled up in a nice Clk.

"No wonder you didn't want to use one of my whips."

"Come on, let's get outta here."

"A'ight follow me."

"Do you think we can hit a few clubs while we down here?"

"By clubs, do you mean body tap?"

"I mean clubs that we can get a party on in."

"Of course."

"Where we going tonight?"

"Jeezy and T. I performing at Visions."

"Say no more you know them my peoples."

"I hope you don't mind puttin' or shoes tonight?"

"Not really, but I rather put on some boots."

"It's a dress code tonight."

"I don't care. I just wanna get drunk and enjoy my freedom."

"We better get dressed."

"You still haven't talk to Jah'ceer?"

"No, you?"

"Unh, Unh."

"I hope nothing happened."

"I'm sure he's Ok; he's probably wit Nya."

"I'll get wit his ass tomorrow."

I could tell Roc was really upset about Ceer not coming to see him on his first day out.

"Jah'ceer, what took you so long we were about to go in my moms car."

"I told you I had to handle something that couldn't wait."

"That was an hour ago."

"I'm here now and that's all that matters."

"Come on Mom, let's get in the car before I hurt him."

"Yeah right."

"Yeah, Tae called to see if we were already there."

"Why she didn't just hit my phone?"

"She did, twice."

I took my phone out to see I had two missed calls.

"Damn."

"What's wrong?"

"I had it on silent."

"I'm glad it wasn't a life or death situation."

"I better hit her up."

After three rings, she picked up.

"I tried to call you twice."

"I know my phone was on silent."

"We on our way to tha party."

"So are we."

"You know your uncle is pissed wit you."

"I know he is, but he'll be OK once he sees me at tha party. Did you give him tha necklace?"

"No, I'm a give it to him when we get to tha club."

I could hear Uncle Roc asking who she was talking to.

"Sissy, I'll see you at tha club." All I could do was laugh.

"We'll be there in 15 minutes."

"Ok, if you get there before us, wait."

15 minutes later, we were pulling up at the same time as Jizz and Tisa.

"Hey Miss Sissy."

"Hello Tisa."

"Yo Ceer is Roc already inside?"

"There they go," Nya said as they pulled up and in this pretty cranberry 600.

"Damn, you can come to tha club but couldn't bother to be there when your uncle get out tha gates?"

"I had a lot of stuff to take care of; that's why I told Aunty Tae I would meet y'all here tonight."

"She didn't tell me all that," he said, looking at Aunty Tae. "Must of slipped my mind."

"Yeah I bet."

"Boy, shut up and put this on."

It was tha same chain he had made for me, but his was a little more icier.

"Roc you hurting 'em wit that new 600."

"I know it just hit tha showroom floor, so I'm tha first Nigga wit one."

"As you should be."

"Are we gonna sit out here all night or go get our party on?"

"Girl, I'm wit you on that."

"Me too."

"Y'all in a rush to sweat."

As soon as we walk through tha door tha smell of weed and tha sounds of Drake's "Miss Me Hit Us like a 10 Pound Weight to tha Face"."

"Yo, what up Roc?"

"Hey Roc."

"My Nigga Roc."

"Well, Well, Well, they finally let a real Nigga out."

Those were a few of tha comments people were saying. The DJ stop tha music, "I like to welcome my boy Roc; welcome home Big Homie." He then put on Welcome Back by Mase.

"I need a drink; let's hit tha bar."

"Come on, we in the VIP section."

"Damn, Aunty Tae you hooked this up."

"Van did it, I just told him what I wanted."

"Wow Baby, you had all this done for me?"

"Yup, me and Jah'ceer."

"Hey we had to throw you a big welcome home party."

The night was going good until some dude came up to Uncle Roc talking half-ass slick.

"You finally made it outta there, I see."

When I saw Uncle Roc's face, I knew something was about to go down.

"No dap for an old friend?"

I couldn't believe this Nigga had tha audacity to show up to my party; then again, why wouldn't he? He has no ideal I know what he did. I did not want to show my hand, so I remained calm.

"What you plan on doing now that you're home?"

"I don't know."

"Well, a lot has changed since you've been gone."

"What's that supposed to mean?"

"I run these streets now."

"When this happen?" Sharky asked, walking up?

"Been, I just let you eat on them outta respect for ya boss."

"I'm my own boss and ain't nobody let me do shit!"

I looked at Uncle Roc and Sharky to give me tha word and I would've aired this nigga out right here in front of everybody. Uncle Rock just shook his head no.

"Listen, I just came back home and don't plan on going back."

"Is that a threat Roc?"

"Ain't nothing change; I still get down you, know my work or have you forgotten?"

It took everything in me not to slump his bitch ass right there on tha spot.

"Roc, you'd be fighting a fight you couldn't win."

"Is that right?"

"Yeah, it is, I got it for tha low; take my number and get at me."

"Matter fact, I think I will take ya number so I can get at you; I respect tha game."

"Make sure you hit me."

"Oh, I will."

"Bartender four bottles of ya best."

"You don't have to do that."

"It ain't bout nothing, from one friend to another."

As soon as he stepped off, I looked at my Uncle Roc.

"What?"

"Jail made you soft."

There's a reason for everything, Ceer never let your enemy see you coming."

"I knew you wouldn't go out like that."

"It took a lot for me not to kill him right there."

"Who is he? I've never seen him before?

"I'll tell you about it tomorrow. I don't want to spoil ya night."

"A'ight."

"Roc, let's have a drink please."

I took that as a sign that she wanted to talk to me.

"What's up Tae?"

"Why did you let that bastard get away like that?"

"He's not getting away. I had to do it like that so it won't come back to me when he just happens to disappear. Tae never ever act on emotions because when you do it always turns out badly."

We partied for tha rest of tha night enjoying ourselves.

"I wanna thank y'all for throwing me this party."

"Unc, you don't have to thank us this goes wit out saying."

"I think I better drive," Aunty Tae said, taking Uncle Roc's keys.

I didn't say anything I just handed Nya my keys.

"Jah'ceer."

"What up Unc?"

"Hit my phone when you get up in tha a.m."

"He gets up early."

"So do I, I'll be up."

"Aunty Tae I love you."

"I love you too Jah'ceer."

"Tisa, can y'all drop my mom off since y'all going that way?"

"Sure, come on Ms. Sissy."

"Nya, don't forget we have that hair appointment at 9:30 tomorrow morning."

"No Bitch you don't forget."

"Damn Heaven, this block is doing numbers."

"I told you he had a goal mine."

"How come he hasn't opened up another block?"

"Good question, I don't know; let's ask him."

"Wiz come here for a sec."

"What up Cuz?"

"How come you don't open up another block?"

"I'm not ready for a war wit Jizz and his peoples."

"Who tha Fuck is Jizz?"

"Him and his man pretty much run tha A."

"So, what you do to get this spot?"

"Catch a couple bodies."

"Seriously."

"I am."

"So what's tha problem then?"

"We called a truce, but they gotta lot of Niggaz runnin' wit 'em now."

"I can have some real shooters down here by tha morning."

"I'm kool wit this block."

"That's tha problem you're content wit just this."

"It's bringing in a lot of doe."

"I know, but just imagine what you would be bringing in wit a few blocks instead of just this one."

"I never thought about it like that."

"Just think about it over tha next few days and let me know."

I couldn't front tha idea of opening up another block or two was very tempting but did I want to start a bloodbath.

"Wiz, I think we should take them up on it."

"Khalil, you know that will end tha truce and start a war."

"As long as they send those extra hands, we'll be straight."

"I don't know."

"Man Fuck Jizz!"

"This city could be our biggest breadwinner."

"Yeah, if my cuz do it."

"Even if he doesn't we'll set up our own team and do it."

"It's What ever you know I got ya back."

"On second thought, let's not involve Wiz; let's just set up shop."

"I was thinking tha same shit."

"We can let Wiz know when we meet him at tha club tonight."

"I don't know about you, but I'm hungrier than a slave."

"I know the perfect spot."

"As long as tha food is good, I don't care where we go."

"Boy, Aunt B's is one if not tha best soul food joint in the A."

When we arrived at Aunt B's, it was crowded as usual.

"Yo, what up Ceer," some dude said as he was walking out.

I looked at Heaven.

"Do you know him?"

"Nah."

"Well, he sure knows you."

"I don't know; maybe he was in the same foster home."

"It will come to you when you least expect it."

We sat down and looked over tha menu.

"I want tha fish and chicken dinner wit mac, greens and cornbread."

"I'll take the same wit a side of shrimp."

"You must really be hungry?"

"I told you I was."

"How many people do you think we need to bring down?"

"Maybe six or seven."

"That's all?"

"Yup, we gon' get ya uncle to give us his best men until we can get poppin'."

"He'll do it cause that means more money for him."

"Yo Heaven, you wasn't lying this food is jumpin'."

"I told you that."

"Hello."

"What up Unc?"

"Shit, where you at?"

"In route to ya crib."

"A'ight hit me when you get close."

"Sure will Playa."

Fifteen minutes later, I was calling to let him know I was a block away.

"I hope you don't mind riding in my hoopty for tha day?"

"If this is ya hoopty, I'd love to see ya real car."

"This my trap car, I hope you don't mind; I have a few stops to make first."

"No problem, I wanna see how you conduct biz-ness anyway."

"So who was dude last night?"

"That was Robby."

"I heard him say Sharky was eating because he let him."

"Imma find out about that."

"I don't see how because Sharky has shit on lock and what he doesn't, I do."

"Listen Jah'ceer, what I'm about to tell you is going to really piss you off."

"Well, I think I need to pull over then."

"Nah, just handle your biz-ness; we can talk over lunch."

Four drop-offs and 72,000 later, we were pulling up to Ed's for lunch.

"Oh Shit, is that my boy Roc?"

"The one and only what it do Ed?"

"I heard this morning that you was home."

"Yeah I touched down yesterday."

"I can't believe Fish set you up."

"Ed some Niggaz ain't built for this game."

"Lunch is on tha house."

"Gotta put this in my mental Rolodex Ed ain't never give me no free lunch."

"Cut it out Ceer; I always make sure you good."

"Yeah, you do, but it ain't never been free."

"Well, it's free today."

While we waited for our food Uncle Roc started talkin' bout my brother Nah'ceer.

"Unc, I think about him all tha time."

"Me too and now that home, I can really use my resources and try to find him."

"I wonder if he knows I even exist?"

"Not if he grew up wit foster parents like you had."

"Not to get off the subject, but I need to tell you about Robby. While I was doing my time, there was this guy name Pete that told stories all the time."

"What kind of stories?"

"About all tha jobs him and his man did."

"Dumb ass nigga don't he know not to talk."

"Especially in jail, it's always a Nigga trying to get out on another Nigga."

"He's probably doing a life bid now."

"Nah, he's in tha boneyard courtesy of me and my boy Rich."

"I'm guessing one of tha stories involved you?"

"Not me personally, but it did involve Ash and Zeke."

"My mom and pops?"

"Yeah."

"Hold up, please don't tell me he has something to do wit them getting murdered."

As soon as he shook his head I instantly became angry."

"Hold on there's more; the guy Robby was tha one who actually pulled tha trigger."

"Dude from last night?"

"Yeah, it took all I had not to slump his bitch ass last night."

"You should have gave me tha Ok when I asked you."

"Not in front of all those people."

"That explains why you all of a sudden back down and took his number."

"Yup."

I thought jail had made you soft."

"Come on, nephew never that."

"I need to be tha one to kill him."

"You can, but first, we need to find out who he's connected wit."

"Fuck who he's connected wit Unc!"

"First mistake, Jah'ceer you never and I mean never, let your emotions override your intellect; it could get you killed."

"I know, but this is tha Mafucka that deprived me of knowing my mom and dad and twin brother."

"Believe me, I know, I wanted to kill him so badly last night but I had to put my emotions in check."

When Jodeci's Forever My Lady started playing, I knew it was Tae.

"What's up Baby?"

"I just saw Robby at tha mall."

"What he say?"

"Nothing, he didn't see me."

"Good, I'll see you later."

"Love you."

"Love you too."

I went to my contacts, found his name then pushed send. After three rings, he picked up.

"Yo who dis?"

"Roc."

"Oh shit, I wasn't expecting to hear from you so soon."

"I don't have time to play no games. I need to get at this cheddar."

"I feel you on that; what was you trying to do?"

"Depends on tha numbers."

"Why don't I just front you something?"

"Nah, I don't need no handouts."

"So, how much are you willing to spend?"

It was taking everything in me not to cuss his punk ass out.

"I told you it depends on tha numbers."

"26,000."

I knew he was trying to play me.

"Damn, that's too high Imma get at Sharky, see what his numbers look like and hit you back."

"Check it out; if you get at least five, I can do 22,000 apiece."

That was still high, but it was a lot better than tha first price.

"What if I buy three?"

"24,000."

"Damn, I know you probably only paying 18,000 at tha most."

I actually was paying 19,000, but he would never know.

"Nah, Roc, truth be told, I'm paying 21,500."

"I might be able to get you a better number than that."

"How tha hell you gonna do that and you can only afford to cop three?"

I been down 15 years and still got more doe than this nigga; who tha fuck he think he talkin' to.

"Just let me get 10."

"Ten?"

"Yeah, ten, you can handle it, right?"

"Of course, I can handle it, but how you go from 3 to 10?"

"I need 5 and my nephew needs 5."

"You ain't workin', are you?"

That was it, "Mafucka don't ever disrespect me like that. I just did a 15-year bid for somebody else and didn't cry or complain about it, so don't ever in ya life come at me like that again!"

"No need to get upset; I just need to be sure."

"Nigga either you want this money, or you don't."

"Call me in an hour."

"You good, Unc?"

"That bitch nigga had tha nerve to ask me if I was Po-Po."

"Nah."

"Fuck, he didn't. So can he handle tha order?"

"I guess, he said, hit him in an hour."

"Unc I say we off him on sight."

"Ceer I want to kill him just as bad as you do, but we have to do this tha right way."

One hour later, Robby was hittin' my phone.

"What up Playa, you still want that?"

"Yeah."

"A'ight meet me at tha old pavilion in 20 minutes."

"Robby don't have me waiting."

Who tha hell he think he is? He needs me I don't need him! Me and Jah'ceer sat there for 30 minutes; as I was about to pull off, Robby was pulling up.

"Going somewhere?"

"I'm not none of them other cats you use to dealing wit. If you tell me to be here at a certain time, I expect you to be on time as well."

"Nigga you not tha only person I have to meet."

"Let's get this shit over wit."

"You got tha money?"

"Yeah and tha work?"

"Get in."

Jah'ceer got in tha back while I got upfront. When I looked at tha work, I could tell that it already been cut.

"What's this?"

"10 bricks."

"Man, this shit is all stepped on."

"Roc, this tha best work out there."

"Yo, let me see that Shit Unc."

"Nigga you ain't gotta watch me in ya rearview, I'm not going to steal none of this bullshit ass Coke; in fact, I'm not even buying none of this garbage."

"Fuck,you mean you not buying none?"

"Just what tha fuck I said!" He turned to look at me.

"Robby, I don't know who you're use to dealing wit, but you're not selling us no bullshit!"

"Listen Roc, I don't have time to be playing no games either you want it or you don't!'"

"Unc who tha fuck he think he talking to?"

No disrespect Roc but you need to tell ya, nephew, to respect his elders."

"Fuck this shit," Sptt, Sptt, "that's for killing my mom."

Sptt, Sptt, Sptt "That's for killing my pops."

"Damn Ceer, you definitely are your father's son next time, give me heads up."

"My bag Unc but I was tired of his mouth."

"A'ight make sure you wipe down everything you touched and let's go."

"Oh shit, let me grab that work; no sense in leaving it."

"Yeah, not like he'll have any used for it." I checked our surroundings to make sure no one has seen was just took place. Once I was sure there were no potential witnesses, we got into a car and pulled off.

"I see this is not your first kill."

"What makes you say that Unc?"

"Poise."

"Huh"

"You're to poise; if it was ya first time, you wouldn't be so poise."

"You're right, Unc it's not my first time and I'm pretty sure it won't be my last."

CHAPTER 18

"Damn, Cuz you got this block Jumpin' more than ours."

"We could take over this whole city if we want it, but we are cool with the two blocks we have."

"I know that Jizz is going to be on some bullshit once he hears about this."

"So let him come; we can handle him and whoever he brings wit him, trust me."

"I always do, Cuz, I always do."

"Where's Murder at?"

"He had some other biz-ness to deal wit, so he didn't make tha trip this time, but he said to tell you what's up."

"Damn, I had some bad chicks lined up for him."

"I'm sure he'll be disappointed about that."

"Ya man K.K he cool peeps."

"Everybody we deal wit is cool peeps."

"What tha deal is Heaven?" Khalif asked, walking out tha house.

"I can't call it, just trying to stay afloat."

Ever since Wiz told me what he said about liking me, I always made sure to flirt wit him.

"Heaven, when you gonna let my boy take you out to dinner?"

"I never mix biz-ness wit pleasure."

"I respect that."

"He would've asked me hisself if he really wanted to go."

"He doesn't know I asked. In fact, he doesn't even know I told you he likes you. My man is throwing a party for his girl tonight you trying to go?"

"Nah, I'm a be on tha block."

"They don't need you out there they've been doing a'ight for tha past few weeks."

"I guess you're right; count me in."

"Cool, be ready by no later than 9 o'clock."

Meanwhile, back in Philly…

"So, I understand that you now have a piece of North Carolina and two blocks in Atlanta lockdown."

"Yeah I had to take my show on tha road."

"I have somebody in Atlanta that I've been doing a lot of biz-ness wit for tha past 20 something years; I hope he's not going to mind me cutting in on his biz-ness."

"I doubt it; there's enough doe down there for tha both of y'all."

"Which means more money for you."

"Sure, you're right."

"What I'll do is let him know about you to prevent any drama that may occur."

"Mr. Ross, you don't have to do that. I can handle myself."

"I know you can, but I don't want no problems; Nah'ceer, you're like a nephew to me; it's not just about biz-ness."

"I know."

"I'll handle it if need be."

"A'ight, but they call me Murder down there."

"Very smart, never use your real name when you're out of town."

"Nah'ceer, I'll be retiring in a few years and I was thinking of handing it all over to you."

"What about Heaven?"

"She would never want to take over; she loves tha killing part of tha biz-ness too much."

I had to smile because Ross was absolutely right. Heaven would never want to run tha biz-ness and give up killing.

"Besides, I see how close tha two of you have become so I know she'll be ok wit you in charge."

"Heavens like a sister to me and I'll always have her back no matter what."

"I know you will; that's why I want to groom you on all aspects of my business."

"I'll be ready when you decide to step down in a few years."

"Yeah, about that I'm thinking more along tha lines of six months."

"Six months?"

"Yeah, so that doesn't leave a lot of time, so let's get started."

"Back down in tha 'A'."

"You tell me to be ready by 9 and you're not on time."

"My fault, I ran into a little problem."

"Is everything a'ight?"

"Nothing I couldn't handle."

"I hope you don't mind; we gotta stop and pick Khalif up."

"You're driving, I'm just a passenger."

"Here light this up," I said passin' him a Dutch."

Wiz took two pulls then started coughing.

"Damn Cuz, what's this?"

"Sour Diesel."

"Where you get this from?"

"Up top."

"Next time you send tha work, you need to send me a pound of this."

"This shit ain't cheap."

"I don't care how much it cost. I need some of this."

When we pulled up to Khalif's Wiz, hit tha horn two times.

"I told this slow ass nigga to be ready by 8 o'clock."

"Nigga it's 9:30."

"I know, if I tell him 8, he'll be ready by the time I come scoop him up."

Khalif came out tha house wit out a care in tha world.

"You about to be driving ya own shit. I know you heard tha horn."

"I came out, didn't I?"

"You're worse then a female, slow ass nigga."

"It takes time to look like this."

"Ha! Ha! Ha!"

"What's so funny Heaven?"

"Y'all act like a married couple."

"I see you got jokes."

"What y'all smokin' on that shit smells good."

"Lif this some serious smoke you can't handle this wit those tender lungs you got."

"What ever Nigga let me hit it."

Khalif pulled long and hard and started coughing like crazy.

"I just told you take ya time wit that."

"Yo, this shit right here is definitely some exotic."

"Nah, that's regular where I'm from."

"Don't taste like no regular."

"It's exotic, but we smoke it so much we consider it regular."

"This that Sour Diesel," Wiz said, taking tha Dutch back.

"Sour Diesel, huh?"

"Yup."

"How much is a pound of this?"

"For y'all 9000."

"DAAAAAAMN!"

"Hey, this Shit is top shelf."

"You ain't lying, Cuz they can get 9 stacks from me all day."

"Me too."

"Like I told Wiz, I'll send it wit tha next shipment."

"Is Joker throwing this party for his girl?"

"Yeah, I think it's her birthday or something."

"Did you say Joker?"

"Yeah."

"Is he short, brown skin, curly hair?"

"Yeah, you know him?"

"I sure do," I said, pulling out my phone to call Nah'ceer.

"What up Sis?"

"You'll never guess who I found."

"Who?"

"Joker."

"He's in Atlanta?"

"Yeah, I'm on my way to his party."

"Oh, so that Mafucka in Atlanta throwing parties wit my money?"

"Don't worry; I'll make sure this will be his last party he throws."

"Nah, see if he has my money first. If he does, get it then kill him."

"No problem, talk to you later."

"If you don't mind me ask'n what was that about?"

"Is Joker ya man?"

"He a'ight we were buying weight off him before we hooked up wit you and Murder."

"So, he doing good himself."

"Yeah he got Decator on lock."

"I need you to take me back so I can get my piece."

"Y'all got beef wit him?"

"He skipped town owing us some paper."

"It must of been a nice piece of paper."

"Six figures."

"He is hard to get it because he keeps at least five Niggaz wit him at all times and they all holding heat."

"Evidently, you don't know me that well."

"Y'all go ahead. I'll see y'all at tha party."

"Look Cuz, I don't know what you're planning, but I'm not letting you do this alone."

"Thanks for the support, but I work alone."

"Are you sure?"

"Trust me, I got this."

"A'ight we'll see you at tha party."

"Do you see her yet?"

"Nah you?"

"Nah, but I got my strap. I'm not letting it go down like that."

"I got mine too."

"Maybe she's outside waiting on him."

"Would one of you like to buy a girl a drink?"

"Nah, I'm good Ma," Khalif said wit out hesitation.

"What you drinking Shorty?"

"Bombay on tha rocks wit a lemon."

"I'll be right back."

"I guess you do this often."

"Excuse me."

"I said I guess you do this often."

"What's that?"

"Ask guys to buy you drinks."

"It depends if they are cute or not."

"Typical broad."

"You wouldn't know a typical broad if you seen one."

"I'm looking at one."

"Here you go Shorty."

"Thank you."

"Don't mention it."

"Wiz, Khalif, what's tha deal?"

"Same Shit, you know we had to come show some love."

"I appreciate that; I heard y'all got it going on over there."

"We just trying to stay alive."

"Y'all doing a damn good job at it."

"What tha numbers lookin' like?"

"Better than yours."

"I see it's been damn near 8 months since we've done any biz-ness."

"Maybe you should holla at us."

"I doubt that you'll have that much work to fill my order."

I sat there taking it all in, thinking I would get what he owed us plus interest. Wiz went in his pocket to retrieve his phone and all Joker's men pulled out.

"Whoa, no need for that. I'm just try'n to get my phone."

"It's cool fellas."

"Give me ya number and I'll be sure to hit you up tomorrow."

After we exchanged numbers, I offered to buy his girl a bottle.

"Send it over to VIP."

"No problem."

"Shorty wit y'all?"

"Yes," I said, not giving Wiz or Khalif a chance to respond.

"Nah, she ain't wit me," Khalif quickly said.

"She wit me," Wiz said, grabbing my arm.

"A'ight, Imma holla at y'all tomorrow for sure but feel free to join us in VIP.

Thirty minutes later and still no sign of Heaven.

"She ain't coming Wiz."

"I know."

"Ya girl stand you up?"

"None of ya biz-ness."

"Your boy is too damn smart."

"Call me on Wiz; let's check out tha VIP."

I just stood there as they started to walk off.

"Shorty you gonna stand there, or you gon' come wit us?"

"I didn't know I was invited."

"You wit me tonight."

I wanted to laugh but kept it to myself. Joker and his crew were filthy drunk by tha time it was over. Joker had sent his girl home a little while ago it was just him and his boys. When I saw they were leaving, I told Wiz that I was about to bounce.

"Hold up Shorty, we are outta here too."

Everybody was standing around trying to catch as soon as I saw my opportunity. I pulled out my .45 wit tha silencer attached and let off five shots droppin' Jokers boys before they knew would hit 'em."

"Oh shit," Khalif said, pulling his heat.

I had already grabbed Joker. "What the fuck is going on?"

"Nigga shut up and walk."

I looked at Wiz and Khalif, then winked.

"Oh shit that's Heaven."

"Yo ya Cuz is one bad bitch."

"Get tha car so we can follow her."

As soon as we got to my car I knocked him out then put him in tha truck.

"I need to take him somewhere quiet."

"No problem, follow me."

Forty minutes later, we will pulled up to this isolated house. When we got out, I instructed Wiz to hit tha trunk button on tha inside of tha car. As soon as tha trunk opened, Joker jumped up only to be met by my .45 in his face.

"Get out slow."

"Yo, what the hell is going on?"

We walked toward tha house. "Welcome to hell," Khalif said, opening tha door.

The house was set up like a torture chamber.

"Wiz, Khalif, what is this about?"

"I'll be asking all tha questions tonight."

"Who are you?" (SMACK)

"What did I just tell you? I see you still don't listen Joker." Tha look on his face asked tha question his mouth wanted to.

"Where is tha money you owe," I asked while removing tha mask from my face.

"Oh shit!"

"You didn't think we wouldn't find you, did you?"

"I can explain."

"No need to explain to me." I pulled out my phone and called Nah'ceer.

"What up Sis?"

"Somebody wants to explain something to you."

"Fuck all that explanation shit. Does he have that 300 grand?"

"Yeah I got it."

"Well, you know I need 500 grand for my pain and suffering."

"I have it; I just need to get to it."

"No, you tell Wiz or Khalif where it is and one of them will get it."

"Damn Joker, you got yaself in a messed up predicament. I thought you was good people."

"Come on Wiz I always been fair to you."

"You have but this here blood and you know what they say blood thicker than water."

"Where tha money at and don't try to bullshit or that pretty bitch of yours is dead along wit that baby she's carrying."

"Yo, she don't got shit to do wit this."

"Unless you involve her tha choice is yours."

"Ok, I'll tell you where it is."

Once he gave up tha info, I sent Wiz to retrieve it.

"Cuz I'll call you once I have it. Hey, what if it's more than 500 grand there?"

"Leave it," I said, winking at him, making Joker think he would be left alive.

"Joker, let me ask you a question. Why would you run off wit our paper after tha love we showed you?"

"Truthfully Kool said that he was going to kill y'all and I could keep tha doe as long as I use him as my supplier."

"You still ran off."

"I figured if he would kill his best friend wit no remorse then it would only be a matter of time before he killed or tried to do tha same to me."

"Kools dead."

"He is?"

"Yeah, Ali killed him."

"Ali?"

"Yeah he was stealing money and tried to make it seem like it was Ali."

"That Nigga a real snake on some real shit. I buy tha Philly Inquire every day to see if y'all was dead or not."

"Khalif, keep an eye on him. I need to call Murder."

"Hello."

"I got some new info for you."

"I'm listening."

After I told Ceer everything, Joker told me he told me not to kill him that we could use him.

"Joker, what's tha number on them things?"

"26,000."

"Damn you getting raped."

"I know, but I still make a hell of a profit."

"Check this out, I was going to kill you, but we decided you'd be worth more alive. As of now, I can give 'em to you at 22,000 apiece."

"Word."

"Yeah."

"That's right on time. I need to re-up."

"That's Wiz hold up."

"Yo, talk to me."

"Cuz this Nigga holding."

"A'ight, just take tha 500 grand leave tha rest."

"What are you serious?"

"Yeah, I'm not going to kill him."

"If you say so."

"I'm serious, Wiz leave it."

"I'm taking 10 grand for my troubles."

"Khalif untie him."

"When do you think you can get that to me?"

"How much do you need?"

"50."

"Ok, plus we'll throw you 50 at 24,000 apiece."

"Damn right, I'll be a fool to turn that down."

"Let me place a call real quick."

When I finished my call, I let him know that it was on tha way and should be here no later than 3 o'clock this afternoon.

"Can I catch a ride back to my whip?"

"Sure."

I caught Kyleef looking at me so I made sure to throw my hips as I walked away.

"Hey Heaven."

"What's up Khalif?"

"Never mind."

Damn, I can't believe I just froze up.

"Khalif, you drive, I'll get in tha back."

I could tell Joker was skeptical about getting up front.

"Nigga if I was going to kill you, you would already be dead."

By tha time we got to tha club, everything had died down.

"I'll hit you in a few hours."

"Cool."

"And sorry about your boys."

"They weren't on point, so they got what they got."

"Unc what's tha deal wit ya boy House?"

"What you mean?"

"He acts like he scared to get at this paper."

"House is more of a gun than a hustler."

"I need somebody like that around me; sorry, Neph, I already got him on my squad."

"Unc, you ain't gotta do nothing but fall back and let my team handle everything."

"I am, but I still want him wit me just in case a nigga get outta line."

"I feel you."

"I knew it was something I needed to get at you about."

"What's up?"

"Do you know this kid named Murder?"

"Nah."

"Well, my man Ross called me a few days ago and said his nephew had a few blocks down here."

"What that got to do wit me?"

"He wanted to be sure he was straight."

"As long as he's not interfering with my money, I don't care what he does."

"If he does, I need you to holla at me first before you make a move on him."

"Why?"

"Because Ross is my connect, so I owe him that much, not to mention he got at me while I was down."

"In that case, you got that Unc."

"Man, I swear you just like ya dad."

"You know they always say like father like son."

"I gotta pick ya aunt up."

"She need to drive her own self to work."

"She does, I just took her car today so I could get her car detailed."

CHAPTER 19

Over tha last few months, tha money has really been coming in, we had three spots in Atlanta and North Carolina doing major numbers.

"Aye Ceer, Wiz, Joker, Talib, and Sheed all are ready."

"Damn them Niggaz runnin' thru that shit like a fat bitch at an all you can eat buffet."

"Boy you stupid."

"Nah, on some real shit, I think we need to up what we send them."

"If you ask me, I think they good wit what we send 'em."

"You think?"

"Positive, I know it would cut down on tha trips up and down tha highway, but my gut is telling me we good."

"That's all it is then; they'll continue to get tha same order."

"Unc, I need to holla at ya plugs peoples."

"Why, what's the problem?"

"My money!"

"You've got plenty of it."

"That's not the point."

"Then tell me what is."

"He's cuttin' into my money, so now it's a problem."

"Let me give my man a call so we can have a sit-down."

"A'ight, but I'm a keep it 100 if they don't make it soon, there's going to be a lot of bloodshed and it's not going to be mine, I promise you that."

"Slow down, Nephew, slow down; let me get at my man before you go all Rambo on a nigga."

"Unc, I told you we can all eat, but when you start taking food off my plate, then it's a problem."

"I feel you; just let me holla at my man before you do anything."

"Roc, My Man, what can I do for you?"

"We got a little situation."

"I'm sure nothing we can't handle."

"That's what I'm hoping."

"Well, talk to me."

"Do you think you can set up a meeting wit ya nephew?"

"In reference to?"

"His biz-ness is interfering wit my nephew's biz-ness and I'm trying to nip it in the bud before it gets outta hand."

"A'ight, I respect that; let me make a call and I'll hit you back in a few."

"Ok."

"Hopefully, we can resolve this wit out any blood being shed."

"I'm a boss, I'm a boss, I'm a boss."

"What up Mr. Ross?"

"What I tell you about that Mr. Shit?"

"My bag Old Head."

"You got jokes; now I told you just call me Unc."

"That's what we call washed-up old heads that smoke."

"Well, we both know I'm neither of those."

"I'll just call you Uncle Ross."

"Cool, but on a more serious note, I need you to have a sit-down wit my man Roc in ATL."

"I just got back in town, but Heaven is still down there; she can handle it."

"I'm sure she's more than capable to handle it, but you know how her temper can be."

"What's this about anyway?"

"Evidently, your biz-ness is interfering with his."

"Ain't shit to talk about!"

"Just hear them out; maybe y'all can come to an agreement."

"Give me all tha information and I'll pass it on to Heaven."

"Let me call Roc back, then I'll hit you back wit everything."

Twenty minutes later, I was on tha phone wit Heaven relaying everything Ross told me.

"So let me get this straight these Niggaz want to have a sit down because we suppose to be taking food off their plate?"

"You got it."

"Fuck 'em!"

"Same thing I say, but Ross wants us to do this for him."

"So what you coming back down?"

"Nah, I want you to handle it."

"A'ight, I'll take Capone and a few other niggaz wit me."

"Here's his number, his name is Rock."

"Hello."

"Is this Roc?"

"Who's asking?"

"I understand you want to talk."

"This doesn't sound like Murder."

"I'm his sister."

"I prefer to talk to him."

"Well, what you prefer and what's going to happen are two different things. Do you want to talk or not?"

I had to bite my tongue so not to start off on tha wrong foot.

"Do you know where tha old pavilion is?"

"I'll find it."

"Be there in an hour."

As soon as I hung up, I called Wiz so he could take me.

An hour later, we were pulling up to this old building.

"I'm not going in there wit out my pistol."

"Me either."

There were two guys coming out tha door when we got out tha car.

"No need to pat us down we all holding and we're not going in wit out them."

"Yo, go let Roc know."

Three minutes later, he was back, letting tha other guy know it was cool for us to come in. Even though we were outnumbered I like our chances if anything went down.

"Hello, you must be Heaven?"

"And you must be Roc?"

"Yes I am."

"So can we get to tha matter of this meeting."

"Sure, as you know my nephew controls…"

"Excuse me not to cut you off but where is your nephew?"

"He had another meeting that he needed to attend, but he sent his right hand. As I was saying, he controls majority of this city."

"To my understanding, he let Wiz control one of tha blocks."

"He didn't let me do anything; we had to go through a lot of Shit to get that block."

"Be that as it may, you still have a block too at that."

"I don't see what that has to do wit ya nephew."

"Roc if I may."

"Go ahead Jizz."

"Long story short, we have no problem wit ya blocks, but when you change tha size of what they get for 10, 20 or 50 dollars, that cuts into our pocket."

"How?"

"Word spreads and of course now everybody wants tha dime that's really a 20."

"Listen, we can sell what we want on our blocks if you're losing money, I suggest you step up tha size of ya work."

I didn't say shit, but I did agree with what she was saying. I could tell Jizz didn't like what she was saying, so it was only a matter of time before he snapped out.

"Listen Bitch I will shut down both those Fuck'n blocks y'all got!"

I wanted to see how far this would go before I stepped in.

"First off, don't get it or me twisted!"

"You said that to say what?"

"Just what I said, don't let this pretty face fool you."

I could tell he was about to reach for his pistol so I beat him to the draw.

"You'd be dead before you even got to pull that."

"Hold up, no need for all of that."

"No disrespect to you Roc, because my uncle speaks very highly of you, but when you are ready to talk, you know tha number."

She was like Ross in a lot of ways.

"I should've put a bullet in that bitches head."

"Nigga she had tha drop on you and you ain't even know."

"Never judge a book by its cover; it could get you killed."

I could tell Jizz wasn't trying to hear what I was tellin' him, but it was tha truth.

"How did tha meeting go?"

"That nigga sent his sista."

"His sista?"

"Yeah his Fuckin sista and that bitch got a smart ass mouth."

"You should've shut it for her."

"I went to pull out and she already had her shit in my face."

"Oh, so this bitch wants to play a grown man's game?"

"When I said something about tha size of their work, do you know what tha bitch told me?"

"What?"

"Step up tha size of our work."

"Hold up, and where was Unc when all this was going down?"

"Right there."

"Hell Nah, let me hit him up."

He picked up after tha fourth ring.

"What's up Nephew?"

"I don't know you tell me Unc."

"I take it Jizz filled you in?"

"Yeah he did."

"Imma set up another meeting so you can be there."

"Unc, I don't want to be there. I might slump that bitch!"

"You need to be there this concerns you."

"I know, but trust me, you don't want me there."

"A'ight, that's up to you, but Imma work out tha best solution to this problem."

"As long as it's not no bull, I can live wit that."

"Come on Ceer, I'm not going to let nobody get over on you you're blood and that's first and foremost."

"I'm glad we're on tha same page."

"So it was a waste of time?"

"Yeah."

"Fuck 'em we gonna keep doing what we doing and if they get in the way of that they'll see a side that they really don't want to see."

"That's all it is then; you know I got ya back."

"Wit out a doubt."

"I was about to push that nigga Jizz shit back."

"Why?"

"He has a big mouth."

"He thought he could talk to you like tha average broad."

"He found out real quick he couldn't; if it wasn't for Roc, he'd be nothing but a memory."

"So this Roc nigga he was cool?"

"Yeah, in a way, he reminds me of you."

"How's that?"

"Cool, calm and quiet. I could tell that he was agreeing wit everything I was saying. The problem I have is if they would've said something from tha door instead of waiting until they start losing a few customers."

"You know how tha game goes Ceer you ain't just start hustling."

Before he could respond, my line beeped.

"Hold on Ceer."

"Hello."

"Hello Heaven, this is Roc."

"What's up Roc?"

"I was wondering if you would be free for a sit-down tomorrow?"

"Sure, as long as you don't bring that loud mouth Nigga wit you."

"No, just me and you."

"A'ight, I have no problem wit that."

"Cool, I'll call you tomorrow." (Clicked back over)

"Ceer."

"Damn, I thought you forgot about me."

"Nah, that was Roc; he wants to meet tomorrow, just me and him."

"I'll fly in."

"No need, I'll handle it."

"Are you sure?"

"Yeah, I'm already down here."

"You down there more than you're up here."

"I know Wiz was just saying tha same thing."

"Well, hit me after tha meeting tomorrow. I'm bout to meet Ross."

"Ok, tell him I said hi."

"Will do."

"Did you get everything settled at tha meeting?"

"Nah, but Heaven and Roc set up another meeting wit just tha two of them for tomorrow."

"What happened at tha first one?"

"Heaven said some loud mouth Nigga was talking stupid."

"He still alive?"

"Yeah thanks to ya man Roc."

"I'm sure Heaven and Roc will come to a mutual understanding."

"If they do or they don't, it doesn't matter either way cause we not shutting down shop."

"I just don't want any unnecessary bloodshed."

"Listen, I respect you to tha fullest and even though I don't know Roc, I respect him because you do."

"That's why I'm trying to prevent any blood being shed; although I respect him, blood is thicker than water."

Hearing Ross say that made me feel good because I now know if a war breaks out, what side he'll be on.

"If Heaven can't get them to come to terms, then we gonna let the ball bounce where it may."

CHAPTER 20

"I talk to your uncle today and he feels tha same way I do."

"How's that?"

"We both want this resolved wit no bloodshed."

"That depends on ya nephew Roc; we had these blocks for close to a year and now it's a problem."

"Heaven Imma be honest wit you, tha problem is the size of tha work."

"We're not trying to step on nobody's toes that's just how we do it."

"I agree wit you when you said they need to step tha size up."

"I always believe that you out do all competition if I pay 20,000 for bird I'm cool wit making 22,000 which is only a 2000 profit, but it's about tha quick flip."

Roc truly reminded me of Ceer; they both had the same logic in hustling. By the time we were done talking, we had come to a mutual understanding and hopefully, his nephew would respect and honor it.

"Heaven, I'm glad we could come to an agreement."

"Me too."

"You have my number; if there's any problems, please don't hesitate to give me a call."

"As long as ya nephew sticks to tha deal, there shouldn't be any problems."

As soon as we were done I called Ceer to update him.

"Do you think we'll have any problems."

"For their sake, I hope not."

"A'ight, I'll be down in a few days, so make sure y'all ready to hang out and have some fun."

"Listen, I'm taking Nya to Aruba for a few days; you and Auntie Tae want to go?"

"It doesn't sound like a bad ideal; let me call and ask her."

I made a few calls while he called Aunty Tae.

"A'ight Nephew count us in."

"I already told Nya to make tha reservations."

"I hope a week ain't too long?"

"That might not be long enough."

"We can always stay longer if we're having too much fun. I'll hit you later. I have to take Nya shoppin'."

"I got a better ideal."

"I'm listening Unc."

"Why don't you send Nya shoppin' wit Tae?"

"I need to grab some stuff too."

"So do I, so we let tha woman shop and we can shop; unless you want to be in tha stores for tha rest of tha night?"

"Hell Nah!" I called Tae and have her pick Nya up.

"Hey Nya."

"What's up Tae?"

"I'm on my way to pick you up so we can go shoppin' for a trip."

"A'ight, just hit tha horn when you get out front."

"Come outside now. I'll be pulling up in a few minutes."

"That was quick."

"I was in tha vicinity when Roc called me."

"Oh, they didn't want to be in the stores all day, huh?"

"better for us."

"We can take our time and not be rushed."

Girl, I hate when Roc rushes me, then he'll say, "This is why I don't like coming to tha store wit you."

"Ceer is tha same way."

We ended up shoppin' until tha stores were about to close.

"Tae, I can't wait to put on this bikini."

"Ceer gonna want to rip it off you."

"As long as he has tha 1500 to replace it, he can."

"Do you need help carrying those bags in?"

"No, I got it."

"What time do we have to be at tha airport?"

"Check-in is at 9 o'clock, so 8 o'clock."

"Ok, I'll see you in tha morning."

As soon as I walked in tha house, Ceer said, "I'm glad I didn't have to go wit you."

"Me too, because I didn't have to be rush."

"Looks like you bought tha whole mall."

"Nope, just what I liked."

"I hate to see what you didn't like."

"Damn Nya, we only going for a week, not a month."

"It's hot in Aruba Imma need to change my clothes at least twice a day if not more."

"Wow, you're something else."

"That's why you love me."

"Let's pack tonight so we won't have to do it in the morning."

"I'm already packed but wit all that stuff you got you're probably gonna need to use tha other luggage."

We ended up wit eight suitcases, three mines tha rest hers.

"Something smells good."

"That would be dinner."

"Oh my, you cooking tonight?"

"Yeah, I decided to cook steak and shrimp. Somebody's getting some tonight."

"You said it like I don't always get some."

"Boy, go ahead."

"I'm just saying."

"You're not saying nothing."

"I must not have given you enough attention today."

"You haven't."

"Awe poor Baby, come to daddy. You better not burn that food."

"Oh shit, I'm glad you said something."

The next morning, we all boarded the plane to Aruba.

"I can't believe Ceer agreed to let them keep selling on those blocks."

"He said they came to terms and it was all good."

"How long is he going to be gone?"

"At least a week if not longer."

"I hope you don't plan on doing nothing stupid."

"What's that supposed to mean?"

"Just what I said."

"Does it matter, either you wit me or you're not."

"Come on Nigga you know I'm with you, I'm just saying."

"I just don't agree with them setting up shop."

"If I'm not mistaken, you're the one who agreed to let Wiz do his thing."

"That was before they started coming between my doe."

"I think we should honor Ceer's word."

"Yeah maybe you're right."

Later that night, I sent Craig Crack through there to cop so I could see what they were giving up.

"Damn Jizz, I don't know what tha quality is like, but the quantity is nice."

"Let me see."

I couldn't front tha work was a nice size for tha price.

"Do you need me to test it for you too?"

"Yeah, but wait till we get back across town I don't want to smell that shit."

"Damn Nigga give me a chance to park."

"Man, I need my wake up."

"I don't give a fuck what you need you better not do that shit no more. Now get tha fuck out my shit."

"My fault Nephew; I'll be right back."

Fifteen minutes and Craig Crack was back.

"So what's it hittin' for?"

He put up his index finger. I could tell he was geeking.

"Nephew, y'all need to get some of this. I ain't had no Coke like this since the early 80s."

"That shit like that, huh?"

"Yeah it's like that Nephew."

"A'ight, good-looking Crack."

"No problem Nephew, anytime."

I knew my next move was more than likely going to start an all-out war, but I didn't care.

"Wow, tha water here is beautiful."

"I know I haven't seen anything this beautiful only in tha magazines."

"At tha rate, you're going you're be out of pictures by tomorrow."

"No, I won't," Nya said, pulling out another digital camera, "this one holds 379 pictures, so I'm good."

"Ha! Ha! Ha!"

"What's so funny Roc?"

"He's laughing because I bought two digital cameras too."

"What can we say? Great minds think alike."

"Tell us about it," they both said, putting on their Prada shades.

Once we arrived at our hotel, I was trying to check-in so I could find some weed. The bellhop that was taking our bags up must've sensed it because he let us know if we were interested; he has some good weed for sale.

"How much do you have and what's tha price?"

"As much as you want and 1500 American dollars a pound."

"Is it any good?" Nya asked.

"The best."

"Well, we'll take two pounds."

"I'll bring it to your room in 20 minutes."

"A'ight."

"I'm sure 1 pound would have been more than enough to last for tha week."

"The way Roc smoked, I don't know."

"Damn Unc, you blowin' like that?"

"I'm still makin' up for lost time."

"Come on Unc, you was blowin' good in there probably better than a lot of Niggaz on tha street."

Twenty minutes later, the bellhop was knocking on tha door.

"Come in."

He walked in and sat tha weed on tha bar.

"This look like some good weed."

"It's tha best."

I counted out 3000 and handed it to him.

"Thanks."

"No problem, there's plenty more where that came from."

"I'll keep that in mind." Before he left, I asked if there was any way to get some of this back to the states?

"Definitely."

"I'll definitely be in touch if this is as good as you say it is."

"Here's my number."

Me being a hustler I was, I knew that Ahmad was big time. This bellhop gig was just a front. It would be later confirmed that Ahmad was major in tha weed game and he owned tha hotel we were staying at.

"Now Baby, who would've thought Ahmad was tha man?"

"Me."

"Besides you?"

"That's how it's suppose to be low-key under everybody's radar."

I wasted no time rolling up; I was anxious to taste this weed. There was a knock on tha door. I knew it was Jah'ceer because it was tha adjoining door.

"Whew, that smell like some funk."

"Ahmad damn sure wasn't lying this tha best weed I've ever smoked."

"Let me hit that Unc."

"Roll ya own," he said, handing me a pound.

"Whew, this shit fluorescent green. How much I owe you?"

"It's on me."

"Feeling generous?"

"Come on Neph, that shit ain't bout nothing."

"I'm just saying, I know this cost some doe."

"You would not believe me if I told you."

"That much."

"Nah 1500."

"Bullshit."

"Seriously."

"1500 and it's that good; we need to get some of this back to tha states."

"Already on it." I took one pull and started coughing.

"Let me find out you can't handle it."

"I didn't know it was that smooth."

"Tell me anything."

"Only tha truth Unc."

After we finished smoking we headed down to tha lobby to see what they had to offer tha tourists.

"I'll be glad to show you around if you like."

"What time do you get off Ahmad?"

"Whenever I want."

"Tae looked at him then said, "Your relatives own this."

"No, I do."

She turned to look at me; I didn't say anything, I just gave her a look that said, I told you. I could tell Ahmad knew I was about a dollar and he wanted to see how we could benefit of one another.

CHAPTER 21

"Are you sure you want to do this Jizz?"

I didn't respond; I just pulled my mask down, cock my pistol and started down tha block. As soon as we rolled up on our targets, I let my .50 cal sing, leaving no one standing.

"Heaven, Heaven."

"What's up Sal?"

"Wiz got shot along wit Jay and 5 others are dead."

"What, who did it?"

"I don't know; they wore mask."

"Where were tha shooters."

"We were all coming from a meeting Wiz called."

"I don't give a shit. I told them to keep shooters on tha roofs at all times!"

"Wiz had called an emergency meeting."

"I don't give a fuck if tha president called a meeting!"

"Somebody could have relayed tha information to them."

"We were just following orders."

"Where was Wiz shot?"

"In his back."

"Are tha police there?"

"Yup."

"Shit!"

"Don't worry, by tha time they got here, it was just a call about shots fired; we had it cleaned up."

"Good, Good."

"Once tha police leave, we will continue biz-ness as usual."

"A'ight, keep me updated."

For some reason, I knew that Roc's nephew was behind this, but when I tried to call Roc, it went straight to voicemail. I tried again wit tha same results.

"Hello."

"What up Sis?"

"We ran into a little problem down here."

"What kind of problem?"

"Wiz and Jay got shot."

"How?"

"A couple of niggaz wit mask came through shooting."

"Where tha fuck were tha shooters?"

"Wiz called an emergency meeting."

"I don't give a fuck; there should always be shooters on tha rooftops!"

"That's what I just told Sal. Also, five people are dead."

"You need to come home until tha heat dies down."

"Ain't no heat. Sal had it all cleaned up before tha police got there."

"Sal's very dependable as well as loyal he needs a promotion."

"Already ahead of you."

"I'll be down next week. Do you need me to bring you anything?"

"Nah, I'm good."

"Ok, keep your ear to tha street, see if you can find out who is responsible."

"I'm pretty sure it was Roc's nephew and if it was gloves are off, I'll talk to Ross."

"You do that."

"Heaven, I think this is about to get messy, so Imma send some more people down just in case."

"I think that's a good ideal."

"I'll hit you up later after I talk to Ross."

"A'ight."

"Heaven."

"Yeah."

"Be safe."

"You know I'm trained for this shit."

"I know, but still be safe."

"Don't worry; I will."

As soon as I hung up, I called Ross to see if he could get some clarity on tha situation.

"I don't think it was Roc or his nephew."

"Why you say that?"

"Because they took a vacation to Aruba, he called to let me know he would need me when he got back."

"Maybe they back by now."

"They just left yesterday."

"I am a head down there for a few days."

"I'm sure Heaven can handle it."

"I know, but I just want to make sure she straight."

"You two have become real close over tha years."

"She's tha sister I never head."

"Nah'ceer, at the end of the day, always remember to put family first."

"That goes wit out saying; you never have to worry about that."

"A'ight, hit me when you get down there and let me know what's going on."

"Will do."

"We might need to stay for another week."

"I'm wit you on that, this week went by too fast."

"Let me call Jizz and make sure all is well."

After six rings, he picked up.

"Yo who this?"

"It's me Nigga."

"Oh, what up? I didn't recognize tha number."

"I'm on a burnout."

"You home?"

"Nah, we're going to stay another week. I'm just checking to make sure you good."

"I'm straight."

"So everything is cool?"

Damn, I wonder if he knows about tha shootings.

"Yeah, you know Imma whole shit down to tha fullest and do What ever has or needs to be done."

Something in the statement told me Jizz was up to something, but I just downplayed it.

"A'ight Homey, I'll talk to you next week."

"Just make sure you come back next week cause I'll need more work by then."

"We'll definitely be back by next week."

"Damn Nigga, who was that one of your bitches?"

"Nah, that was Ceer."

"What he talkin' bout?"

"They staying another week."

"They must be having a ball over Jamaica."

"Nigga they in Aruba, not Jamaica."

"You should've told him about tha hit we did on Wiz and his peeps."

"I didn't want to ruin his vacation."

"Yeah, I feel you."

"Is everything straight?"

"I don't know."

"What do you mean?"

"Jizz said everything was good, but something in his voice told me it wasn't."

"I'm sure Jizz has it under control; let's just enjoy another week of fun in tha sun."

"Yeah you're probably right."

"Let's go join Tae and Roc at tha pool."

"Sounds good to me."

"Are you going to change first?"

"I wasn't."

"So that means you're not swimming wit me?"

When Nya came out tha bathroom in her bikini, I couldn't take my eyes off her.

"Wow, on second thought,, I think I might just go for a swim wit you."

"Thought you change your mind."

"What happened to your other bathing suit?"

"Nothing, I just wanted to put this one on; why is there something wrong wit it?"

"Hell Nah, you should have been put that one on."

"Wasn't nothing wrong wit tha other one."

"It wasn't, but that one there would make tha strongest man week."

"Ha! Ha! Ha! Boy you something else."

"A'ight, come on, I'm ready."

"Grab tha towels off tha shelf."

"I didn't think you two were coming."

"Don't blame me," I said, pointing to Nya.

"He was on tha phone, not me." "It's Jizz a'ight?"

"I think."

"What do you mean you think?"

"I don't know; something in his voice alarmed me."

"You want to leave?"

"No!" Tae and Nya, both of you.

"Nah, we good Unc."

"You sure?"

"Yes, he sure," Tae added.

"I'm talkin' to Ceer."

"We cool I'm not going to jump to conclusions, I'm just making sure biz-ness before pleasure."

"I know Unc I know."

I didn't want to ruin Aunty Tae and Nya's trip, so against my better judgment, I chose to stay.

"Listen, Nephew, we can always come back; if you think we need to get home, let's go."

"We straight Uncle Roc."

"I don't care about Tae being upset if we leave; she'll get over it."

"Jizz can handle it; I trust him."

"I'm glad you do."

"You don't trust him?"

"Not on tha biz-ness aspect because he'll let his pride get in tha way; I saw that firsthand at tha meeting wit Heaven.

If it hadn't been for me, we would've been making funeral arrangements."

"Unc, I've been telling Jizz for years not to let his pride get in tha way of biz-ness. I just don't want his pride to be your downfall."

"Sorry I'm late; traffic was messy."

"You only 5 minutes late, besides my plane just landed."

"You know I hate not being on time."

"So, what's tha deal on tha shootings?"

"Nobody has said anything, but I'm pretty sure Roc's nephew was behind it."

"I told you Ross said they're in Aruba."

"Well, he probably gave tha order to his bitch ass sidekick."

"We'll find out."

"You better believe when I do, there be a few T-shirts made. What are you smiling for?"

"Just glad I'm on your side. How long you're staying this time?"

"About a week."

"Damn, that's all?"

"I have to maintain tha biz-ness up top."

"You've been down here so long it's like home to you now."

"I was just telling Khalif tha same shit."

"What's tha deal wit y'all?"

"Ain't no deal."

"Come on Sis; it's me."

"Seriously, I don't look at him like that can't say the same for him though."

"He's not a bad-looking dude and he gets at a dollar."

"I came down here for money, not love."

"Everybody could use a little love."

"So why haven't you found it yet?"

"I get all tha love I need from you; besides, I'm just not tha settling down type."

"That's right, you are playa playa."

"Nah, I just like to come and go as I want; wit a girl you can't do that."

"Let me find out my big bad brother is afraid of c-o-m-m-i-t-m-e-n-t," she said, spelling it out.

"I'm not afraid of anything."

"Are you sure about that?"

"Positively."

"I don't know about you, but I'm starving."

"Me too, let's go to Aunt B's."

"Who do you think shot you?"

"Ain't no thing, I know it was Jizz bitch ass."

"What you wanna do about it?"

"My cuz said to fall back until we're 100% sure."

"I told you a long time ago that nigga was suspect."

"You did, didn't you?"

"I wonder why he waited so long to show his true colors?"

"Probably because these blocks wasn't seeing money like they are now. One thing for sure two things for certain once I find out it was him, he's gone."

"You know I'm wit you."

"No doubt."

"Oh shit, is the Murder wit Heaven?"

"Yeah, she said he was coming down for a few days."

"Shit definitely about to get real."

"What up Big Homey?"

"What up Khalif?"

"Hey Lif, hey Wiz."

"What up Cuz?"

"Hey Heaven."

"Anything new on tha bullshit that when down?"

"Nah, but I know bitch ass Jizz had something to do wit it."

"That's what I'm thinkin' too."

"Don't worry; we'll find out soon enough I'm offering 20 grand to anyone wit information."

"That'll definitely get us a name or two."

"So you gonna let us show you a good time for once?"

"Yeah, I'll do that."

"My man is having a party at Visions tonight."

"I will be back thru later."

"Make sure your back no later than 9:30."

"No problem."

"I better take him to tha mall since he didn't come wit any luggage."

"You'll just make sure you're back by 9:30."

CHAPTER 22

"You know that boy Spit is having a party at Visions tonight?"

"Yeah, but I'm not messing wit it."

"Me either then."

"No nigga go ahead and enjoy yaself."

"What I look like going wit out you?"

"See, that's why I fucks wit you."

"Damn!"

"What?"

"Wifey calling."

"Nigga you better answer it."

"Man, ever since she got knocked up, she call for every little thing."

"Nigga answer ya phone."

"Hold up Jizz."

"Hello."

"Damn, why I gotta blow ya phone up before you answer?"

"Tessa, I was taking care of something."

"I don't care what you was doing; when I call you answer."

"So, what was so important?"

"My cousin said there's a 20 grand reward for any info about tha shooting involving Wiz and his peoples."

"Oh yeah."

"Yeah, do you know anything about it?"

"Nah, I wish I did. I could use that doe."

"You mean we could use it."

"Yeah, yeah What ever."

"Well, I'll call you if I hear anything else."

"I'm sure you will."

"What? What you say?"

"I love you; that's what I said."

"You must of been getting tha biz."

"Nah, she was just telling me how much she misses me."

"When my girl was pregnant, I couldn't deal wit all tha emotions."

As Jizz continued to talk, I was thinking about tha 20,000 Reward Tessa just told me about.

"Yo Nigga."

"What up?"

"You ain't hear nothing I just said."

"My fault, I was just thinking about my son, that's all."

"Kids are expensive; trust me, I know."

"You got eight; you should."

"Nigga I got two."

"That you claim."

"Tha blood test say tha other ones ain't mine."

"We was about to leave y'all."

"You could've I know how to get there."

"Well, get in."

"We gon' to drive."

"Well, we could've just met y'all there instead of driving all tha way back over here."

"I didn't know I was driving until I got a call from one of my young jawns."

"You should've called us and told us to meet you there."

"My fault Cuz."

"Are y'all going to talk all night or go to this party?"

"Let's roll."

"Spark this up," I said, passing Ceer tha Dutch of Sour Diesel.

We pulled up to tha valet and it was packed. After paying the valet, I looked at Wiz and kindly let him know I wasn't the one to be standing in no long ass line.

"Come on now Cuz, what I look like standing in this line?"

We went straight to tha front of the VIP line.

"What up Wiz?"

"Same shit Josh."

"You a'ight, I heard about that bullshit that went down."

"I'm straight."

"Spit is already inside."

"Cool, they wit me."

As soon as we walked in, we were met by tha sounds of Kelly Rowland's Motivation featuring Weezy.

"Come on, let's head to VIP." Tha VIP was jumping. Spit had bottles everywhere.

"I see ya man is doing it big."

"Yeah that's Spit for you, always over tha top."

"Wiz, My Nigga what's up?"

"I can't call it."

"I didn't think you was gon' make it."

"You know I wouldn't miss this for tha world."

"Damn shorty bad as a Mafucka she wit one of y'all?"

"Yeah."

"Who's tha lucky one?"

"All of us."

"Oh, like that?"

"Nah, she family."

"Does that mean you're available?"

"Actually, I'm wit Khalif."

Tha look on Khalif's face said it all; he was surprised just like me that I said that.

"My bag Lif, no disrespect intended."

"None taken."

"Spit these my cousins' Murder and Heaven."

"Well, ya name definitely fits you."

"So does mine!" Ceer let him know wit an attitude.

"Whoa, Whoa Homey, no need to get hostile that's his sister."

"Shareef, bring three more bottles."

"Imma slide to tha bathroom."

"What's up Ceer?" some dude said, walking past me.

By tha time I turned around dude was in tha crowd somewhere. I couldn't help but wonder who that was since nobody in Atlanta knows me, especially not by my real name.

"Damn what you had to shit?"

"Ha Ha very funny." I explained to Heaven what just took place.

"You didn't ask him where he knew you from?"

"I told you by tha time I turned around, he was gone."

"It might have been somebody from home."

"Maybe you're right."

For the next hour, I scanned tha crowd from VIP, hoping to spot dude. By now, Wiz boy Spit was drunk as hell talking reckless.

"Never do biz-ness wit that dude."

"You don't gotta tell me we're all be cased."

"Nothing worse than a talkative Nigga who can't hold his liquor."

"Wiz, you might want to tell ya man to shut his big mouth. I can see him now at tha A.F.D.C. (Atlanta Federal Detention Center).

"Diarrhea in tha mouth."

"Cuz you might want to reevaluate ya friends."

"Not might need," I added.

"Hey Wiz, make sure you get at me. I can make you rich like me," Spit said, throwing a wide of money in tha air.

"I don't know about y'all, but I've had enough. I'm ready to route."

"Me too."

"Damn, it's still early."

"We can go somewhere else. I just need to get away from ya boy."

"A'ight let's bounce."

We made our way to tha exit. "You not gonna tell him you out?"

"He'll be a'ight Fuck 'em!"

"So where to Magic city?"

"Nah, I don't feel like no strip club."

"Well, let's hit 112."

"Lead tha way."

By tha time we got to tha club, it was 1:30.

"Damn, tha line is still long."

"We're not going to have no problem getting in."

We walk to tha front of tha line, where Khalif passed tha bouncer some money to let us in.

"Y'all enjoy yourselves."

"No doubt, if you get a chance, come in first rounds on me."

"This is where we needed to be."

"I know; look at all these broads."

"I'm surprised you noticed."

"What's that suppose to mean?"

"You've been watching my cousin all night."

"Damn, put a nigga on blast Wiz."

"He ain't putting me on blast because I ain't been watching her all night."

"Yeah What ever Nigga."

"Come on, let's get a couple bottles."

"Stop trying to play me like that."

"Nigga I'm not playing you; I'm just keeping it 100."

"Don't even worry about it; I got you."

"What's that suppose to mean?"

"You'll see."

"I turned just in time to see Tash walking towards us."

"Hey Wiz, Khalif."

"What's up Tash?"

"Y'all didn't go to Spit party?"

"Yeah but we left."

"So did we that nigga was drunk as hell talking reckless."

"There she go, Wiz tell her."

"Tell me what?"

"I don't know what he talkin' bout."

"Nigga stop playing, just tell her you wanna holla."

Tash started blushing, then said, "Is that true?"

"I don't know what he's talkin' bout."

"Nigga stop fronting; you know damn well what I'm talking bout."

"Man up Wiz."

"She know I was feeling her."

"No, I didn't."

"Well she knows now."

"I sure do."

"Come on y'all, let's let them talk."

"So, how long have you been feeling me and why didn't you say anything?"

"Cause everybody be try'n to get at you and I know that shit be getting on ya nerves."

"Only when they come wit some lame wack game which most of them do."

"So, if Khalif didn't say nothing, you would've kept quiet, huh?"

"Yup."

"Well, I guess I would've had to be tha first one to holla, huh?"

"Huh?"

"You heard me; I been waiting for you to get at me. At first, I thought maybe you had a girl. You don't have no wifey, do you?"

"Nah, I'm single, no strings attached."

"That's what they all say."

"Yeah, but they all not me."

"Point taken."

"So now what?"

"Now, we exchange numbers and go from there."

"Imma tell you now I'm not for no games."

"Yeah I see you use to dealing wit lames."

"What ever take my damn number."

"Such hostility, would you like a drink?"

"Sure, why not."

"Let me guess, Long Island Ice Tea."

"Boy pleeeeease Bombay and orange juice."

"Wow I'm impressed."

"I'm not allowed to drink something stronger than a Long Island?"

"Of course, I just wouldn't have pegged you for a Bombay type of girl Hennessey or Remi maybe but definitely not Bombay."

"Are you gon' order tha drinks or not?"

"What you drinking?"

"Let me have a Bombay and orange juice and another double shot wit pineapple wit a twist of cranberry."

"Let me find out you drink Bombay too."

"That's all I drink."

"I'm liking you more already."

"Now you got me blushing."

"I don't want to hold you hostage."

"My cousin looks like she's busy."

I turned to see her all up in Murder's face.

"Who's he? I've never saw him before?"

"That's my cousin from Philly. He's visiting for a little while."

For tha rest of tha night, we kicked it and I really knew Tash was something special.

"Hey Cuz, I'm going wit murder you gonna be a'ight?"

"Yeah, I'm good call me tomorrow."

"I will."

"Wiz, Imma need a ride since Murder is leaving."

"I'm bout to bounce too."

"I'm not ready to leave yet."

"Me either," Khalif said smiling.

"Well, I was about to leave; maybe I can give you a lift."

"Sure, if you don't mind."

"I wouldn't have offered if I did."

"Y'all gonna be OK?"

"You know we straight, go head."

CHAPTER 23

"That was tha best two weeks of my life."

"Tell me about it."

Once I dropped Nya off, I headed over to one of my stash house, where I knew Jizz would most likely be.

"Damn Homey, you look like one of those dark skin Dominican Niggaz."

"Two weeks in tha hot Aruban sun and you'll be black as hell too."

"I can't afford to get no darker."

"You right about that."

"Fuck you Nigga."

"So, what's been going on since I've been gone?"

"Same shit, M-O-N-E-Y."

"Everything been cool?"

"Yeah Nigga."

"I'm just asking because when I called, you sounded like something was up."

"Shit been good wit us."

"What's that mean?"

"Somebody shot Wiz block up last week."

"Anybody get hurt?"

"Wiz got hit in a couple Niggaz got killed."

"You don't know who did it?"

"I heard some Niggaz from Southwest."

"I knew that Jizz had something to do wit it my gut was telling me he did."

"I'm glad you came back because I got a 3 brick sale and no more work left."

"I'm about to go pick up tha shipment now."

"Do you need me to go wit you?"

"Nah, I'm straight. I'll hit you when I'm ready."

"A'ight just don't be all night."

"Ross."

"Hey, My Friend, how was your trip?"

"Relaxing and stress-free."

"We always need to get away every now and then."

"We do, but now it's back to biz-ness."

"I'm already two steps ahead of you; ya shipment is already there."

"Did Sharky hit you wit tha bread?"

"Yes, and if he didn't, I know you're good for it."

"You know I always believe in C.O.D. (Cash On Delivery)."

"I don't know if you're aware, but there was a shooting that took place while you were gone."

"Nah, I wasn't aware of it."

"Well, my niece thought your nephew was involved, but I assured her that he wasn't."

"Was she shot?"

"No, but my nephew was and a few people were killed."

"I don't know why but I had a feeling Jizz has something to do wit it."

"I'll find out what tha hell happened and deal wit it."

"A'ight, I'll talk to you in a few weeks."

Soon as I hung up, I called Jah'ceer to let him know I needed to see him A. S. A. P. 30 minutes later, we were sitting in my living room.

"So, what's tha deal Unc?"

"I talked to Ross and he informed me that while we were away, there was a shooting which his nephew was shot."

"I know Jizz told me he heard that some Southwest Niggaz did tha shooting."

"Bullshit!"

"Huh?"

"Why tha fuck would some Southwest Niggaz shoot up their block? I'm telling you now, if I find out that Jizz had anything to do wit it Imma kill him myself!" I looked at my Uncle Rock and knew he was dead serious.

"Ceer, one thing about me is if I say something, I honor it."

"So do I Unc."

"Good."

Leaving, I could not help but think that Jizz would end up losing his life behind his stupidness.

"Hello."

"Can I speak to Murder?"

"Who' dis?"

"You don't know me, but I have information about tha shooting you have tha $20,000 reward for."

"I'm listening."

"Not until I have my money."

"Where can we meet?"

"How bout Daddy's Soul Food."

"Cool, I'll be there in 20 minutes."

"I'll be wearing a red Braves fitted."

"How do we know this dude ain't trying to stiff us?"

"Let me worry about that."

Twenty-five minutes later, I see dude walk in wit his Braves fitted on. I motioned for him to come have a seat.

"So, who's Murder?"

"I am."

"Do you have my doe?"

"Hold on Cowboy, before I hand over 20,000, I need to know a few things."

"Ask away."

"How do I know your information is legit?"

"Because I was wit tha nigga that did it."

"Oh, so you don't have no loyalty?"

"Actually, I do; that's why I'm here."

"You lost me wit that."

"I had no ideal he was hittin' Wiz had I known I would've never went wit him."

"If that's tha case, why did it take a reward for you to come forward?"

"It didn't, I've been trying to get in touch wit him but haven't been successful."

"So, it's not about tha money?"

"No, but it was a bonus and I could definitely use it."

"Well, let me ask the most important question whom did the shooting?"

"Jizz."

"I knew it was that Mafucka!" Heaven said, raising her voice and causing everybody to look at us.

"Here's ya money and thanks for tha information."

"No problem."

"And don't worry, I won't mention ya name."

"I don't care if you do or don't Jizz don't want no smoke wit me."

Little did he know Jizz wouldn't be a bother to anybody else when I was done wit him.

"I think we should've killed him too."

"Nah, he said he didn't know it was Wiz until it was too late."

"And you believe him?"

"Yeah, I do, and I'm pretty good judge of character."

"Next question, when are we going to take care of Jizz bitch ass?"

"In tha next few days."

"You know this is going to start a war?"

"I know, that's why I'm going to take a few days to bring some more people down."

"I say we do tha same shit to him that we did to Kevy-Kev."

"Now, that's not a bad ideal."

"Don't worry; I'll put everything in motion."

"You just be safe."

"I always am."

"Yo Jizz I saw that chick Heaven and she asked about you."

"Man fuck that bitch!"

"Nigga say what you want she bad as a mafucka; not to mention fat to death."

"She got too much mouth for me."

"So if she let you you wouldn't smash?"

"Of course."

"I know you would."

"Let's hit the mall. I need to grab Tessa some maternity clothes."

"Oh no, not mister, I'm not buying her no clothes."

"Man go ahead, her clothes are getting too small and I'm not going to have my baby mom's looking all crazy."

"I feel you Playa."

"Damn, it's a lot of broads in here today."

"Who you telling?"

"Aye yo ain't that Heaven over there?"

"Where?"

"By tha pretzel stand."

"That's her."

"Jizz she's a bad bitch."

I had to agree. I couldn't stop staring at her.

"How many broads do you know, 5'6", caramel skin tone, long pretty hair, gray eyes wit an ass that would put Beyoncé to shame that's T.T.G. (Train to Go)?"

"Not many."

"Shiiit, I don't know any."

"Oh shit, Jizz she's coming over here."

"Nigga calm down; she probably just walking pass."

"What's up Jizz?"

"I can't call it."

"I thought I'd come speak since you were staring so hard."

"Damn, I was that noticeable," I thought to myself.

"Actually, I was checking out tha chick that was behind you."

"They said you'd say that."

"They who?"

"Just a figure of speech."

"Right, that's that up top slang."

"Next time, just speak," I said, turning to walk away, making sure to make my ass bounce.

"Nigga you scared of all of it."

"Yeah, right."

"Well, why didn't you ask for her number?"

"We didn't actually see Eye to Eye tha first time we met."

"Looks like she got over it; maybe you should do tha same."

"I'll say something next time."

"Next time?"

"Yeah, next time."

"You a fool, I'll be right back."

"Where are you going?"

"To help you out."

I watched as he talked to her, wondering what he was saying. I wouldn't have to wonder long because she started walking back wit him.

"Why couldn't you just ask me yaself?"

"Ask you what?"

"If you gonna play games."

Nah, Nah, he ain't going to play no games," Tommy said, cutting her off.

"Can he speak for himself?"

"Of course, I can. So can I get ya number or what?"

"Only if you gon' use it."

"I'm definitely gon' use it."

After giving him my number, I walked off, thinking how easy that was.

"So, how did everything go?"

"It was easier than planned."

"Most Niggas think wit tha wrong head."

"Who you telling, show 'em a little cleavage, a phat ass and you got 'em every time.

"Only a dumb nigga cause ain't no real nigga going to fall for that, especially after you put a gun in my face."

"Well, everybody ain't as smart as you."

"If there were, less Niggas would be set up. Give him a few days he'll call."

"A few days, tha way he was drooling, he'll call tonight."

"I hope so; let's grab something to eat."

"You gonna call her tonight?"

"Nah, Imma wait till next week."

"Nigga you keep trying to play hard; you better hit her up tonight."

"You think I should? She just gave me tha number. I don't want to seem thirsty."

"Nigga call."

"Fuck it," I said, pulling out my phone to call her.

After four rings, she picked up.

"Hello."

"What's up Heaven?"

"Who dis?"

"Damn, you give ya number out that much?"

"Listen, I don't have time for games."

"It's Jizz."

"Oh hey, I didn't think you would call till next week."

"Why put off till next week what you could do today?"

"I hear you."

"So, do you have plans for tonight?"

"No."

"Would you like to have dinner?"

"I guess we can do that."

"I'll pick you up around 8 o'clock."

"Sounds good, see you then."

"I take it that was Jizz?"

"Yup, we'll be able to take care of him tonight."

"A'ight, I'll be at tha spot waiting."

"I'll hit ya phone when we're on our way."

"He got to be tha dumbest Nigga."

"Well, that's a good thing for us."

"Don't get me wrong; I'm not complaining at all."

"I'll have Wiz follow you just in case."

"Ceer all he thinkin' bout is a shot of pussy."

"You're probably right, but we gonna make sure he ain't still holding on."

Later that night Jizz called to ask where he could pick me up from. I told him to pick me up at tha house that would be his death. He hit my phone to let me know he was out front. I asked him to come in for a minute so I could finish getting dressed. When I heard tha front door, I yelled down for him to have a seat.

"Do you need some help up there?"

"Sure, come on up."

I knew I could get him, but I had no idea it would be this easy.

"Where are you at?"

"In tha back room."Damn was all I could say as she was standing in a pair of thongs and bra.

"You better close ya mouth before a fly goes in it."

I was in a daze.

"Don't just stand there; take ya clothes off."

"Who me?"

"Ha! Ha! Ha!" I had to laugh, "you're the only one standing there."

He took his clothes off so fast I had to laugh again.

"Hold on, let me use tha bathroom real quick."

"Go ahead, take your time we got all night."

I walked out tha room wit my robe on because I knew Wiz, Khalif, and Ceer was outside.

"Is he ready?"

"If you consider being butt naked on tha bed ready."

"Wiz, you and Khalif can handle him but take this."

"What we need this for?"

"Make sure you get him talking about what he did just in case Roc don't believe it."

"Main man, what it do."

Jizz jumped up and tried to reach for his pants.

"Unh Unh, I wouldn't do that," Khalif said wit his .45 aimed at his chess.

"What tha fuck is going on?"

"Nigga you know exactly what's goin on?"

"No, I don't."

"You didn't actually think my cousin would let you hit after you shot me in tha back, did you?"

"I don't know what you talkin' bout."

"That's not what ya boy Kenny said."

"Kenny's a mafuckin liar."

"A liar wit 20K for telling us it was you."

"I'm not feeding into that."

"Why did you do it?"

"I didn't."

"That's ya story and you stickin' to it."

"We were suppose to be cool Jizz."

"We are cool."

"If this is what you do to people you cool wit I'd hate to be ya enemy."

"Heaven y'all got it from here. I'm going back to tha room."

"You must got something set up?"

"You know me too well."

"Just make sure you strap it up."

"I always do Lil' Sis, I always do."

"A'ight, y'all do what y'all gotta do, just make sure you get rid of him when you done."

"Now you disrespecting and insulting me."

I walked back in tha room to find Jizz wit his hands and feet taped up.

"You Fuckin' Bitch!"

"Thank you."

"I knew I should not have trusted ya skank ass."

"I don't blame you for wanting some of this." I dropped my robe and slid my Seven Jeans back on.

"Come on, Heaven next time, give us a heads up."

"Boy, we use to take baths together."

"Yeah, when we was kids, we grown now."

"Khalif didn't mind, did you Khalif?

"Huh what?"

"You got Lif mesmerized."

"Fuck you Wiz."

"For being honest."

"Let's not get off track," Lif said, switching tha subject.

"Did he say why he shot you?"

"He said Kenny's lying."

"Jizz, I knew you was a coward when I first met you."

"Fuck you Bitch!"

"No Fuck ya mom!"

"Bitch Imma kill you!"

"We all know that ain't gonna happen."

"Cuz his aim is trash; that's why I'm still breathing."

"Nigga tha only reason you still breathing is because I didn't want to kill you."

"Look at ya other peoples."

"So you did shoot me?"

"You damn right I did."

"After Roc put a stop to a war that was about to happen?"

"You just said Fuck him, huh?"

"He's tha reason you're still alive."

"Fuck this nigga we got what we need," Wiz said, pulling his .40 cal out.

"I'll see you in Hell nigga."

"You just might."

"I hope y'all know Ceer ain't gonna let this shit ride."

"Pop, Pop, Pop" three shots to his head put him to sleep.

"Damn Wiz, you moving all fast; I wanted to ask him how he knows

Ceer."

"Who's Ceer?"

"That's Murder's real name clean this mess up and hit me when you done."

"We'll take care of it."

CHAPTER 24

"What's up? Did you get what you needed?"

"Yeah, but before Wiz killed him, he said Ceer ain't gonna let this ride."

"How does he know my name and what did he mean by that?"

"I don't know. Wiz shot him before I could ask."

I didn't have to say anything to Heaven because she knew me so well she already knew what I was thinking.

"Don't worry about it; a dead man tells no tales."

"That's true but ain't no telling who he was talking to."

"Imma call Roc and set up a meeting."

"No need."

"I just want to put them on tha same page, so this won't turn into a full-fledge war."

"Since when did you care about a war?"

"I don't."

"Well then, don't call him."

"Fuck it, I won't."

"Are you gonna stay in all night, or do you want to have a few drinks?"

"We can have a few drinks; I'll call you in a little bit."

"A'ight."

"Unc, let's get out of here."

"I'm wit you on that one."

"I been hittin' this nigga all night."

"Who?"

"Jizz."

"Nephew I know that's ya man but on some real shit he dead weight."

"Unc you don't like Jizz, do you?"

"Nah, because he doesn't think before opening his mouth."

"I try to keep him under control."

"Imma tell you something ya pop used to always tell me."

"What's that?"

"If you have to monitor a person, then they don't need to be a part of tha team."

"Question for you, how can you keep a person under control if you're not around them 24-7?"

"You can't; I had a guy just like him on tha team he ended up dead. Just like you and I know he was responsible for that incident wit Heavens people."

"I hope not Unc."

"For your sake, I hope not too."

"I knew that Roc wouldn't hesitate to rock him to sleep."

"Let me try his phone again."

"Still no answer, huh?"

"Nah, he did say he had something lined up. If that was ya dad calling me, I would have answered because if he keeps calling, it must be important."

"I knew what my Unc was saying was true, but I didn't want him to know it even though I'm sure he does because he said it."

"That's just food for thought nephew."

Jizz was reckless, but he was still my boy.

"Jah'ceer, I know you ain't and don't wanna hear it, but it's real and

I've been giving you real ya whole life, so I'm not going to stop now."

"I feel what you saying, but Jizz is my best friend. If it was my dad would you cut him off?"

"Ya dad would never put me or himself in a situation plus we always about that dollar no if's and's or butts about it."

"Can we just agree to disagree on this one?"

"If you say so."

"Imma call it a night nephew ya Aunty Tae said I couldn't hang out late tonight."

"Tell her you wit me."

"I told her that tha other nights and she told me Nya might let you stay out all times a night, but she ain't having that."

"A'ight I'll get wit you in tha morning."

After dropping Roc off, I decided to go body tap. I pulled up to tha light and there was this bad chick sitting there. I didn't say anything and because of my tint, I knew she couldn't see me staring at her. I pulled off when tha light turned wit out, thinking twice about her.

I must be tired because that dude looked like Nah'ceer.

"Hello."

"I'll be there in 10 minutes."

"I'll be out front waiting on you."

Sure enough, when I pulled up, he was waiting.

"What's up Sis?"

"I was at tha light and I thought I saw somebody that looked just like you."

"Are you sure you wanna get some drinks instead of some sleep?"

"I know, but I'm good."

"You just want to hang out wit ya big bro."

"I rarely get to spend time wit you anymore."

"That's because you made this ya home."

"Nah, I'm just overseeing our money."

"Wiz can handle it."

"Let me find out you miss me."

"I do."

"Then stay a little longer."

"I can't; I have a meeting wit Uncle Ross and a few other people tomorrow afternoon."

"He's probably stepping down tomorrow and turning tha reins over to you."

"That's what I was thinking since he just called and told me to be back by tomorrow afternoon."

"Imma go back wit you."

"You don't have to."

"Yes, I do because I want to let everyone know disrespect will not be tolerated."

"They already know that."

"I'm going and that's all it is."

"Say no more, our flight leaves at 8 AM."

"I'll be ready."

When the plane landed, Nah'ceer had to wake me up.

"Damn, I must of dozed off."

"Dozed? Heaven, you were snoring, so I know you was tired."

"I know; I only snore when I'm tired or sick."

"Ceer, Heaven over here."

"What up Big Mike?"

"Mr. Ross sent me to pick y'all up."

"That's what's up."

"Actually, he didn't say Heaven was coming."

"It was a last-minute decision."

"Well, it's nice to see you; it's been a while."

"She's from Atlanta now."

"Nah, I'm always Philly bred just getting money in Atlanta."

When we pulled up in front of Uncle Ross's mansion, Ceazar and Buck were posted out front. They both ran up to me, almost knocking me down.

"Buck, Ceazar, get over here."

"They a'ight Uncle Ross, they miss me."

"So do I, but I'm not knocking you down."

"They're just dogs Uncle Ross."

"Come give ya uncle a hug."

"What brought you back?"

"Nah'ceer said you called for him to come back for a meeting."

"I did."

"Well, if I know you and I do you're probably turn it over tha reins to him today."

When he just smiled and didn't say anything, I knew I was on tha money.

"Let me guess you came to lay down tha law?"

"Your guess would be accurate."

"There's no need for that everybody at this meeting knows their position."

"Maybe, but we're gonna make sure they do because there's always one person who tries his or her hand."

I caught Uncle Ross smiling at Ceer, who returned his smile wit a head nod.

"Heaven, you're ya mother all over again."

"Only difference is I won't get caught slippin' like she did."

"She wasn't slippin'; she just followed her heart."

"No disrespect to you Uncle Ross, but she was slippin' her heart made her make a bad decision. You don't have to say nothing because I know I'm right." And she was.

"Are you two hungry, or did you eat?"

"I don't know about Ceer, but I'm starving."

"I could use a bite to eat also."

"A'ight, let's go grab something from Miss Tootsy."

"Now you're talking."

"Big Mike, pull tha car around."

Once we were done eating, we headed to where tha meeting would be taking place.

"Well, I see just about everyone is here except K.G."

"Boss, he's always late."

"We're not going to wait on him. Everybody, please be seated. I know you're wondering why I called you here today on such short notice," they all nodded in agreement, "as you know, I'm stepping down, I've been saying this for tha past year, but today is tha day."

"So who's going to take over?"

"I decide to let my nephew run tha biz-ness unless any of you object."

I looked around at tha faces to see if I could detect any hate, envy, jealousy or animosity but saw none.

"We're all OK with it; we assumed it would be Nah'ceer anyway."

"Hey, Hey, Hey, I know you ain't start wit out me."

"K.G., you need to make this ya last time arriving late to a meeting."

"Ross, no disrespect to you, but you better tell him to stay in a child's place."

"K.G., you might wanna rethink that."

"Because Ross just step down and put him at tha head of tha table."

"What!"

"You heard him; now sit ya bitch ass down!"

He started walking towards Heaven; before I could react, Ross grabbed my arm. By tha time K.G reacted Heavens .45 was in his face.

"Please give me a reason."

"No need for that Shawty."

"Well, sit ya punk ass down."

K.G looked at Ross.

"I'm no longer in control, he is."

"Let's get this meeting started. I've decided to lower tha price."

"I'm liking you already."

"You might wanna let me finish first. If you buy 50 or more; if not, tha number will increase."

"Hold up Cowboy, slow ya roll."

"It's not open for discussion; if you don't like it, you can always go elsewhere. But 9 outta 10 it's still comin from me."

"Man Fuck this Shit, y'all gonna go for that?"

"We love that we can up our orders."

"I'm outta here. I ain't goin for this bullshit."

"See you."

"I'm bout tired of ya Fuckin mouth."

"You know what? I'm tired of yours too, so how bout I shut it for you."

"Shawty, you not built for this shit, so stay in ya lane before you find yaself in trouble."

Pop, Pop, Pop, Pop, Pop "You talk too much. Anybody else gotta problem they want addressed?"

They all quickly nodded no

"I told that nigga his mouth would be his downfall."

The cleanup crew did what they do while we finished up wit our meeting. After everybody left, Uncle Ross let me know that he knew he had made tha right decision. I explained to him why I lowered the price for 50 or better.

"I already knew why you did it and it made a lot of sense. Nah'ceer I support What ever you do no matter what it is."

"Uncle Ross, I don't know how you put up wit him for so long."

"Heaven, I use to ask him tha same thing," Big Mike said.

"Big Mike you might as well come work for me."

"Nah Nephew, he still wit me."

"I need somebody to ride shotgun since my wingman is always outta town."

"I think he misses you Heaven."

"You think?"

"It's all right to miss me Ceer I miss you too."

"Uncle Ross, did you put ya man Roc down?"

"Yeah he'll probably give you a call in tha next few days."

"Y'all just talked him up."

"Hello."

"Heaven, how are you doing?"

"I'm good."

"Do you think we can meet somewhere and talk?"

"I'm not in town right now, but I'll be back in a few days."

"A'ight just give me a call when you get back in town."

"I'll do that."

"Oh yeah, would you mind giving me ya brother's number? Ross gave it to me, but it somehow didn't store in my phone."

"He's right here; hold on."

"Hello."

"What up Murder?"

"I can't call it."

"Ross told me you runnin' tha biz-ness now."

"Yeah."

"We might need to talk face-to-face."

"Is your line secure?"

"My line straight."

"Well, I need to let you know that tha numbers will decrease if you buy 50 or more, but if not, then they will increase."

"There's no need for me to worry about that. I'm sure Ross told you tha deal wit me."

"He just said that tha two of you have been friends for a long time and ask me if I would continue to have ya shipment sent to you."

"Well, I buy 100 to 150 kilos."

"Me knocking off 1500 should help you out."

"It'll help both of us out me cheaper prices, you more bricks being dumped."

"Heaven told me you were everything Uncle Ross said you were."

"All I have is my word; that's why I never go back on it."

"I'm tha same way."

"Then we should have no problems."

"I don't want you to think that because I'm 19, I won't fill my uncle's shoes."

"Check this out; if you weren't capable, we wouldn't even be having this conversation right now."

"Well, you can send me 200 A.S.A.P."

"Consider it done."

"Hopefully, we can meet face-to-face soon."

"I'll be down that way in tha next three weeks."

"A'ight, tell Heaven to make sure she calls me when she gets back in town."

"Gotcha."

"Uncle Ross, I see why you like him so much."

"I'm usually a good judge of character."

"Heaven, he said make sure you call him when you get back down there."

"I'm on a flight in tha morning." "

Damn, you aren't even staying for a few days."

"Biz-ness is taken care of."

"In and out like a robbery, huh, Sis?"

"Unless you need me to stay for something else."

"Nah, I'm good; go head back home."

"Fuck you Nah'ceer!"

"Maybe Khalif would, but we family."

Uncle Ross, Big Mike, even Heaven had to laugh at that.

"Come on, let's get outta here."

"Sure Boss."

"Come on Unc, cut that out."

"You better get use to it."

"Besides tha people in tha meeting and Roc nobody will know I'm runnin' nothing."

"Uncle Ross, you know he likes to fly under tha radar."

"That's tha only way to fly."

"I thought First Class was tha only way to fly."

"First Class under tha radar."

"What tha fuck? I been trying to reach this nigga for two days."

"He probably got Shawty hostage somewhere."

"Yeah, he still should answer his phone when he see my number."

"I was beginning to think my uncle was right about what he was saying."

"Hey Bishop, did you find out about that shooting?"

"Which one?"

"Wiz and his people."

"Nah, but between me and you, my cousin told me Jizz had something to do wit it."

"What do you think?

"Honestly, I don't know, but my cousins' info be on point."

"Do you think they retaliated?"

"I don't know Ceer."

"Do you know Wiz?"

"I know Khalif, his right-hand man."

"Do you want me to holla at him see if they got him?"

"Even though I know he's not going to tell you, hit him up."

"Klalif what up Homey?

"What it do Bishop?"

"I need to ask you something."

"I hear you."

"Did y'all do something to Jizz?"

"Why you ask me that?"

"Come on Lif, you know we always keep it 100 wit one another."

"I don't think you want to know the answer to that."

"So, I'll take that as a yes."

"All Imma say is when you do something as serious as he did, you have to be Ok wit tha consequences that come wit it."

"A'ight Lif, thanks for tha info."

"Bishop, I hope this doesn't ruin our friendship."

"Me either."

"Yo, what he talkin' bout?"

"Let me put it to you this way Jizz swimming wit tha fishes."

"NOOOOO Fuck NOOOOO!"

"These Mafucka's want a war. Imma give 'em a Fuckin war. I put that on my mom and pops!"

"What you want me to do?"

"Nah, you fall back. I don't want you involved in this."

"Jah'ceer you sound stupid."

"I know that's ya man."

"Nigga you my man."

"Say no more. When do you want to handle it?"

"As soon as tha sun goes down, we gon blow thru there like Hurricane Katrina leaving nothing but dead bones from our wrath."

"Imma a get everybody together."

"I'll meet you back here at 8 o'clock sharp."

As I was pulling off, Nya was calling my phone.

"Yo."

"Yo, is that how you answer ya phone now?"

"I'm not in tha mood right now for no bullshit."

"Let me hang up and try this again."

Before I could say anything tha line went dead. I started not to answer when she called back, but I did.

"What's up Nya?"

"I'm sorry if you're not having a good day, but Ceer please don't take it out on me."

"You're right and I do apologize."

"Well are you busy?"

"At tha moment, no, but I do have some important biz-ness to handle. Why, what's up?"

"I wanted to treat you to lunch."

"I guess I have enough time for that besides, I'm starving anyway."

"Where are you?"

"On tha block."

"I'll be there in 10 minutes."

When I pulled up Ceer had this look on his face that I have never seen before and it scared me.

"Hey Baby," I said while reaching over and planting a kiss on his cheek, "what do you feel like eating?"

"You're treating, so I'll let you decide."

"I think I'm in tha mood for Aunt B's."

"Aunt B's it is then."

We rode in silence tha whole ride. I wanted to tell him my news but decided to wait and tell him over lunch.

"What are you eating?"

"I've been craving fish, mac, greens and fried shrimp."

"Sounds good, but I want chicken breast instead of fish."

After we placed our order, I started up a conversation.

"Ceer you know Tae's birthday is coming up."

When he didn't answer, I yelled his name, "Ceer!"

"Huh?"

"You didn't hear nothing I just said."

"My bag, I just got a lot on my mind right now."

"Anything you want to talk about?"

"Not really."

"So when we start doing that?"

I knew she was right, but I also knew if I told her, she would either try to talk me out of seeking revenge or call my uncle Roc and at this point, I wasn't trying to hear either. I decided to just tell her I'd been thinking about my mom, dad and brother, which wasn't a lie.

"Ceer, I'm always here for you no matter what."

"I know you are."

"Jah'ceer, there's something I need to tell you."

By tha look on Nya's face I knew it was serious.

"Jah'ceer I'm pregnant."

"WHOOOOOO!" Everybody turned to look at him.

"I'm sorry, but I'm gonna be a dad." They all clapped and congratulated us.

"How do you know?"

"I had a doctor's appointment today."

"Why didn't you tell me?"

"Because it was just a routine physical."

"Aren't you on tha pill?"

"Yes, but remember I ran out and you wanted some that night, but I tried to tell you to wait till tha next day."

"Damn, this shit I got is pure."

"Boy you stupid."

"You do want this baby, don't you?"

"Of course I do, tha question is, do you?"

"I would love to have a little me runnin' around."

"How do you know it won't be a girl."

"It's not, but if it is ain't nothing wrong wit a diva runnin' around."

"I don't know if tha house will be big enough for two divas."

"Don't worry, will get a bigger house to make sure there's enough room."

Judging by tha smile on his face, I could tell that a little of his stress was now gone.

CHAPTER 25

"I'm glad to see you could make it today Heaven."

"And vice versa. My uncle sends his hello."

"I'm going to miss doing biz-ness with him, but I'm definitely looking forward to dealing wit you and ya brother."

"As do we you."

"Hopefully, I'll get to meet him soon."

"He'll be down in a few weeks."

"Roc, I want to be the first to tell you ya man Jizz ain't right."

"Let me be tha first to tell you I don't like Jizz, I deal wit him because he is my nephews' boy."

"Well, you don't have to worry about him anymore."

"Why not?"

"He's dead."

"You killed him?"

"No, my cousin did."

"Heaven, this is going to start a war."

"Roc, you might want to listen to this," I said, sliding tha tape recorder across tha table.

I watched his face expression as he listened to the tape.

"Would you mind if I made a copy of this tape?"

"You can have it; I got it for you."

"Let me call my nephew."

"Sure, go ahead."

"Yo, I was just getting ready to hit you, Unc."

"I have something I think you might want to listen to."

"I just found out I'm gonna be a daddy."

"Oh word, that's what's up, congrats."

"Thanks, so what do I need to listen to?"

"Where are you at?"

"At tha crib wit Nya."

"A'ight give me an hour and I'll be by."

"Where are you at now, Unc?"

"Having a meeting wit Heaven."

"About what?"

"You'll find out when I get there."

"Cool, I'll see you in an hour."

"Is everything a'ight?"

"Yeah, I just want to make sure there won't be any more bloodshed behind this."

"Roc, I don't want to beef wit ya nephew because it will only end badly for one of us and it won't be me. I can promise you that."

"Heaven, that's why I like you because you don't bite ya tongue despite tha fact that's my nephew you're talkin' about."

"Roc, not to brag, but I'm tha real deal you might want to ask my uncle about me."

She had no idea that I already knew about her; once Ross told me who her mother was, I knew she was tha real deal. Me and Zeek had used her mother on plenty of occasions.

"Heaven, I'll give you a call after I talk to my nephew and let you know what it is."

Thirty minutes later, I was knocking on Jah'ceer's door.

"Hey Roc, come on in."

"I hear congrats is in order."

"Thank you."

"Are you excited?"

"Yeah, but not nearly as excited as Ceer is."

"Where is he?"

"In tha basement, ya wife said don't be out all day."

"Tell her I said I'll be back when I leave here."

"Unc, is that you?"

"Yeah."

"Come on down."

"Look at you, tha baby ain't even here yet and you smoking cigars."

"Just getting some practice. Unc, I wasn't going to say shit, but it's going down tonight."

"What's going on?"

"Wiz and Khalif killed Jizz."

"How do you know?"

"Bishop talked to Khalif and he confirmed it."

"So what's ya plan to go through there and just shoot up everything?"

"Yup."

"Now your emotion is overriding ya intellect."

"That was my best friend."

"Ceer, ya boy was reckless; he didn't care about how his actions would affect you or anybody else. I squashed tha beef only to have him kill a few people and shoot Wiz."

"Unc, we don't know if he did that."

Wit out saying another word, I pushed play on tha recorder so he could hear it for himself.

"Where did you get that from?"

"Heaven."

"Come on Unc, how do you know that bitch didn't force him to say that?"

"Nephew, let me put you up on something."

"I'm listening."

"Heaven is cut from a good cloth. Me, ya dad and her mother were real good friends."

"Oh, so you and my pops was knocking her mom off?"

"Nah, she did hits for us or as you kids say, she was a hired gun."

"Her mom?"

"Yeah, she was tha best in tha biz-ness."

"What she do, retire?"

"She was killed."

"How did that happen if she was as good as you say she was?"

"Love."

"Love?"

"Yup, tha nigga she was in love wit used it against her for money."

"Damn, he did her dirty; I know he's dead."

"Yup, Heaven killed him."

"Heaven?"

"Yeah, it was her dad she found out he set her mom up and killed him.

She was 10 when she got her first body."

I could tell by tha look on his face he was surprised.

"So you not wit me Unc."

"Jah'ceer, let's get one thing clear you're blood so I'm always wit you, but Jizz got tha hand he was dealt. When you do dirt, you get dirt; he made me look like my word wasn't shit. So do I feel bad that he's in tha boneyard, hell Nah."

I knew what Roc was saying was tha truth, but I wasn't even feeling it.

"Jah'ceer, you're no longer living for yourself; you have to think about ya child that's on tha way."

Now he had me. I didn't want to be dead or in jail before I had tha chance to see or get to know my child.

"Ceer tell me you'll at least think bout what I'm saying."

"I'll think about it, but I can't make any promises."

"If not for me, then for Nya and ya child."

"You know what? Unc set up a meeting wit Heaven and her brother."

"Heaven's here, but her brother won't be down for another two weeks."

"Well, I'll give them two weeks no more, no less."

"I'll let her know."

"I need to make a phone call too."

After hanging up wit Heaven, I listen to Ceer tell his boy to hold off.

"I'm telling you Unc, they got two weeks."

"I swear you're just like Zeek."

"Uncle Roc, I want to find my brother; he's been on my mind a lot lately."

"I've been thinking about him too."

"What's up wit Pete?"

"I talked to him earlier today; he said he might have some good news this week."

"I hope so; it's been 19 years. What should I get Tae for her birthday?"

"I'm still trying to figure out what else to get her."

"What have you gotton her so far."

"The new Audi A–8."

"Man, those things are fire."

"Who are you telling."

"Unc she don't want nothing but that Honda she's been driving for tha past five years."

"Every time tha commercial come on, she keeps saying how nice they are."

"She always do that when she see a nice car."

"Oh well, too late it's already bought wit rims and system."

"You'll be lucky if she drive it."

"Hey if she don't, I will."

"You probably got it for yourself anyway."

"Come on Ceer, I would've just cop two for all that."

"I hear you."

"Heaven."

"What up Nah'ceer?"

"Did you talk to Roc?"

"Yeah he was cool. I don't know if you know this but him and his man use to deal wit ya mom real tough."

"Uncle Ross told you that?"

"Yeah. He said his nephew wants to have a sit-down wit us when you come back down."

"I won't be down till tha week after next."

"He knows Roc said he's not going to retaliate."

"That shipment will be back at the usual spot by morning."

"That's what's up because everybody is ready."

"There's an extra 20 in there for y'all."

"Ok Ceer, you a'ight?"

"Yeah."

"You sure, seems like something is wrong."

"Sis, I been thinking about my brother a lot lately."

"Tha lawyer still didn't find out anything?"

"Nah, not yet."

"You might need to throw him some more money to motivate him."

"I done hit him with damn near 300 grand."

"Damn, they might need to find him slumped over his desk."

"Nah Sis, we ain't gonna do nothing to him."

"Let me find out my brother gettin' soft on me."

"Come on Sis, ain't nothing soft on me but shoes when I put them on."

"That's right, talk that talk."

"Walk the walk to if I have too."

"A'ight Big Head, I'll hit you up in tha morning once I get that shipment."

"Ok, oh yeah, I put a couple pounds of weed in there too."

"Bout time, had me down here blowing this backyard boom boom."

"You were smokin' it cause you wanted to."

"Bullshit, I been told you to send some of that sour diesel down."

"No, you didn't."

"Just say you forgot Ceer it's a'ight."

"Sis, I'm telling you."

"You have a lot on ya plate so you probably just forgot."

"If I did, why didn't you remind me?"

"I got a lot going on."

"We both do."

"When this is resolved, I'll be back to hold you down."

"Do you want me to send some more people down."

"Nah, Roc is a man of his word."

"Yeah, but his nephew might not be."

"The way Roc speaks highly of him, I think he is too."

"He better be because as much is I like doing biz-ness wit Roc, I'm pretty sure me killing his nephew would put an end to that."

"You think?"

We both had to laugh at that. "Heaven, I love you and I'll talk to you tomorrow."

"A'ight, I love you too Big Head."

I couldn't believe how close me and Heaven had gotten in tha past five years. She's like tha little sister I never had. There's nothing I wouldn't do for her and I know she feels tha same way because she's already proven it.

"We still hustle till the sun comes up."

"What up Ali?"

"What time you coming thru?"

"I'm in route now, so I'll be there in less than 15 minutes."

"I'll be waiting."

"We were gonna shoot to King of Prussia, so we could grab something to wear to tha Don's Vs. Divas party tomorrow night."

"Come on Big Homie, this how you do it?"

"This is this my hoopty," I said, referring to my Dodge Magnum wit 22s on it.

"Big Homey when you get this whip?"

"Two years ago; it's my work car."

"Damn, I need to upgrade cause I got a hoopty for real."

"Ali ain't nothing wrong wit that Delta 88."

"My shit is a real hoopty this ain't nowhere near no hoopty.

Then again, when you use to driving Benz and BMWs, I guess this would be a hoopty."

"Nigga it ain't like you can't afford one of them."

"I know. I just don't want to focus, that's all."

"Ali, don't cheat yaself treat yaself."

"I am, that's why I'm bout to spend a nice grip on my outfit."

"This shit don't count; you do this on a regular."

"Nah, not really."

"Come on Ali, all you wear is Gucci, Prada, Ralph Lauren."

"A'ight, a'ight point taken."

"So then treat yaself."

"I do like that 750 and A-8."

"My uncle just bought my aunt one of those for her birthday."

"Damn Big Homie your auntie going to be deucing on all tha females wit that."

"I know and once Nya sees it she's gonna want one or something better."

"So get her one."

"Oh, did I tell you I'm about to be a dad."

"Yeah, right Nigga"

"Nah, seriously, she told me a few days ago."

"Congratulations Big Homie."

"Thanks Man."

"Are you excited?"

"Man, I don't think words can describe how much I'm excited."

"I don't have no kids, but I remember how I felt when my sister had my niece. I'm telling you Big Homie, I can just imagine how are you gonna feel."

"Ali, I'm so excited now, so I know how I'm gonna feel six months from now when I'm able to hold him."

So it's a boy?"

"I don't know, but I'm pretty sure it is."

"Wow, a little big homey gon' be runnin' around."

"Ali, you just don't know. Imma do all tha things I never got to do wit my dad."

I could see tha pain in big Homie's face when he spoke about his dad. We both ended up dropping a nice piece of paper at tha mall. Ali was a major asset and I was lucky to have him on my team. Even though I was only 19, Ali was my young boy. He's 17, I've been grooming him since he was 14. When he killed Kool, I gained a lot more respect for him. He didn't care what tha consequences were because Kool was my man. I could have easily killed him for that, but because Kool was trying to burn me, I didn't care. Tha funny thing is I could see Ali tha jealousy and envy he was showing me. I just acted like I didn't.

"Big Homie, Big Homey."

"Yo."

"Damn, you was deep thought you ain't hear nothing I said."

"I was just thinking about something, my bag."

"I wasn't saying nothing important anyway."

"Let's stop on South Street. I need to go to tha Net."

"Good cause I needed to grab a bite to eat from Fy'Heed's."

"Yo, that's my spot Big Homie."

"Man, I been eating from there since they opened a few years ago."

There was a guy pulling out as we were pulling up.

"Right, they are Big Homie."

"Now that's what I call good timing."

"He Ali."

"Hey Malissa."

"I haven't seen you in a while."

"If you come to work more often, maybe you would."

"You know we just opened a store in Jersey. I've been up there working."

"Come on, Lis it's me, I know where you've been."

"Keeping tabs on me, are you?"

"I was just checking on my future wifey."

"If you were a few years older."

"What age got to do wit it?"

"Who are you?"

"Liz, this is Big Homie."

"Big Homie?"

"Nah'ceer, but you can call me Ceer."

"I haven't seen you in here before."

"Don't take this tha wrong way, but you probably won't see me in here after today."

"Oh, you got long money, huh?"

"Nah, that's tha thing I can't afford this stuff Ali is treating me."

"Ali is a nice guy."

"So why are you playing tha young card?"

"Because I'm 25 and he's only 17."

"That shit don't mean nothing; he's more mature than most grown men."

I didn't want to commit to him, but he was right. I've never messed with anyone that was younger than me. "Sometimes you have to take a chance in life."

"Last time I took a chance, I got my heart broke."

"Does he look like the kind of guy that would break ya pretty little heart?"

She turned around to look at Ali, who was checking out a pair of jeans.

"I'm telling you don't let one bad decision stop you from finding happiness."

"Don't you sound like Dr. Phil?"

"Ha! Ha! Ha! You got jokes too."

"If you don't mind me asking, what ethnic are you?"

"Hispanic and Dominican."

"That's what I thought."

"Lis was 5'5, bronze skin, gray eyes, pretty shoulder-length hair in a butt like tha broad Key Toi from the old Outkast video.

"Ali better be lucky he's my people."

"Damn Big Homie, are you going to grab some stuff or talk to Lis?"

Just as I was about to say something, I thought my eyes were playing tricks on me.

"Close ya mouth; that's my twin sister Clarissa."

"WOW, God was feeling good tha day he made tha two of you."

"Hey Ali."

"Hey Ris."

"Who's this Lis?"

"Nah'ceer," I said, not giving Lis a chance to introduce me.

"I know you not throwing moves on Ali's future wifey?"

I tried not to laugh as I caught the look Lis gave her sister.

"Girl, I don't care nothing about you looking at me like that especially tha way you kept calling asking if Ali was in tha store that day."

"Yo, let me find out you was checking up on a nigga."

"Yes, she was on a regular."

"Damn, you really got me blushing now."

"I never saw a Black man turn red before."

"First time for everything."

"Nah'ceer, you're cute; how old are you?"

"I'll be 20 in a few weeks. Let me guess you're 25 too?"

"Well, since we are twins, I say that's correct."

"So you're both comics?"

"I'm not a comic; I just keep it real."

"That's what I like, a woman who keeps it 100."

"You'll love me then."

The only difference between Lis and Ris are their eyes. Lis's are gray while Ris's are green Everything else is identical.

"What's your number Nah'ceer?"

"And you're bold."

"If I see something I like, I go after it."

"That must mean you don't have a man?"

"If I had a man, we wouldn't be having this conversation, that's for sure."

"Faithful too. Wow, that's rare in a woman."

"Not wit me."

"So you mind if we take y'all to dinner tonight, our treat?"

"I can't speak for Lis, but I'll be more than happy if you take me to dinner tonight."

Ali looked at Lis then asked if she wanted to go.

"Since you asked, sure I'll go wit you."

"A'ight, let me pay for this stuff so we can go."

"So what time do we need to be ready?"

"8 o'clock and dress formal."

"Boy bye will see you later."

"Lis, why are you keep playing games wit Ali? You know you want to mess wit him."

"Ris, he's only 17; he's a baby."

"Unh, Unh, you gon' to mess around and miss out on something good."

"Now you sound like his boy Nah'ceer."

"Papi is sexy as hell."

"You are a mess."

"Bitch you know he's sexy."

"He is."

"I've never seen him in here before."

"Me either; he said I probably won't see him back in here after today either."

"I wouldn't bet on it," Ris said, winking.

"Damn Ali, why you ain't never put me onto Clarissa?"

"I don't know."

"Malissa likes you; she doesn't know how to tell you."

"Man, all she got to do is say it."

"Well, since she played tha two young card, she's trying to stick to it."

"Since she's so bad, I'll play tha game wit her for a little while."

"Not to mention fat to death."

"Don't worry, when I get her, she'll be hooked like a fish. Let me call and make these reservations."

"Aye, get separate tables."

"Already on it."

"I don't know about you, but I am hittin' Ris tonight and taking her to tha Dons and Divas party tomorrow."

"Nigga you crazy."

"She's a diva; why wouldn't I showcase her on my arm."

"Fuck it; Imma see if Lis want to go. If she say yeah, we can take them to get something to wear."

CHAPTER 26

"Sharky, did you handle it wit Joshua yet?"

"Yeah, I took care of it yesterday."

"Did you hit him wit tha extra five I told you to give him?"

"Yup, plus I put tha tax on it."

"Of course, he already knew tha deal."

"I wasn't messing wit tha work; I let Jah'ceer and Sharky deal wit that."

"Honey, I'm home."

"I'm in tha kitchen." I walked up behind her and kissed her on tha neck.

"OOOH, you better stop; you know that's one of my spots."

"My bag. Smells good what you cooking?"

"Barbecue chicken, collard greens, mac & cheese, corn and honey biscuits."

"Daaaaaaamn what's tha occasion?"

"You know I cook every Sunday stop trying to play me."

"Baby, I would never try to play you."

"What you doing home so early anyway?"

"I'm not allowed to spend time wit my wifey?"

"Of course, you are. I would love for you to do it more often."

"Tae."

"Yes."

"Just in case nobody has told you today or you just need to hear it, I love you."

"Awe ain't that sweet; I love you too."

"Have you talk to ya nephew today?"

"As a matter of fact, I invited him and Nya over for dinner tonight."

"That explains all this food you cooked."

"Don't I always cook a lot so we can have leftovers tha next day?"

"Now that tha food is done, could you do me a big favor?"

"What's that Baby?"

"Take me upstairs and blow my back out."

"I certainly can."

"Jah'ceer, Jah'ceer."

"What's up Nya?"

"What time are we going over to Tae and Roc's?"

"About 5 o'clock."

She looked at her watch, "That's three hours from now; I need a snack. I'm hungry now."

"Well, make a sandwich or eat one of those microwavable dinners."

"Can you make one of ya famous turkey clubs?"

"Yeah, that doesn't sound like a bad idea."

We ate then ended up falling asleep if my phone didn't ring, I would've never woke up.

"Yo, what up Bishop?"

"Damn Nigga, you been in tha crib all day; you coming out?"

"Nah, I'm bout to head to my uncle's spot for dinner."

"A'ight hit me up tomorrow."

"Everything straight, right?"

"Yeah we good."

"A'ight then, I'll get at you tomorrow."

"Ceer let's go. Tae just called me."

"I'm ready; I was waiting on you."

"Here I come; let me grab a snack."

"I'll be in tha car."

When Nya got in tha car, she had a pickle on top of an oatmeal cream pie, which was her favorite snack.

"My son got you eaten crazy."

"I keep telling you it's a girl Brazil NaJa Abrams."

"Damn, you already got tha name picked out. So that means I don't get no say so."

"If it's a boy."

"Nya, you already know he gonna be a junior."

"J.J, huh?"

"Nah, Lil Ceer."

"I'll probably call him J.J."

"No, you not, you're going to call him Lil Ceer."

"Okay What ever, no need to get upset besides, we ain't got to worry about that."

"Would you like to put a wager on that?"

"How much?"

"One dollar."

"Boy you stupid."

"I'm serious."

"You must know you gonna lose since you only betting a buck."

"Just trying to save you some money."

"Really, let's bet 500 then."

"How about 500 and a month of massages?"

"That'll work for me."

"Those massages are gonna feel real good."

"They sure are," Nya said, getting out tha car, "you're going down Jah'ceer Abrams."

"What are you two talking about?" Tae asked, opening tha door?

"We just made a friendly bet about tha sex of tha baby."

"I hope you said, boy Nya."

"No, she said girl."

"Well, I hope you didn't bet too much."

"500 and a month of massages."

"Tae, you not co-signing that, are you?"

"Nya, look how low ya stomach is."

"That don't mean nothing."

"When do you get ya ultrasound?"

"I had my first one, but she kept moving, so they couldn't determine tha sex."

"She goes back in two months."

"They will be able to tell then."

"Nya, I'm with you, is probably a little diva."

"Not you, too Unc."

"Hey, I wouldn't mind lacing a little diva up wit all that high-end stuff I be seeing in tha stores."

"Hate to be tha bearer of bad news, but it's a boy."

"Are y'all gonna keep talking about tha sex of tha baby or eat?"

"I don't know about y'all, but me and Brazil are hungry as slaves."

"She even got tha name picked out."

"So does Ceer."

"Mine is a no-brainer; of course, my first one would be a junior."

"Ya dad was thinking about naming both you and ya brother after him."

"How was he going to do that?"

"Easy, just name y'all after him."

"Then one of us would have been a junior while tha other was tha third."

"I'm not mistaken. Zeek said it would have been Junior for who came out first and tha third for who came out next."

"Uncle Roc, my pops sounds like a thurl dude."

"Sounds, Jah'ceer ya pop was more than thurl."

"I can only imagine seeing how you are."

"What's that suppose to mean?"

"Unc you down to earth, not to mention you schooled me to a lot in this game."

"Ceer, I knew that you would eventually get in this game. So I had to make sure you knew all tha end results as well is tha ins and outs."

"Roc, you and Ceer come sit down and eat before it gets cold."

"Daaaaam Aunty, you put ya foot in this."

"I know Tae, this mac & cheese is off tha chain."

"Thank you."

"Why y'all pump her head up?"

"They didn't tell me nothing I don't already know!"

"It's Ok."

"Roc please, you love my cooking." I didn't say anything; I just smiled.

"No comment?"

"Nope."

"I didn't think so."

"Ha! Ha! Ha!"

"What you laughing at Ceer?"

"It's just funny how you so tough in tha streets, but when it comes to Aunty Tae, you a straight-up punk."

"Yeah, just like you are wit Nya."

Nya immediately looked at me, waiting to hear my response. I chose not to respond.

"Not tha big bad wolf wit nothing to say."

"Don't feed into that Ceer."

"Aunty, I know when not to say something."

"He better not say nothing or Nya gonna get wit him."

"That's right, take tha focus off yaself."

After we ate, me and Ceer went into tha basement to talk privately.

"So Unc, did you talk to Heaven?

"Yeah, her and Murder will be ready to meet wit us next week."

"I hope so because I want to meet them."

"You still have ya dogs on a leash, right?"

"Yeah, but they hungry they wanna eat."

"Jah'ceer ya boy started this, not them."

"I know; that's why I gave them a few weeks for a sit-down."

"We don't need any bloodshed especially not wit our connect."

"Uncle Roc, I'm not trying to mess up our biz-ness; believe me, I'm not but if shit hit tha fan then that's all it is. Besides, Ross shouldn't let beef override biz-ness."

"When it comes to family, nothing else matters but Ross has retired from tha game."

"So, who's in control?"

"His nephew Murder."

"Murder? Isn't he my age?"

"I think so."

"Ross must have a lot of trust in him to let him take over his empire."

"Look what he's done wit those two blocks."

"Yeah, he did turn them into a gold mine."

"Truth be told, I couldn't wait to meet him; it seemed we have a lot in common."

"She moves like a tiger in tha woods hunting for prey."

"Hello Heaven."

"Hey Roc, I was just calling to confirm our meeting next week."

"We still on Baby girl. Make sure your nephew comes. I want to meet him."

"He wants to meet you and ya brother too."

"A'ight, I'll holla at you next week."

"I guess we talked her up."

"Yeah, she was just making sure we were still on for next week. She wants to meet you too." "Unc, I'm not Jizz; if she get out of pocket, I will push her shit back!"

"Don't go in there on no dumb shit Jah'ceer I'm telling you now."

It kinda caught me off guard hearing my uncle talk to me in that tone. Maybe that was his way of letting me know he was serious. As bad as I wanted to snap, I didn't say shit. No one and I mean no one, has ever talked to me like that before; if he was anybody else, he be dead.

I wanted to laugh; looking at Ceer, I knew he was mad because his jaw clinched tha same way Zeek's did when he was upset.

"Calm down Playboy, no need to get mad."

"I'm cool."

"No, you not; I've seen that look too many times from Zeek to know you're pissed off." All I could do was smile because he hit it on tha nose.

"Why are you smiling?"

"Cause you right Unc."

"I know."

"For a sec, I almost forgot who you were."

"Well, lucky for you that you did remember."

"What's that suppose to mean Unc?"

"Jah'ceer, I get down too in case you didn't know."

"Uncle Roc, I heard all about you and my pop. You know tha streets talk, especially when they found out you was my uncle and Zeek was my pops."

"Wow, I can imagine what they were saying."

"Let's just say y'all gotta lot of respect in this town."

"We earned it; it wasn't just given to us."

"So you think mine was?"

"Not at all; if anything, you had to work harder because of me and

Zeek." "I just wanted people to know I'm my own man. Unc ain't nobody give me shit; everything I got I had to get on my own."

"That makes it much better knowing you got it on ya own."

"Unc ain't never lied about that."

"Nephew, I don't lie about nothing!"

"Wiz, you need to check Rala."

"Why, what he do now?"

"He coming up short again."

"So why didn't you handle it?"

"Because you know I don't like him and if he would of said something crazy he'd be dead."

"Nigga you mad at him trying to holla at Heaven."

"How Imma be mad she ain't my girl?"

"That's what I'm trying to tell you."

"Nigga you ain't telling me shit!"

"God damn, no need to get upset Baby Boy."

"Wiz, you be on some straight bullshit."

"Nigga I just keep it 100, which you already know since we been boys since tha sandbox."

"I'll tell you what I do know."

"What's that Lif?"

"You always trying to save Rala."

"He a'ight."

"Nigga Banks came short one time and you kicked his ass like he stole something."

"Banks was trying to be slick."

"And I guess Rala ain't?"

"Leave it alone Lif."

"Leave what alone?"

"Nothing."

"Now I know it's something because you answered to fast."

"Don't worry about it; Heaven and I got it all under control."

"I don't think you do," Khalif told me what was going on and I snapped

out.

"Wiz you too soft!"

Ain't nothing soft about me!" he said, raising his voice.

"Nigga you better pipe down!"

"I ain't trying to hear that shit Heaven!"

"Wiz family or not you better check yaself."

"Yeah I hear you."

"Khalif, let me holla at you for a sec."

"I followed Heaven to her car."

"What up Heaven?"

"Bring Rala to the warehouse in an hour."

"A'ight I gotcha."

"Yo, what tha fuck was that about Lif?"

"She wanted to know what was up wit.you."

"Ain't shit up wit me, I'm just sick of her talking crazy to everybody."

"She only talk crazy when tha money and coming up right."

"I run this block."

"Well, you might need to get niggaz back on tha same page."

"I need to handle something. I'll hit you later."

"A'ight, cause I need to take care of something too."

I waited for Wiz to leave then I walked over to Rala.

"What up Lif?"

"Heaven want to holla at you asap."

"Oh, it's probably about what I asked Wiz to do for me."

"Probably, I'm headed over to see her as well. Do you want to ride wit me?"

"Sure, why not."

On tha ride to tha warehouse, I smoked a blunt wit him to keep him at ease.

"Do you think that Heaven would let me fuck her?" I almost swerved into another car when Rala asked me that.

"Damn Nigga, you better pass me that," he said wit his hand out for tha blunt.

"It went down tha wrong pipe."

"I hate when that happens."

"You never answered my question."

"I don't know; you have to ask her and find out."

"Nigga is you crazy? I'm not asking her for nothing like that."

"Why not?"

"Even though I've yet to witness it I've heard about her mean streak."

"Awe Nigga you tough."

"You right I am, but I've never had to check a broad."

"You'll end up in a box," I thought to myself.

When we pulled up tha warehouse Heaven was already there.

"Yo, leave ya phone in tha car."

"Why?"

"Didn't you just say you never saw her mad?"

"Yeah."

"Well, unless you want to see her mad, I suggest you leave ya phone here."

"A'ight if you say so."

"Trust me, leave it here."

"I said a'ight now let's go."

"I can't stand this punk ass nigga," I thought to myself.

"I was beginning to think y'all wasn't gon' to show."

"Nah Ma, that's this driving Miss Daisy Ass nigga."

"What tha fuck you just say?"

"I don't stutter, so you heard exactly what I said."

I could see murder in Khalif eyes, so I quickly switched gears before it got out of control.

"So Rala Wiz tells me you ready to step up."

"Yeah Ma, I'm trying to advance in tha game."

"I see that's what's up."

"Listen Ma."

He was really working my last Fuckin' nerve wit this Ma shit, I can't stand when Niggaz use that Ma bullshit.

"Would you be an asset or liability?"

"Come on Ma, you see my numbers I'm putting up."

"Well, since you mentioned that, that's why I told Khalif to bring you here."

He started smiling like if I had just told him, he could get some of this pussy.

"I'm putting up LeBron and D-Wade numbers Ma."

That was it I lost it.

"First of all Nigga don't you ever in your miserable life call me Ma again! Secondly, LeBron and D-Wade don't flatter yaself more like Greg Odom numbers. Third, you been skimmin' doe that's why ya shit keep comin' up short."

"Hold up, I know you didn't go runnin' ya mouth?"

"He ain't have to say nothing I can count real good. Why do you think everybody has a different color of rubber bands?"

"I never paid attention to that stuff."

"Maybe if you did, you wouldn't be here now."

"Yo, y'all trippin'."

"Nah Nigga you trippin' you owe about 10 grand give or take."

"I ain't come short no 10 grand."

"Yes, you have; I just wanted to see how long Wiz or Khalifa was going to let it go on."

"Real talk Heaven; if it was up to me, this cocky ass Nigga would have been a memory."

"Nigga you could never be on my level."

"I would never want to be on ya level."

Rala acted like he wanted to reach for his pistol, but Heaven already had hers pointed in his face.

"Whoa Whoa no need for that."

"Put ya Fuckin' hands up. Khalif get his gun."

"What's this all about I thought we were here to discuss biz-ness?"

"We are and this is biz-ness!"

"I think we need to call Wiz."

"Nah Playboy, Wiz ain't gonna save you this time."

"Khalif you a bitch!"

"Rala you all mouth Nigga."

"Put tha gun down and I'll show you a thing or two."

"Handle ya biz Khalif."

"Heaven, I'm not fighting this punk; I'll hurt him."

"Nigga you scared."

"Yup, you right scared of what Imma do to you."

"Like I thought you a bitch Nigga!"

"Hold this Heaven."

Wiz said Khalif used to box for years. I'm about to see how good he is. Rala put his hands up and I could tell he had a little bit of training, but It didn't faze me being an ex-lightweight Golden glove. He caught me off guard with a straight jab that hit me on tha chin. When he threw his hang maker, I sidestepped it and caught him wit a right hook that set him on his pamper. Long story short, I beat tha brakes off him.

"A'ight, A'ight that's enough."

"I don't think he want no more anyway."

Rala's face look like he just got jumped on by a bunch of Niggaz.

"Now that is over, how long is it gonna take you to pay that 10 grand you owe us?"

"I don't know because I don't feel like I owe y'all no money."

Boom! Boom! Boom! Three shots to tha face close range.

"Wrong answer Nigga."

"Damn, you could've just let me do that from tha door."

"And take tha fun out of watching you kick his butt?"

"It's been a while since I've fought anybody."

"Wiz wasn't lying when he said you can fight."

"Wiz always runnin' his mouth. So you really knew Rala was coming up short?"

"Yeah I was just waiting until one of y'all said something about it."

"Wiz kept letting him ride."

"He kicked Banks butt for coming up short a few times."

"That's what I was telling him when you walked up earlier."

"I swear if Wiz wasn't family, he'll be on a T-shirt."

"Do you want me to get rid of tha body?"

"Nah, we got people to handle that for us. But I do want you to keep Wiz in line; he starting to slip."

"No problem Heaven."

"Thank you Khalif."

"No need to thank me. I'm sure if tha shoe was on tha other foot, you would do tha same for me."

"Of course, I would."

CHAPTER 27

When I pulled up to tha block, my phone began to ring. When I checked, there was no missed calls. When it started again, I realized it wasn't my phone.

"Shit!" I looked at tha caller ID and saw it was Wiz. I quickly turned it off then dropped it in tha drain when I got out tha car.

"What up Wiz?"

"Lif, have you seen Rala?"

"Nah, he said he was going to holla at some young girl before I left."

"I told him that I needed to see him when I got back."

So you finally gonna say something about that change he keep messing up?"

"Lif, don't start it."

"I'm just asking. Let me try his phone again."

"He's not going to be answering his phone no more," I thought to myself, which caused me to smile.

"What tha fuck you smiling for?"

"Cause you always letting him slide and as long as you do, he's gon' to keep coming wrong."

"That's my young boy Lif."

"Then that's even more reason to check him and guide him right. Because if you don't, he'll just be another nigga that can't get right."

Even though I knew what Lif was saying was tha truth, I didn't want to admit it to him.

"Uncle Roc, are we still on for this week?"

"Yeah, everything is still ago."

"A'ight, just making sure."

"How is Nya feeling?"

"She's Ok. She just had a little morning sickness."

"I heard Tae talking to her on tha phone this morning."

"Aunty Tae was supposed to be picking her up so they could do some shoppin'."

"That's all they do is shop."

"Who are you telling?"

"When is tha next doctor's appointment?"

"In two weeks."

"It's not even my baby and anxious to know tha sex."

"Unc already told you it's a boy."

"That's what you keep saying. Would you like to lose some of that doe you holding?"

"Nah, I'm good."

"Come on Unc, I know you ain't scared to bet some of that long money you got?"

"Truth be told, I'm trying to save you some doe."

"Don't save me no money; help me get some more."

"Bet 2,500 then."

"It's a bet; I'll be buying my son some new clothes thanks to his Uncle Roc."

"No Nigga you'll be buying ya aunty this bracelet she's been wanting."

"Nah'ceer when you go to your meeting wit Roc, let him know I said hello."

"I got you Uncle Ross. Uncle Ross do you miss being in tha game?"

"Truthfully, no, I don't, I actually wish I could've gotton out a little sooner than I did."

"Why did you wait so long?"

"I didn't have anyone to turn tha reigns over to."

"Why didn't you just let Heaven take over?"

"Because I didn't know she was in the biz-ness until a few years ago. I knew about tha bodies she had which let me know she was just like her mother in every aspect."

"She's definitely a killer, but she's also biz-ness smart as well."

"You two always talk so highly of one another."

"Uncle Ross, we've taught each other so much over tha years."

"Believe it or not, I've learned from you both too."

That made me feel so good knowing I taught Uncle Ross something. What I don't know what he says I taught him something.

"Just make sure tha two of you be safe and stay outta trouble."

"Come on Uncle Ross, us get into trouble."

"Don't act like your sister isn't hot-tempered; we all get a little hot-tempered at times.

I've never seen you upset."

"Uncle Ross, I get upset; I just keep it under control."

"I see."

"I learned that from you."

"From me?"

"Yup, I always know when you're upset because you start whistling or you crack your neck."

All he could do was smile because he knew I was right.

"That's one of the things I love about you."

"What's that?"

"Your observation, Nah'ceer you're very observant."

"I have to be Unc."

"What time is ya flight departing?"

"7 o'clock."

"I'll drop you off so you won't have to drive."

"I'm cool Unc."

"I'll have Bear pick you up when you come back if that's what you're worried about."

"A'ight, I'll just call and let you know what time my flight will be landing."

"No problem, I'll pick you up at 6 o'clock."

"Cool."

"Hey Cuz."

"Wiz."

"What time is Murder plane coming in?"

"I don't know he's gon' call me wit all tha info."

"When is tha meet?"

"In a few days."

"I'm coming along I want to meet Jizz people, tha man who never shows his face."

"It's just going to be us and them."

"Why?"

"Because I don't want them to get tha wrong impression."

"What's tha wrong impression?"

"Ain't no need to go into all that we are going by ourselves."

"Yeah, you are, but are they?"

That was a good question, but I had no reason to believe they wouldn't come alone.

"A'ight, you can come."

"Thanks Cuz."

"Did you ever get that situation straight with Rala yet?"

"I haven't talk to him in a few days."

"So, who's been holding his shift down?"

"Alex stepped up."

"I hate to say it, but I told you Alex was the one you should've put under ya wing."

"Rala was good folk."

"Then why is Alex running his shift for him?"

Now that is a damn good question.

"Fuck 'em, he was messing up paper anyway. I had to put 15,000 of my .own paper up to make up for tha doe he owes now. Imma just out my losses wit Rala he's dead weight."

"He owes me and he'll pay one way or another."

"Hello."

"Hey Little Sis."

"A Big Head."

"My plane will be landing at 8:15."

"I'll be at the usual spot waiting."

"A'ight make sure you got some of that good green for me."

"Don't I always?"

"True, I'll see you in a few hours. I haven't seen Ceer since I went home a few a few weeks ago and I missed him. After this meeting, if everything went well, I planned on going back wit Nah'ceer to Philly.

I spotted Ceer before he spotted me.

"Over here, Big Head."

"I saw you when I first came in."

"No, you didn't."

"Yes, I did; you had ya glasses on, then you took them off."

"That was about 15 minutes ago."

"This is me; Sis, come on."

"You right; I should've known ya plane was landing earlier than you said."

"So, are we going to stand here all night or leave?"

"Come on, since you in a rush."

"I'm not in a rush. I just don't want to be in tha airport all night. Can we stop and grab a bite to eat I'm starving, Sis?"

"We can do What ever you want."

"Good cause I want to go out tonight."

"We definitely can do that; Joker having a party tonight at Third Level. Oh shit, before I forget, look in the glove box and get that box."

He went to hand me the box.

"It's for you."

"What is it?"

."Open it up and see."

"WOW! Now, this is what I'm talkin' bout."

My Lil Sis had gotten me an iced out Jager-Lecoultre watch. Tha same one I was telling her about a few months ago.

"Thanks Sis."

"You're welcome Big Head."

"Now I feel bad I didn't even buy you anything."

"You didn't have to; you spent enough on this," she say, holding up her diamond ring I bought her last time I was down here.

"You still got that thing?"

"Of course, why wouldn't I?"

"I don't know."

"You see, I got it on my ring finger."

"I don't need to ask why already know why."

"Why?"

"So No Niggaz don't try to holla at you."

"Yup, but some still try anyway."

"If I was them, I would too."

"So, what's the deal with Khalif?"

"What do you mean what's the deal with Khalif?"

"You still ain't give him no airplay?"

"No, and I'm not."

"Why not?"

"Ceer, I don't look at him like that."

"Sis ya shit gonna have cobb webs by tha time you get some."

"How you know I'm not getting none?"

"Come on, it's me you talking to not some other Nigga."

"Well, for your info, I have had some, as a matter of fact, I flew my young boy down just last week."

"Who Melo?"

"Who else would I fly down?"

"Heaven you so mafuckin' sneaky."

"I know that's why I'm so good at what I do."

"I can't argue wit that and speaking of which, we have a flight to catch first thing in tha morning."

"Where and why?"

"Miami and tha Santos brothers, but I'll fill you in over dinner."

We pulled up to Daddy's House and it was packed as usual.

"Yo, what up Ceer."

"Me and Heaven both looked at each other while discreetly placing our hand on our pistol.

"Do you know me?"

"Not personally, but I do know you got the 'A' on lock."

"Yeah how you know that."

"Come on, who don't, you tha man on tha streets."

"A'ight Homey you be cool."

"You too."

"How tha hell anybody know my real name down here? He, not tha first person to say my real name."

"I don't know; that's a damn good question."

After we ate and I put Heaven up on tha situation wit tha Santos brothers; we decided to get some rest instead of hittin' tha club. As soon as I hit tha pillow, I was out for tha count.

Tha next morning, I woke up to find Little Sis standing over top of me.

"Boom," she said wit her hand in tha form of a gun.

"You better stop slippin', or you might find yaself slumped."

"Nah, I was just tired; I heard you come in 30 minutes ago."

"How you know it was me?"

"Who else is going to come in and go in my fridge."

"Then maybe you ain't slippin'."

"Sis, I'm never slippin' maybe tired but never slippin'."

"Get on up and brush ya tongue so we can get to tha airport."

"I need to shower and tha whole nine yards."

"Well, what you waiting on?"

"You don't have to rush me. I got this."

Thirty minutes later, I was dressed and ready to go. When we got to tha airport, we had 25 minutes until boarding.

"I'm hungry; let me hit this sandwich spot before we have to board."

"I'll wait here."

"You're not hungry?"

"No, I ate before I left my house this morning."

"A'ight, I'll be right back."

"Nah'ceer."

"Yes."

"You can get me a pack of gum and orange juice."

"A'ight, anything else?"

"Nope."

"Flight 352 to Miami is boarding at gate 7 in five minutes, flight 352 to Miami is boarding at gate 7 in five minutes."

"That's us, Big Head; let's go."

"I'm right behind you."

Ceer slept tha whole flight. I was too anxious to sleep. I hadn't put any work in in a while and I was long overdue.

"All passengers, please fasten your seatbelt and prepare for Landing."

"Nah'ceer, Nah'ceer."

When he didn't answer tha second time, I shook him, which caused him to grab his waist.

"Nigga you ain't got no gun, so what you're reaching for?"

"Habit."

"Nigga you better start getting some rest."

"I know."

Once tha plane landed, we headed to tha rental spot to grab a car.

"I'll get our bags and meet you at tha entrance."

(Beep-Beep)

"I see you."

"Well, come on."

I threw tha bags in tha back but not before grabbing my Jeezy CD out.

"What CD is that."

"Jeezy."

"I should've known that's all you listen to."

"Look up in tha sky tell me what you see, clouds Nah Nigga, not me, I see opportunity I'm a opportunist."

"How can you Fuck wit Jeezy?"

"Oh yeah, you a Nikki Minaj type of girl."

"Boy, you stupid, where to?"

"Any hotel or South Beach."

"I know tha perfect low-key spot."

"I bet you do wit your sneaky ass."

"Ain't I suppose to enjoy myself?"

"I never said you wasn't; I just called you sneaky."

I'm good at what I do, so be thankful I'm sneaky. All I could do was smile.

"Hello, welcome to the Embassy Suites."

"Hi, could I have a luxury suite?"

Once all tha paperwork was done and we had our keys, we went to our room.

"Imma take me a nap. I'm still tired."

"You must got somebody knocked up sleeping like that."

"I don't sleep over wit out my sleeping bag."

"Glad to hear I'm not ready to be an aunt yet."

"That's tha last thing you have to worry about Sis."

"A'ight, well get some sleep. Imma do a little bit of shoppin'."

"If you see something, I might like grab it, please."

"You know I got you Big Head."

I decided to hit tha gun shop to grab a few items that I knew would come in handy for tha jobs we had to do. When I got to tha mall, I went crazy in all tha stores they had. When my phone started ringing, I realized I had been shoppin' for a few hours.

"Hello."

"Damn, what you got lost?"

"Nah, I'm bout to leave now."

"I know you ain't still shoppin'?"

"That would be correct."

"You must of bought up tha whole mall?"

"I might have if you didn't call."

"Well, come on, we got work that needs to be done."

"Give me 20 minutes. I'll be there."

"I'll be in tha lobby."

"I need to take these bags up to tha room."

"No problem, I'll be in tha lobby waiting on you."

When I pulled up to tha hotel tha busboy offered to help take tha bags to my room.

"Sure, why not."

Once he had all tha bags on his cart, we made our way inside only to be greeted by Nah'ceer."

"You don't need my help, so I'll be in tha car."

"OK, I'll be right down."

After I put tha bags in tha room, I tip tha busboy $20 and made my way back to tha car where Nah'ceer was behind tha wheel waiting.

"So did you get everything you needed."

"Yeah, I think so."

"I know you got me a thing or two."

"Of course I did, so where we headed?"

"To meet wit some friends of mine."

CHAPTER 28

We pulled up to this gated mansion.

"Hello."

"Nah'ceer here to see Pedro."

Two seconds later, tha gate opened up. When we got to tha top of tha hill to Armen wit two German shepherds were waiting.

"Nah'ceer My Friend, you can get out; they won't bother you."

Once we were out tha, two men went to search us, but Pedro stopped them.

"Hey, never disrespect Nah'ceer and his lovely wife."

"Ha! Ha! Ha!"

"What, did I miss tha joke?"

"Pedro, this is my sister, not my wife."

"Oh, I'm sorry, I shouldn't have seen tha resemblance."

"Funny thing is a lot of people say the same thing. I've just come to tha conclusion that we've been around each other so long we started looking alike."

"Please follow me."

Pedro escorted us to his backyard, that was filled wit people lounging around.

(Clap, Clap) Pedro clapped twice and everybody dispersed. "Have a seat. Would you like a drink?"

"No, thank you."

"Nah, I'm good."

That was a rule neither of us would ever break having a drink during biz-ness.

"Shall we get down to tha reason for this meeting?"

"We're listening."

"We have a problem wit tha Santos brothers."

"What kind of problem would that be Pedro?"

"A reliable source informed me that they no longer want to play by tha rules."

"Well, in that case, set up a meeting wit them."

"What time and where at?"

"Same place at 8 o'clock."

"Do you want me to let them know you'll be joining us?"

"No, just tell them you want to be a part of their plan What ever it is. Pedro, bring me my phone."

"Hello."

"What do I owe this call Pedro?"

"I need to meet wit you and your brother ASAP."

"About what?"

"Come on Luis, don't insult my intelligence."

"I don't know what you speak of."

"Luis, I don't have time to play games; you want to play call your kids."

"Please explain what you speak of."

"Tha situation wit Nah'ceer I want in."

"Where do you get your info Pedro?"

"Can we talk or not?"

"Where, what time?"

"Sacko Warehouse at 8 o'clock"

"Will meet you there." (CLICK)

"Pedro, you need to have ya men surround tha warehouse but outta site."

"We'll get there at 6 o'clock so we can find a place to hide."

"Ceer they'll probably be there at 7 to do tha same thing."

"I know, but 7 o'clock will be too late; we'll already be in position."

"Pedro, I want you to come at 7:45, so they don't suspect anything."

"No problem My Friend."

"Just like I thought they're early."

"I do tha honors and take his men out."

"Let me get tha tape recorder."

"Where are you going?"

"Closer so I can get it all on tape."

"Be safe, I don't want to have to go mid-evil in this bitch."

"I think you're about to do that on your own wit out my help."

"Boss Pedro is pulling up."

"How many men is wit him?"

"Three."

"You sure?"

"Positive."

"A'ight stay out there and make sure nobody else shows up."

"Will do Boss."

"Answer ya phone."

"Hello."

"Hey Hector, what's tha deal?"

"Same shit."

"I was in town thought I'd give all my friends a call."

"I'm about to meet wit Pedro. I'll give you a call when we finish."

"A'ight."

"Hector, Raul."

"Hello Pedro."

"So what's tha deal wit Nah'ceer?"

"Me and my brother get 60 to 100 bricks, so we figure we would have him send us 200 and not give him a dime."

"Yeah and if you do tha same thing, that'll give us 400."

"If we do that, will need to find another plug."

"Already got it tooken care of."

"Well, I'm with it."

"A'ight, you know he's in town."

"Is he?"

"Yeah, he said he called you."

I pulled up my phone to play it off.

"He did call. I don't know how I missed it."

"Boss, you put ya phone on silent before we left."

"Oh shit, I did, didn't I. I better call him back."

"I told him we would hit him after our meeting."

"Hector, is Nah'ceer not good to you and Raul?"

"Not as good as he is to you; if it was up to me, I'd kill tha bastard."

"You never bite tha hand that feeds you."

"I don't think they heard you Pedro; tell them again."

Hector and Raul turned in total shock, but before they could pull their weapons, Heaven had hers drawn on them.

"You might want to think about that."

Hector started looking around. "You don't have to worry about them they're all dead."

"I've always treated you guys right, so why would you try to steal from me?"

"We didn't steal anything from you."

"But you were gonna if I had given you an extra 100 bricks."

"You got it wrong Papa Pedro was tha one who suggested it."

I just smiled and played tha tape back for them.

When I pulled my gun out, they instantly started begging for their lives.

"Please spare me at least die wit some dignity."

"Fuck you Papa!"

Pop, Pop, Pop "Nah fuck you."

"Do you have any parting words you like to say?"

"Fuck you!"

Putting my gun to his head, I pulled tha trigger causing his head to explode like a watermelon being dropped from a building.

"Pedro My Friend, today is your lucky day."

"Why is that?"

"You now control all of Miami."

"Nah'ceer My Friend, you just made me tha happiest man."

"I respect ya loyalty because you could have not said anything and went along wit their plan."

"Only to end up like them."

"Yeah, you do have a point."

"Have someone dispose of all these bodies."

"Now, we can have that drink you offered us earlier."

"We'll go out to celebrate my newfound success."

Our flight landed in Atlanta just after 8.

"Do you wanna go to ya crib or across town wit me?"

"I'm wit you."

"I need to check on Wiz."

"Don't tell me Wiz been fuckin' up."

"He ain't been fuckin' up, but he has been making some stupid decisions and I mean stupid."

"I know he's family, but if his decision-making is interfering wit our money, then maybe Khalif needs to be in charge."

"I got Khalif running tha other block."

"So you saying he can't run both?"

"He could."

"When are we having that sit down wit Roc and his nephew?"

"Day after tomorrow."

"What up y'all? Glad to see y'all made it back in one piece."

"Why wouldn't we?"

"Because when y'all left, I thought y'all was on a serious mission."

"We was but nothing we couldn't handle."

"I heard that."

"So, what's up with you?"

"Same shit, these dead presidents."

"That's good but don't let them dead Presidents cloud ya judgment."

"Now you lost me."

"Well, I suppose you find me."

"Heaven, what you done told him now?"

"Nigga I told him about those fucked up decisions you've been making."

"I don't think they were fucked up."

"That's obvious because you made 'em."

"Heaven, you been on some bullshit as of late."

"Nah Nigga I just been on point."

"Murder, you need to talk to her."

"He don't need to talk to me."

"Maybe you need a hug."

"What I need is for you to get back focus; stop letting all this doe go to ya head."

"If you think that's what I'm doing then I'll definitely take a good look at that."

"Nigga save tha program bullshit."

"It ain't no program bullshit; it's me keeping it real."

"Wiz, I just don't want you to lose focus."

"That's one thing you never have to worry about like Hov said, I'm a Focused Man."

"Ya action sure ain't showing it!"

"Murder put a muzzle on her."

"Mafucka if you wasn't blood."

"If I wasn't blood, what?"

"Make that your last time you disrespect me I said, walking toward him."

"Hold up, hold up, no need to go there."

"This Nigga smelling his own piss."

"Nah, I'm just tired of you talkin' to me all crazy."

"Well, get ya shit together and you won't have to hear it!"

"Imma holla at you later. I got shit to handle."

"Ceer, I swear if he wasn't family, the cleaners would have been picking him up."

"Heaven, you need to understand he's never had this much money before."

"Neither have I, but I don't let it go to my head and you don't either."

Heaven, we been getting this kind of paper for a while now."

"So has he, stop making excuses for him."

"I'm not."

"Khalif, don't act tha way he does."

"I see a lot of me in Khalif that's why I'm putting him in a higher position."

"What position is that?"

"He'll be tha one picking up tha money and dropping tha work off."

"Thank you, I was trying to find somebody to handle that since Wiz has been on his dumb shit."

"Well, you can stop looking. Khalif will handle it from here on out."

"Handle what, Big Homey?"

"I need you to take over tha picks and drops."

"Are you serious?"

"Of course, unless you don't want to do it."

"Damn right, I want to do it. I just thought Heaven was gonna let Wiz take care of it."

"Wiz got too much on his plate and this is a serious job, no room for error."

"Big Homey, you don't have to worry about that wit me, I promise you."

"I know that's why I picked you for tha job."

"What about Wiz?"

"What about him?"

"This is all he's been talkin' about."

"Wiz has his priorities messed up."

"I'm just saying I don't want to step on his toes."

"Khalif, how can you do that? I came to you."

"True, I just know how he is."

"Look, if you worried about what Wiz is going to think or say then don't take tha position."

"I don't care about none of that."

"Well, that's all it is. Heaven will take you around so you know all the spots."

"Uncle Roc, what time is tha meeting?"

"4 o'clock."

"A'ight just making sure."

"I'll swing by around three to pick you up."

"Cool, I'll be here. I ain't going nowhere."

"Oh, Nya on her spend some time wit me shit?"

"How do you know?"

"That's how your mom used to do Zeke."

"Unc any news on Ceer yet?"

"Nah, I just talked to Pete."

"For some reason, tha past few days I been feeling him like he real close."

"Maybe that's a good thing."

"I hope so; I want to meet my brother."

I could hear tha sincerity in his voice and I definitely felt his pain.

"Baby you Ok?"

"Yeah," I said, wiping tha long tear out of my eye before I turned around to face her.

"You sure, you seem a bit distant these past few days?"

"My mind has been elsewhere."

"Thinking about your other half again?"

"A lot."

"You'll find him."

"I hope so; I really do."

"Trust me; you'll find him when you least expect it."

"Look at you lookin' like you about to blow any minute now."

"I feel like I'm about to blow."

"I wish we would've gotton tha ultrasound."

"I want it to be a surprise."

"I know it's a boy."

"You better hope so; all of those clothes you bought are for a boy."

"Well, if it's not, she'll be rocking all this stuff."

"Yeah right, you not gonna turn my baby into no Tom Boy!"

"Well, it's a good thing we never have to find out then."

"You're just so sure it's a boy. I know you think about ya other half and I don't blame you. I would do tha same if I had a twin sister who I knew existed but never got a chance to meet her. I would wonder if she likes tha same things as me."

"I'm pretty sure he's somewhere getting money like me."

"He might be in college or working one of those white-collar jobs."

"I doubt that."

"And why is that?"

"Because we share tha same DNA."

"I don't know about Jah'ceer, but we are hungry," I said, rubbing in my stomach.

Y'all always hungry."

"Let's order some pizza."

"A'ight, but Rock will be here at 3 o'clock to pick me up."

"I thought you were staying in wit me today?"

"I am, but this meeting is very important and it's been scheduled for a minute now."

"As long as you ain't out all day and half tha night."

"Nah, I'll be gone about two hours tops."

"Ok, order tha pizza."

"What kind do you want, pepperoni?"

"Yup, wit onions, green peppers, and extra cheese."

After I ordered the pizza, I went to take a shower and change my clothes.

"Nah'ceer, are you ready yet?"

"No, you can go I'll meet you there."

"Are you sure?"

"Yes."

"I'm gonna take Khalif wit me."

"A'ight, I'll hit ya phone when I get close."

"I got Sal and Pip in position just to be on tha safe side."

"Do you think we need them?"

"No, I just like to be cautious."

"You just make sure you strapped."

"Come on Ceer, when ain't I."

"Good point."

"Well, I'll see you in a little bit."

"Ok."

(BEEP-BEEP)

"That's Roc. I'll be back in a few hours."

"Jah'ceer."

"Yes."

"Be safe."

"Always."

"I love you."

I love you too Nya.

Uncle Roc was sittin' in his 645 CI wit tha Philly boy Meek Mills blaring out of his speakers.

"Damn Unc, you think you a young boy."

"You only as old as you feel and I definitely don't feel nowhere near old."

"I feel you Unc."

"Nephew, you better hope you look this good when you get my age."

"I hope I do look that good at 50."

"Ha! Ha! Ha! You are a funny dude."

"You know they say laughter is tha best medicine."

"So I've been told."

"You holdin' right?"

"Yeah, but we're not going to need our pistols."

"You never know Unc stop by Shizz house."

"We don't Shizz; I already have it covered."

When we pulled up to tha warehouse, there was already a car there.

"Unc go head; I'll be in I need to make a phone call real quick."

"A'ight hurry up."

Heaven was already inside when I walked in.

"Hello Heaven."

"Hello Roc."

"This is isn't ya brother, is it?"

"No, he's just called; he should be here any minute. I see ya nephew didn't make tha trip wit you."

"He's in tha car on tha phone he'll be right in."

A few seconds later, Ceer came walking in.

"Hey Ceer."

"Do you know me?"

"Boy stop playing."

"I'm not; where do you know me from?"

"Are we really playing this game right now?"

"I just need to know how you know me?"

"Did you hit your head in tha shower or something?"

Before he could respond, I heard Khalif say, "What tha Fuck," and pull his pistol out.

"Whoa, Whoa, no need for that."

When I turned around, I was in total shock. Nah'ceer at tha mention of his name Roc and Jah'ceer immediately turned around.

"Well, I'll be damn," Roc said, walking toward Nah'ceer, "we have been searching for you for tha past 16 years."

"Nah'ceer nor Jah'ceer said anything they just stood there looking at each other.

Finally, Jah'ceer said, "I knew you were close I felt you."

"I felt you too." They embraced.

"A'ight, A'ight enough wit all tha mushy stuff."

"Do I detect jealousy Unc?"

"This is Uncle Roc, him and dad were like brothers."

"Correction we were brothers."

"This is my sister Heaven; we have been a big part of each other's lives for a long time now."

"Damn, so my brother is tha man controlling tha East Coast?"

"Yeah my Uncle Ross handed it down to me."

"Because of your leadership qualities," Heaven quickly said.

"You're not doing too bad yaself."

"We do enough to get by."

"I can't believe how much y'all look alike."

"Maybe because we're twins."

"Go head wit your big head self."

I could see tha brother and sister love Heaven and Nah'ceer had for one another.

"Wait til auntie Tae sees you."

"Who?"

"Aunty Tae, she's Uncle Roc's wife and mom's best friend."

"Yeah, ya mom tha one who hooked us up."

"We still need to discuss biz-ness."

"Yeah, but now it's on a whole nother level; we can discuss it over dinner."

"Oh Shit."

"What?"

"That's how those Niggaz at tha club knew my name. They thought I was my brother."

"Come on, let's get outta here."

"I have an idea."

"I'm listening."

"We'll talk on the way."

"Aunty Tae."

"Boy, why you yelling my name like that?"

"No reason."

"Look at that, Nya, let you come out tha house like that?"

"She didn't feel like doing it?"

"Nah."

"Well, go get tha comb and grease out of tha bathroom. Where is Roc? He said he was picking you up when he left."

"He had to handle something."

"Your hair is growing."

"I know."

"Ceer, I had a dream about ya mom, dad, and brother last night like they were trying to tell me something.

"Aunty l have a strong feeling we're going to find Nah'ceer soon."

"Jah'ceer y'all should've never been separated; there's not a day that goes by I don't think about him or pray that we find him."

"Aunty, are there days you just want to give up looking for me?"

"What?"

"Looking for him. Hell no, I made a promise to Zeke in Asia that would find him no matter how long it takes me."

I could hear tha seriousness in her voice and it made me feel so good to know that they were looking for me the same way I was them.

(Knock-Knock)

"Ceer, get it while I wash my hands."

"I open tha door for Roc and Ceer."

"Who was it?"

"AAAAAHHH!"

We all had to cover our ears; she screamed so loud.

"How, when, where? Please tell me dreaming."

"I'm afraid we can't do that Aunty."

"But how did you find him?"

"Aunty, I'm tha one who found them."

"Hold on, so you're Nah'ceer?"

"Yup, we wanted to see if you would know tha difference."

"Well, that explains why ya hair was longer."

"Oh My God, look at you."

"You already knew what I would look like," I said, pointing to Jah'ceer.

"Yeah, but it's not tha same as this. So tell me what have you been doing wit ya life?"

I looked at Jah'ceer and Roc, who both nodded.

"I've been gettin' at a dollar."

"Why am I not surprised it's in tha bloodline."

"Nah Aunty Tae, he's tha one who's been supplying us."

She looked at Roc, who just shook his head yes.

"You have been pretty busy if you're supplying those two."

"I do a'ight."

"Tae, he got tha East Coast on lock."

"You are definitely your father's son. So tell me, besides hustling what have you accomplished?"

"I graduated and I own my own beauty/barbershop."

"What's the name of it?"

"Za-Za's."

"Oh Shit!"

"What Baby?"

"That's tha shop everybody talks about."

"I do have a wide clientele."

"Baby, that's tha shop I was telling you about."

"You mean tha shop you told me you was going to in two weeks."

"That's true."

How did you come up wit that crazy name Bro?"

"I named it after mom and dad."

"Oh shit Zeke and Asia Za-Za for short."

"So Aunty you was going to fly all tha way to Philly to get ya hair done?"

"Was, I still am."

"What ever you want done it's on me."

"I can take care of my tab Nah'ceer."

"I'm sure you can, but this time it's on me."

"Yup, you definitely got Abrams blood."

"What that's suppose to mean?"

"Y'all do not like to be told no."

"I got no problem being told no just not by family."

"How about we go out for dinner tonight?"

"No problem, but I have to invite my sister."

"Sister?"

"Yeah, her name is Heaven."

"Is that tha same Heaven you told me about Roc?"

"Yeah, that's tha same one."

"Well, I can't wait to meet her."

"I'm sure you love her just as much is I do."

CHAPTER 29

"Hello, Heaven is so nice to finally meet you to actually put a face wit tha name I've heard so much about."

"Well, I hope it's been all good."

"Don't look at me. I didn't say nothing about you except how much I love you."

"I'm sure you did."

"Now have I ever lied to you before?"

"No."

"Well, why would I start now?"

"Boy, no need to get serious on me."

"That's what I'm trying to say to you."

"Ok, Ok, point taken."

"Wow, you to act just like sister and brother."

After dinner, we all went back to Roc' to have a drink.

"Heaven, I need to know why you killed Jizz?"

"Jizz was a snake when I wouldn't do biz-ness wit him he decided to shoot up our block leaving dead bodies along tha way. So I did what needed to be done."

"I ain't gon' front I wanted to go to war behind that shit."

"Well, it's a good thing you didn't because you two would've never had tha chance to meet."

"You think?"

"Ceer, I'm good at what I do, I was taught by the best."

"I have to agree wit her on that nephew."

"Well, it's a good thing we are on tha same team now."

"I knew that I would find you one day; I made a promise to mom and dad."

"Jah'ceer, we are Bound by DNA, so we were destined to find one another."

"Nah'ceer, I never gave up looking for you wit all my resources, I was bound to find you."

"I know that y'all are twins, but I really can't tell tha two of you apart."

"We could've been knocking down all tha females."

"Listen to you."

"Nya gon' whip his ass if she hear him talkin' like that."

"Oh, you got a wifey?"

"Yeah and she due any day now."

"Damn Bro, you've been gettin' it in."

Aunty Tae excused herself so that we could talk biz-ness. When it was said and done, I filled them both in on my day-to-day operations.

"Imma a let y'all take care of business here so I can take my Sis back to Philly wit me."

"Back to Philly?"

"Yeah, I can't stay here, but I'm only a flight away."

"You don't have to leave right away, do you?"

"Nah, I'm here for a few weeks."

Over the next few months, Nah'ceer and Jah'ceer made up for all tha years spent apart.

"Nah'ceer would travel to Atlanta and vice versa."

Nya and Jah'ceer had a baby boy who she named after his dad; everybody called him baby Zeke and spoiled him like crazy. At tha end of the day, Nah'ceer and Jah'ceer were Bound By DNA

ABOUT THE AUTHOR

My name is Jerz Toston, and I reside in Wilmington, Delaware. First, thanks to my fans for your continued support. This is my 8ᵗʰ book titled Bound By DNA. My other seven books are titled Wht U Don't Kno Can Hurt U, Trust is Ery Thing, Compromised, Street Dreamz: Ery Thing Ain't What It Seems, Da Game Ain't Fair, Betrayal & Deceit and Who Can U Trust? are available now on all on-line-bookstores. Also, you can call my publisher directly at 877.782.5550 x1001 and have them shipped to ya door.

Writing books is my passion and I'll continue to give you page-turners. Just call me Ya Fav Author.

YA FAV AUTHOR BOOKS

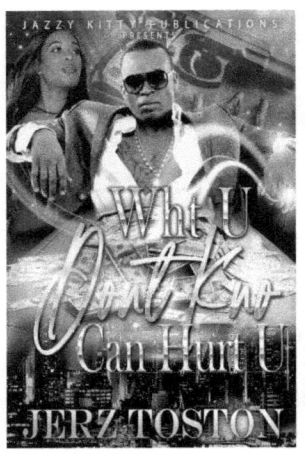

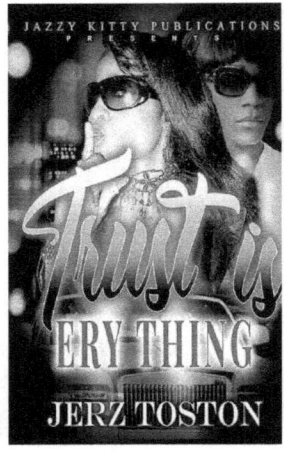